I am enough

CHANGE OF HEART

HAILEY EDWARDS

Edited by Sasha Knight
Copy Edited by Kimberly Cannon
Proofread by Lillie's Literary Services
Cover by Gene Mollica
Illustration by Leah Farrow

CHANGE OF HEART

The Potentate of Atlanta, Book 3

When a lethal drug targeting paranormal citizens is unleashed on the streets of Atlanta, Hadley hits the clubs to pin down the dealer. The party is just getting started when a mysterious fae with his own agenda offers her a taste of power she can't refuse if she wants to purge the evil from her city.

Hadley already owes Natisha seven beating hearts to satisfy their bargain, but the price the fae demands from Hadley might as well be her soul. He strips away her tiny spells, her necessary illusions, and leaves her bare to face judgement from the one person she never wanted to see her truth.

Now Hadley's fate rests in Midas's hands, and all she can do is hope the future she glimpsed for them doesn't slip through his fingers.

ONE

A young girl, maybe eight or nine, greeted me at the only unlocked door. Her dark hair was braided tight against her skull, the tail tucked into the collar of her shirt, and she wore a fitted tee with two crossed cartoon swords appliquéd on the front. She paired it with loose pajama bottoms, tiny bare feet, and a feral glare that dared me to underestimate her.

Warg.

Definitely warg.

"What do you want?" She blocked the entrance to the gymnasium the Lollybrook Women's Shelter rented once a month with her small—but fierce—body. "Well, lady?" She jerked her chin toward the sidewalk. "If you're looking for Thin Mints, there's a Girl Scout troop with nothing better to do than take your money three doors down."

A smile tickled the corner of my mouth, but I kept it off my face. "I'm looking for Midas Kinase."

"Ugh." She rolled her eyes. "You're one of *them*."

Though I could guess, I still asked, "Them?"

"We call *them* his fan club." Her laugh was short and mean and made her hard eyes glitter. "They come to watch him teach and hope they'll get chosen as his partner."

The shadow at my feet coiled in response to my unexpected spike in temper. "I see."

"You're wasting your time." She bared her teeth. "And mine." She glared. "The class is almost over."

"He left his phone at my place." I reached into my pocket. "I need to give it back to him."

"Sure, he did." She shook her head. "Like I haven't heard that one before."

Pushing out a slow exhale, I tried again. "Tell him his girlfriend is here."

I almost choked on the word, but it was guaranteed to snag his attention. It sure got hers.

"You really want me to embarrass you like that?" She glanced behind her, inviting me to do the same, as if I might have somehow missed the standing-room-only basketball court layered in thick mats. "In front of all these people?"

All those craning necks, scrunched brows, and thinned lips curious about me? All those yearning hopefuls praying he would tap their shoulder and ask if he could put his hands on them? All those women without a single shadow darkening their eyes who made a mockery of his dedication because this space was open to the public?

Heck yes.

"Yeah." I bared my own teeth. "I do."

"All right." She propped the door open with its built-in kickstand but held up her hand. "Wait here."

"Sure thing."

The girl pivoted on her heel and marched into the packed gymnasium with starch in her spine that made my chest ache. She was a tough kid, and I respected that. But it made me want to break the world's face for roughing her up so young.

Without her barring my access, I got a clear picture of the chaotic scene and wished I hadn't.

No seats were available in the bleachers. Not a one. Women stood shoulder to shoulder on the polished floor, their shoes pressed into the mats as they shuffled closer and closer to the action.

Most of the crowd wore flashy clothing and carefully applied makeup. Jewelry. They weren't dressed to participate. They were here for one reason, and one reason only.

One blond-haired, blue-eyed reason dressed in a sweat-soaked wifebeater and loose jogging pants.

Midas paused in leading a group of rail-thin girls with lank hair and haunted eyes through a kata when he spotted the pint-sized bouncer en route.

"Midas," she said, her voice loud enough to carry. "Your girlfriend is here."

An invisible hand pressed a cosmic mute button, and the chatter in the gym died a swift death.

Nostrils flaring, Midas whipped his head toward the doorway where I stood.

And he smiled.

Like I was the only person in the world.

Like the dozens of onlookers no longer existed for him.

Like I had made his whole night by showing up out of the blue.

A tremor in my knees warned me I was in over my head with him and sinking fast, but I held my ground.

"Wait." The girl scrunched up her nose. "She's really your girlfriend?"

The kid looked me up and down, a frank assessment of the results from running five miles after I woke at dusk.

Sweaty blonde hair curled beneath a discount Atlanta Braves ball cap. Stains darkened the underarms of a thrift store tank top. Bleach splotched my ripped leggings. Mismatched socks peeked out above the ratty heels of unbranded sneakers with holes in both toes. A rusty safety pin kept the left strap on my sports bra from unraveling. And, the pièce de résistance, a pimple dead center in my forehead, large enough to be my third eye.

This level of sexy couldn't be taught. Either you were born with it, or you died trying.

Dozens of gazes fell on me, assessing and dismissing me as a potential rival, as the women waited for him to blow me off and get back to teaching.

"You forgot your phone." I held it up, pinched between two fingers. "Figured you might want it back."

With the debt we owed Natisha hanging over us, our phones were our lifelines.

Ford was worth the astronomical debt we incurred with the vicious old fae, but I dreaded paying up.

Seven hearts.

Still beating.

Goddess.

"Excuse me," Midas told the girls, then appointed one to continue the exercise. He raked his long fingers through his damp and wavy hair then loped over to me. "You didn't have to bring it all the way down here."

"I was in the neighborhood." I bit the inside of my cheek. "Like two-thirds of the women in that gym."

That dangerous smile of his turned predatory. "Jealous?"

"You're the one with a raging crush on me." I rolled a shoulder. "I keep you around because it's cute."

The flash of his teeth set my stomach quivering as he leaned in. "You think I'm cute?"

"I didn't say *you*." I pricked his princely ego. "Your crush." I watched him deflate. "That's what's cute."

A low growl rumbled through his chest, but the pint-sized bouncer jostled him aside for a better view.

"She's *really* your girlfriend?" Eyes narrowed, she squinted between us. "Like for real?"

"Hadley Whitaker, this is Dani." He squeezed her narrow shoulder, a quick flex of his fingers, but neither looked wholly comfortable with it. "She helps us keep out the riffraff." He didn't hesitate as he locked gazes with me. "Dani Freidman, this is Hadley, my girlfriend."

The title from his lips pooled cold sweat in the small of my back. The coldest. Downright arctic. *Antarctic.*

Midas Kinase was my boyfriend.

Hecate be merciful.

"Hadley. Whitaker." Dani's mouth fell open. "*The* Hadley Whitaker?" She clung to Midas's arm, her nails leaving crescents in his skin. "The next Potentate of Atlanta Hadley Whitaker?"

The clear view of her tonsils freaked me out a little. "That's what it says on my underwear."

Midas wiped a hand down his face, but he wasn't quick enough to erase the beginnings of a smile.

"I'm your biggest fan," Dani gushed, the tough shell around her cracking to reveal the little girl sheltered beneath all that life experience. "I didn't recognize you, I swear, or I wouldn't have hassled you."

"No worries." I tipped the brim of my baseball cap at her. "I'm incognito."

That sounded better than a literal hot mess, given the steaming temperature.

"You're badass." She wriggled past Midas to stand between us. "I saw you fight a chupacabra once."

Wincing at how that ended, with its head at my feet, I really wished she hadn't. "I get that a lot."

"I want to be just like you." That tough outer shell hardened once more, protecting her vulnerable inner self. "No one would mess with me if I carried two swords like you do."

"There's more to being potentate than carrying swords."

A vicious gleam made her eyes shine. "Like cutting off heads?"

"Yes." I palmed my forehead. "I mean, no." I rubbed the spot between my eyes. "That's part of it, but it's not the important part."

"I would protect people too." She left the *duh* unsaid, but I heard it loud and clear. "Would you, maybe, show me how?" She examined her grimy feet. "You're busy and stuff, and way too important, but Midas helps out, so I thought you might come with him."

With a kid this frank, I wanted us on the exact same page. "How to...?"

"Use a sword. Oh! Or maybe two swords. How long did it take you to learn? How long did it take you to get good? Did you cut yourself? A lot? Do you think I'll cut myself? Will you make me sign a waiver? Am I old enough to sign a waiver? I saw Mom working a corner on Peachtree last week. I can probably bribe her to sign with a chocolate bar."

"Breathe, kid." I cut her off before she ran out of oxygen. "I'm working a case right now, but I'll see what I can do after it's solved." I cut my *boyfriend* a sharp look. "Maybe I'll start coming down here with Midas."

"That would be *amazing*." She bounced on her feet. "Do you mean it?"

"Cross my heart." I made the gesture to seal the deal. "Mind if I borrow him for a second?"

"No problem." She backed up a step. "I get it." She made finger quotes. "You guys want to *talk*."

Dani shot back into the gym, closing the inner doors behind her to give us more privacy.

"I like her." I passed over his phone before I forgot. "She's doesn't take crap from anyone, huh?"

"Dani is my first line of defense." He woke his cell to check his messages. "She's a good kid."

A wrinkle formed between his eyebrows, and he angled the screen so we could read the first text and then the second and then the third together.

>>*You two have put me off long enough.*

>>*I expect you and Hadley at dinner.*

>>*Wednesday night.*

When Tisdale Kinase, the alpha of the Atlanta gwyllgi pack, invites you to a family dinner to discuss your intentions toward her only son and heir, you accept. Unless you're me. Then you fake the flu for a week. This gave me three days to relapse or think up a better lie.

"Does that read as attendance optional to you?" I angled my head. "That's how I interpret it."

"Hadley."

"Fine," I huffed. "Tell her royal highness I'll see her then."

Most Atlantans called Midas the pack prince for good reason, so the title wasn't a stretch.

Thumbs flying over the screen, he edited my response to make it alpha—and mother—appropriate.

"Momma's boy," I coughed into my fist then cleared my throat. "Must be those darn allergies again."

Midas didn't rise to the bait, which was a pity, but he did flash me her response.

>> *Steak or chicken?*

"Is this a wedding rehearsal?" I joked then sobered when he didn't laugh. "Midas?"

"We'll go with steak." He fired off one last text then pocketed his cell. "See you later."

"Midas."

"I'll bring home dinner."

"Midas."

"Be safe out there."

"Midas."

He backed through the door and shut it behind him with a soft *click.*

A pathetic imitation of a gwyllgi snarl curled my lip as I raised my fist to pound on the door, or on him.

"Forget Prince Charming," a snarky voice rang out behind me. "I got a hot tip you're going to *love.*"

A hard jerk was as far as I let my startled jump make it before I crushed the impulse flat.

Ambrose, however, glided across the pavement in an oily slick that puddled beneath Remy.

Tonight she paired shredded black tights underneath a sparkly black leotard topped with a frilly neon-green tutu. Her combat boots weighed more than she did, and she had added spiked metal studs to the toes since I saw her last. A lace half glove covered her left hand, and her nails had that glow-in-the-dark murky tint to them. Her makeup matched, and there was a *lot* of it.

"The eighties called." I mimed holding up a phone. "They want Madonna back."

"Midas is right about one thing." She bared her needlelike teeth. "You're not funny."

Ambrose bounced his shoulders in mocking laughter that made me want to stab him.

More than usual.

"He smiles at my jokes." I buffed my nails on my tank top. "He even laughed once."

"He also wants in your pants." She snorted. "I could fake a giggle if it got me laid too."

I almost said *Midas isn't ready for what's in my pants*, but I didn't want to give her ammo to use against him.

Aside from snuggles, nibbles, and smooches that left me hot and him bothered—if the hardness where his hips tucked against my backside were any indication—sleep was all we had done together. So far.

"Walk with me." I waved her on. "I need to get home and shower."

"No time." She mashed a button on her cell that had mine chiming with an incoming text. "You'll have to go as is."

"Go?" After wrestling my phone free of my armband, I pulled up our thread. "Where?"

"I forwarded the deets I got from Seven." She snapped out a mock salute then started walking backward down the craggy side-walk. "I've got to get to work." She grinned. "So do you."

Remy was fae. A macalla, if you wanted to get technical. Or simply an echo in layman's terms. She could split herself into eight sentient halves, or halves of halves, or halves of halves of halves, as the case may be. Make that seven, since Eight had been reabsorbed into the collective upon her death.

In addition to taking over my Peachy Keen Sheets kiosk at the mall, Remy dispatched her other selves on intel-gathering missions across the city to give me more time to focus on nailing my POA apprenticeship.

Goddess knows, I needed all the help I could get with the witch-born fae coven still at large and Natisha's bargain hanging over our heads.

And that became doubly true after I skimmed the information she sent.

"You've got to be kidding me."

From down the empty sidewalk, I swore I heard her laughing.

TWO

Deric Mendelsohn skipped through the Fountain of Rings in Centennial Olympic Park. Five females, his current harem, chased after him. Except for the two who were pregnant. They waddled with determined grunts. Twelve females sat in puddles, some of their own making, laughing hysterically.

They were all nude as the day they were born.

Except for the one wearing a black thong as an eyepatch. She kept yelling *arrr* while slashing her hooked finger through the air.

"Mr. Mendelsohn." I kept a safe distance from the action. "I'm afraid I have to ask you to exit the fountain and put on some clothes."

"You'll have to catch me first." His untamed laughter filled the night. "Better hurry."

No one who had spent five seconds with Mendelsohn would accuse him of being the sharpest tool in the shed. Even if the shed caught fire with him in it and burned to the ground, reducing everything to ashes.

No, wait.

That last part was wishful thinking.

Ambrose cocked his head, his attention focused behind me, alerting me to an approaching presence.

"He's been like this for an hour," rasped a voice raw from yelling. "They've *all* been like this."

Happy for any excuse to look away before the exhibition caused permanent blindness, I cut my eyes and angled my chin toward her in acknowledgment. The others I kept in my periphery, wary of their wild abandon in a public space.

Dim recognition sparked from the late stages of the Bonnie Diaz case as I took in the details of the woman's outfit. She had been wearing a sundress the last time we met too. "Gayle, right?"

"That's me." She worried her top dress button until its fraying thread snapped, and the disc fell into her hand. "I'm the one who called."

The start of a headache throbbed behind my right eye. "Who did you call?"

"The OPA." She produced a creased business card with my information. "I didn't know what else to do."

Yet somehow, instead of Bishop, she had gotten ahold of Remy. No other explanation came to mind for the tip from my employee that would explain why the team at the OPA had yet to update me. Remy had hacked the Swyft database for her own purposes. She might have jacked our forwarding service too.

If that was the case, when Bishop found out—if he didn't already know—he would be *pissed.*

"You did right." I folded her hand over the card, urging her to keep it. A contact inside their pack would be worth cultivating. "We're happy to help in whatever way we can within city limits."

Wargs policed their own. I got the call because this was a situation involving an incapacitated alpha. I was Gayle's best hope for a peaceful resolution, and I had to act fast, before other packs in the area got any ideas. A vulnerable alpha was a dead alpha, and Mendelsohn was out of his gourd. Well, more than usual.

"You were the designated driver?" I noted her clear eyes. "Any idea what they're on?"

Thanks to wargs' higher metabolism, alcohol gave them a buzz, but only if they worked hard for it. Most street drugs fell into the same low-risk category with almost zero addiction rates. That said, there was always something new on the horizon.

"Deric isn't a user, but he'll take favors at parties."

That fit with his *anything goes* outlook on life. "What about his girlfriends?"

"The pregnant ones," she said, taking my meaning, "would never endanger their babies."

Thank the goddess for that. "How about the unpregnant ones?"

Lips tight, she watched her alpha frolic. "They would follow Deric's lead."

"You never said if you drove them here."

"Oh, sorry. No. I wasn't there." She tore her gaze away from him. "I got a call from a girlfriend who works the club district. Jemima tipped me off about the pack. I picked up their trail and followed them here on foot."

"Your friend..." I cast around for anyone else coherent but came up empty, "...she's pack too?"

"No." She shook her head. "Vampire."

"So, they hit a club?" I made a vague gesture toward the gathering. "All of them? Except you?"

"Yeah." She rubbed her thumb in the shallow divot of the button like a worry stone. "I tend to stick close to home, keep an eye on the elders and the kids."

And if that was longing in her voice for it to be otherwise, it was none of my business.

Gwyllgi protocols stumped me on the regular. I wasn't wading into warg politics uninvited.

"Did your friend name the club?"

"Greenleaf." A shudder twitched her shoulders. "That themed bar on Crescent Avenue Northeast."

Clubs weren't my scene, but I was familiar with most by name if not location from my homework.

"Last week, Deric got an invite to an exclusive party. Heavy paper, calligraphy, the works. That's not uncommon, everyone knows he loves to party, but this must have been a special case. He's been pumped for days." Her voice softened. "I didn't recognize the sender's name or the address."

"Do you know if he kept the invitation?"

Gayle worried her bottom lip with her teeth. "He doesn't usually, but if he did, it would be in his tent."

"Check for me when you get home." I tapped the card she had yet to put away. "Call me if you find it."

Her slow, tight nod conveyed her struggle with the request she invade her alpha's private quarters, even for his own good.

"What are you going to do?" Gayle rubbed a pink splotch I hadn't noticed on her forearm. "I tried to get him out of the fountain when I arrived, and he bit me."

Having met Mendelsohn a time or two, that pulled me up short. "He's aggressive?"

All I had witnessed from him so far was a very *tra-la-la* attitude, but I hadn't cornered him either.

"Very." She kept rubbing, but the mark didn't fade. "It's not like him."

Mendelsohn had challenged and killed his father to take over the pack, and he had done the enforcer gig for his old man before that. Rumor had it he executed the coup for the right to knock up every fertile female in the pack. The end result was he tended to choose mating over brawling.

Lashing out at a female, let alone a member of his pack, was out of character for him.

"We need to contain the situation." I woke my phone. "Do you mind if I call for backup?"

Panic brightened her eyes, and her body trembled with the need to shift and defend her packmates.

The spark of magic she exuded barely rated a glance from Ambrose, but the promise of violence set him quivering.

"No..." she gritted out from behind elongating teeth, "...wargs."

"I won't allow any non-Mendelsohn wargs near Deric until he's detoxed," I promised. "Your alpha is safe."

Sweat beaded and rolled down her brow, salting her too-bright eyes. The fine bones in her face shifted and popped. Skin stretched, elastic. Her jaw yawned wide in the beginnings of a horror-movie-style transformation before she regained control of her protective instincts.

"Yeth," she rasped through a misshapen maw. "Do it."

With a tight nod, I walked off to make my call and get me the heck out of Dodge.

"I'm sorry in advance," I murmured to the universe, then dialed.

FORD HOPPED down from his pickup with a pasted-on smile that flaked off once he spotted Mendelsohn.

The courtship with Midas had torpedoed my friendship with Ford, and I absolutely hated it.

Hurt darkened his eyes whenever he looked at me these days, and I wished I could blame it on the coven.

But I had helped put it there.

So had Midas.

"This is a warg matter." Hip against the fender, he tucked his hands under his arms. "I can't intervene."

"Wrong." Bishop exited shadows too thin to conceal his approach, and Ambrose stalked him on his way over with glee. "The wargs are in our city, causing a disturbance guaranteed to draw human attention. That makes it an OPA matter."

"You're slipping." I cocked my hip. "Remy tipped me off like an hour ago."

Bishop ignored me, and the hit to his pride, in favor of staring down Ford.

"I can't intervene," Ford repeated without heat. "I'm sorry."

"You help me and the OPA all the time." I threw my hands up in frustration. "How is this any different?"

"*I'm* different," he said softly, a world of pain spinning through his voice.

The decent thing to do would be to cut him loose now and let him come to me when he was ready.

"Mendelsohn took his harem to a party at Greenleaf," I told him, "and this is the result."

So long, decency.

"Some of these females—" I kept hammering at him, "—are *pregnant.*"

Ford punched the side of his truck hard enough to leave a dent. "I can't intervene."

Unflappable Ford losing his temper dried the spit in my mouth, but that wasn't half as shocking as him raising a hand to his truck. He *loved* that thing. It was his baby, his pride and joy, and he had struck it.

That was not like Ford. None of this was like him. He might as well have been body snatched.

Actually, thanks to the Martian Roaches using him as a host, he almost had been.

"You can go, Ford." Bishop rested his hand on my shoulder. "I've got her back."

Ford flexed his hand, testing it for broken bones, then he climbed into the cab of his truck and sat there.

"I thought I could do this." He aimed the hard words like an arrow straight at my heart. "Be *just* friends with you." His grip on the door handle turned white-knuckled. "I need more time."

"Ford..." I would have stepped closer, but Bishop held me in check. "You *are* my friend."

Before he slammed the door, he murmured, "I'm sorry I can't return the favor right now."

The white pickup sped off before the engine had time to cool from his arrival.

"Give him space." Bishop dropped his arm. "His head is all screwed up, kid."

"I really did a number on him."

"Don't take all the credit," he chided. "More is going on in his head than in his heart."

Afraid of how much I wanted off the hook for hurting him, I asked, "What do you mean?"

"What the coven did to him left a mark that won't fade soon. He's got to make peace with what happened before he can move on. You're just a handy target." He shrugged. "Don't get me wrong, rejection sucks. He's going to be feeling that sting for a while too." He started walking, and I fell in step with him. "Broken hearts mend, eventually. Broken spirits are iffier. Broken minds... Sometimes that's impossible."

Guilt hit me, heavy and hard. "Do you think I should mention this to Abbott?"

"Ford could use a friend." He refrained from pointing out I had cost him his best one. "The more neutral, the better."

Since we were doing the bonding thing, I dared to switch gears. "Are you doing okay? After everything?"

"I've had worse." He brushed me off easily. "That doesn't mean I want to do it again."

Three nondescript vans pulled up behind us and spat out eight women and four men dressed to weather a downpour. They each nodded at my wave, about as much of a *hello* as you could expect from cleaners, who did their best to avoid on-scene interaction for the sake of their impartial reputation.

Moving into position, one man and one woman opened the rear swinging doors on each van, revealing a stainless bench bolted to the wall and the floor on either side.

I stared at the cleaners, and the cleaners stared right back.

Apparently, *everyone* had decided this was an OPA matter.

Where were the sentinels when you needed them? Sheesh. They should have been here by now.

"Come on, kid." Bishop nudged my shoulder. "This is going to be fun."

"And just like that, you've earned a homework assignment from me to you."

A line bisected his forehead. "Oh?"

"Look up *fun* in the dictionary and tell me if Mendelsohn's hairy ass is the picture beside the definition."

"Smartass." Bishop popped his knuckles. "What's our move?"

"We take down Mendelsohn first. The others should fall in line once he's subdued."

"You're the boss." He punched his fist skyward. "Lead us onward to victory."

"Smartass," I grumbled back at him. "There is no victory in this."

With magic off the table, Ambrose lost interest and parked himself on the sidelines. Super helpful, that guy.

"P.S." I gave Bishop a heads-up. "I'm pretty sure Remy hacked into your database."

With a scoff, he brushed me off. "That's not possible."

"All I'm saying is, she answered an incoming call for the OPA." I met his gaze. "From her cell."

"Godsdamn it." He narrowed his eyes in thought. "She must have planted a charm near the CPUs. No one can breach my firewalls through non-magical means, and she couldn't have managed if she didn't have direct access. A magical strike couldn't have gotten through the wards on HQ."

"Well." I patted him on the shoulder. "Have fun with that."

"Oh," he said thoughtfully, "I will."

As much as I hated to narc on her, she had to learn to keep her hand out of the OPA cookie jar. She would always get caught in the end, and Bishop was likely to take off her hand in the process.

"Mendelsohn." I approached the alpha with caution. "You need to exit the fountain."

"Catch me." He whooped, spun in a puddle, and shook his bare ass at me. "If you can."

On cue, lukewarm water jetted from the silver Olympic rings design inset into the bricks and soaked me.

"I'm not paid enough for this," I told Bishop. "There's not enough money in the world for this."

Just as well. Atonement couldn't be bought. It had to be earned. And I was working hard for it.

"You go left." He dodged a pregnant female too exhausted to keep playing tag. "I'll go right."

Mendelsohn spotted us and bolted to the right. I couldn't help the evil grin spreading across my face as I pictured Bishop wrestling with the slippery warg and not me. But as Bishop's grasping fingers glanced off Mendelsohn's wet skin, the alpha dodged left. Right into my waiting arms.

Eww. Eww. Eww.

A precise kick took out Mendelsohn's right knee, and he fell with a crack of bone and a howl of pain. The shock bought me time to bend down and capture his wrists. Sadly, wargs heal quickly, and before I could finish twisting his arms behind him, he mashed his face into my cleavage, such as it was, and motorboated me through my soaked top.

"You're a pig," I spat as he bit the side of my breast faster than I could break free of him. "Not a wolf."

Oinking between snorted laughter, he got his legs under him and lunged at me with inhuman speed. I let him scoop me off my feet, wrap his long arms around me, and pin me against his chest.

And then I crushed his grapes with my knee using every ounce of strength Ambrose could loan me.

"My..." Mendelsohn wheezed in my ear, "...balls."

"They'll drop again," I assured him. "Eventually."

Coughing up slurs and swearing a blue streak, Mendelsohn

leaned all of his considerable weight on me. We both went down and landed on our sides. I was still trapped within the cage of his arms, and he was ratcheting them tighter around me until breathing hurt worse than the alternative.

"Let her go." Bishop hooked his hands under Mendelsohn's arms. "Unless you're done siring offspring."

The threat slid right off him, unable to gain traction in his addled mind.

"Diiie." The alpha thrashed and giggled as Bishop hauled him off me. "Biiitch."

"Calling Bishop names is rude." I got to my feet. "You'll hurt his feelings."

"Ouch," Bishop deadpanned, yanking Mendelsohn's arms behind his back.

I palmed the modified pen in my pocket, almost dropping my pot of emergency ink for more traditional workings, and I drew on the one sigil I used on the regular. The magical restraints clicked into place and locked the insides of his wrists together. With that done, I gave his ankles the same treatment to make escape impossible without assistance.

Together, we lifted the writhing, babbling alpha and carried him to the nearest van.

The cleaners, who were paranormal crime scene techs, not brute enforcers, kept well out of spitting range. They might be in charge of cleaning up messes, but that didn't mean they liked getting their hands dirty.

Only after we dumped Mendelsohn on a bench and traded his magical restraints for silver ones, did the sentinels arrive wearing Atlanta Police Department uniforms. They waded into the fray and helped us herd the more docile females toward their alpha and the waiting transportation.

"We're missing two," Gayle called. "Any sign of them?"

"Hadley," Bishop yelled, jamming his finger toward a flesh-toned streak. "She's making a break for it."

The female clutched her distended belly with both hands and squeezed her thighs together as she ran.

"Ma'am." I jogged after her. "Can you please…?"

Once her feet hit grass, she squatted and…peed.

"I love my job, I love my job, I love my job," I chanted while I waited on her to finish. "Ma'am?"

Unable to stand again, the female toppled sideways, thankfully not into her mess. I helped her upright then escorted her to Gayle, who got her settled. Bishop rounded up the last holdout, who had fallen asleep under a tree, and handed her off to a pair of sentinels.

"That's everyone," Gayle confirmed, then sought out my face. "Thank you."

"You're welcome." I squished when I walked now, and my heels rubbed in my wet shoes. "Take care."

With a tired wave, Gayle sat next to Mendelsohn. He lowered his head onto her lap, finally exhausted, and she stroked his hair with a fond smile softening her expression.

"Come on, heartbreaker." Bishop slung his arm around me. "I'll buy you lunch."

As much as I wanted to go home, shower, and bleach my brain… free food won.

Leaning against him, I rested my head on his shoulder. "From Tex-Mex Momma?"

"Keep eating those ghost chili tamales, and they're going to burn through your stomach lining one day."

"But not today." I straightened and adjusted my soggy top. "I take omeprazole."

"Omeprazole isn't a hazmat suit for your digestive tract."

Flicking water at his face, I cocked an eyebrow at him. "Or *is* it?"

Writing me and my stomach lining off as a loss, he shook his head. "We hitting Greenleaf before or after?"

There was no question we had to investigate. "Before."

We caught a Swyft to the Midtown club, but the street was quiet, and the entrance locked when we arrived. I mashed the buzzer, since it was a private party, but no one answered. I didn't like it, any of it, especially how affected the wargs had been, but we couldn't kick down the door without probable cause.

When no other options presented themselves, we left with the intent to return the following night and try our luck catching it open then.

After Bishop and I ate, which left me sweating in my chair at the outdoor table, we hit the streets for a few hours before I went home to Midas. How weird was it to think about him waiting on me? Weird, but nice. I could get used to it, and that terrified me. Happily, those ghost chilis were guaranteed to burn the fear right out of me, at least for a few hours. It was as good a place to start as any.

THREE

The trauma of the previous night, and the cringeworthy memory of Deric Mendelsohn's hairy butt cheeks shining like twin moons, if the moon was made of moldy cheese, had been dimmed somewhat by spending the remaining hours before dawn enjoying *Their Eyes Are Always Watching* while snuggled up to Midas on the futon with dinner in our laps and chopsticks in our hands.

I woke in much the same position, minus Midas, ready to face the night. As soon as I got my eyes open.

A musical *ting* prompted me to check my phone, and I groaned at being forced to move.

Fingers groping for my cell, I touched paper and pulled the scrap to me where I could squint at it better.

"*Duty calls,*" I read out loud, snuggling into his pillow. "*See you at home.*" I breathed him in. "*Midas.*"

Sadly, the phone didn't see fit to stop ringing while I basked in the giddy thrill of receiving his note.

Clearly, it didn't have the circuits of a romantic.

Unable to ignore the persistent racket, I palmed the blasted cell, read the growing string of urgent texts, then shot upright with a growl on my lips. "Do you believe this crap?"

Ambrose stretched and yawned, faking interest in my outburst, but I didn't waste breath elaborating.

While I struggled into fresh clothes, I called Bishop with a clipped order. "Meet me out front."

Odds were good he would beat me to the sidewalk. He was forever lurking outside the Faraday these days. Like he didn't want me to be gruesomely murdered or something.

Sure enough, I exited the building, too busy to hassle Hank for a change, and aimed straight for Bishop, who waited for me at the curb.

"There's a party spilling onto Crescent Avenue Northeast." A cold knot cramped my gut as I summarized the rest of the text from Remy to him. "A new drug hit the streets tonight." I watched his face as I told him the rest. "They're calling it...Faete."

Ambrose perked at the word *Faete* and slithered closer to hear the rest, his interest genuine this time. The defunct fae club where we found Bishop half dead after the witchborn fae coven finished torturing him had shared the same name.

I doubted it was a coincidence. More like a billboard-sized message.

Bishop locked down his emotions before a single one escaped. "Any idea where it originated?"

"Remy tracked it to Greenleaf." I filled him in on what Gayle told me about the fancy invitation Mendelsohn received from an unknown sender and got a bad feeling he had been invited to enjoy a sneak peek at coming attractions. "With his reputation for partying, I bet his name topped the mailing list."

Clubs in Midtown wooed high profile paranormal clientele with promises of discount booze, new drugs, or sex to keep them coming back for more—and bringing their friends with them.

"But," I had to admit, "given its lingering effect on Mendelsohn and his pack, he might have been targeted for the pre-release bash for more clinical reasons."

"No drug currently on the market affects wargs for more than an hour, tops." Bishop stared off into traffic. "Faete gave those wargs an unprecedented high, *if* that's what did it."

If, because we needed proof before we started making accusations.

Sometimes being one of the good guys sucked. There were so many more rules for us to follow.

"I'll touch base with the cleaners." Bishop dialed them from memory. "We're a day late and a dollar short, but they need to know the Mendelsohns are possible ODs on an unidentified substance so they can pass it on to the medics if they haven't figured it out yet."

Leaving him to tie up loose ends, I walked off for privacy to make a call. To Midas.

"We can't confirm it yet," I said when he answered, "but it looks like the coven made their next move."

"Faete."

A pang slid between my ribs and sharpened my voice. "You knew?"

He would have made the same connection with the name as me, and gwyllgi protective instincts being what they are, he also might have decided I was better off not finding out about it until it came to my attention through other means.

"As of forty-five minutes ago, yes."

Or he could have found out in the last hour, same as me, and hadn't had time to share the deets.

What can I say? Relationships were alien to me. No. Wait. *Alien* was a bad comparison. I watched enough science fiction to feel comfortable with the existence of life on other planets. But to love another person enough to forsake all others and make a life together? Little green men seemed more plausible.

"I'm in Midtown rounding up some of our teens," Midas said when I kept quiet. "We're missing four."

"Bad idea." I gripped the phone harder. "We don't know enough about this—"

Techno music assaulted my ears, and I figured he must have entered a club. The noise made conversation impossible, even before the call dropped with a hiss.

"Bishop," I called to him as I redialed Midas. "We need to go."

No surprise, Midas didn't answer. I told myself he couldn't hear the phone ring over the noise, but I was a good liar and had trust issues. Even with myself.

"Consider us gone." Bishop stepped back up to the curb and flagged down a yellow cab. "Our chariot awaits."

Once he settled in, I slid across the seat next to him and gave the driver Greenleaf's name and address.

Unsure why Bishop had chosen this mode of transportation, I offered, "Remy doesn't work for Swyft anymore."

"She never did," he reminded me. "She was using the app to psycho stalk your boyfriend."

"You're not wrong" about summed up the situation. "But a cab?"

Swyft was cheaper, quicker, and their drivers could handle their passengers, for the most part, if things got ugly. At the very least, they knew who to call—namely me—if that happened.

"We need to quarantine Crescent Avenue Northeast and the surrounding area," he explained. "Until we get a sample of Faete, and a lab analysis on it, we can't be sure who it will affect or how. We don't need to invite more paras to the party."

With a name like *Faete*, the drug must be geared toward the paranormal community. That didn't mean it was safe for human consumption. Likely, the opposite was true. A Swyft driver could be in more immediate danger than our cabbie, but I hadn't registered that either. I had been too focused on Midas.

"Smart." I gave Bishop a pat on the head. "That next-level thinking is why you're my wingman."

"And here I thought it was because you took sick pleasure in watching me wrestle Mendelsohn naked."

"First off, *I* got stuck wrestling Mendelsohn naked. Secondly, has anyone wrestled him not naked?" I wasn't joking. "It's like he's allergic to pants."

The trip to Midtown was short, and I ponied up the cash—or the plastic, as the case may be—for the ride and the tip.

Bishop didn't trust banks, or plastic cards, and he never carried more than twenty dollars in his pocket in the highly unlikely event he was mugged. He preferred the debit card Linus had issued him for purchases, which would be fine. If he bothered carrying it.

"Ever been to Mardi Gras?" Bishop gazed out the window. "All that's missing are the beads."

"Yes. Once. I'm not interested in a repeat." I checked with him. "Are you okay to do this?"

Fae immune systems weren't my wheelhouse, seeing as how good little necromancers avoided them, but his had been compromised recently by the Martian Roach who attempted to use him as its host.

"I'll be fine." He opened the door nearest the sidewalk and exited into the crush. "Watch your step."

The crowd hid what he meant until I stepped out—and onto—someone's twitching hand.

Bodies littered the concrete. Some curled into tight balls, others sprawled with their limbs flung wide.

Most weren't moving, and I couldn't tell if they were breathing.

"Goddess." I accepted the elbow he offered until I found my footing. "Are they alive?"

"Most of them." He nudged the nearest man onto his back and out of his own vomit. "What a mess."

"The drug turned Mendelsohn and his females into giggling children with short tempers who wanted to play in a fountain." As much as I wanted to crouch and examine the nearest victim, I didn't dare. I might fall, and that would get me trampled or worse. "These people are comatose, not manic."

This was either a different faction, or they had it worse for not leaving the area after their first hit.

Part of me questioned how the dealers could stomach lavish festivities after what happened to the Mendelsohns and whoever else had the bad luck to attend last night's soiree. The rest figured they didn't care, or they wouldn't be dealing in illegal substances to begin with.

"I don't recognize any of the partiers." He cut a path to Greenleaf and the bouncer at the door. "We're here on official business."

The tall black man wore a fitted suit in a rich emerald fabric that shimmered under the club lights spilling onto the street. His thin tie, light shirt, and darker shoes were shades of grass, spring, and leaf. He jerked his chin toward the drunken line winding down the block. "I already heard that once tonight."

The silver of Bishop's eyes gleamed bright, hungry. "We're with the Office of the Potentate of Atlanta."

The bouncer flicked a glance past Bishop to me, took in my bleached jeans and holey tee, and smirked.

"Sure, fella." He pointed out the queue, in case we missed it the first time. "End of the line."

"Hadley." Bishop stepped aside and shoved me front and center. "Assert your dominance."

Assert my dominance, my foot. "Look, just because I'm dating Midas doesn't mean—"

"He's the pack prince," Bishop said flatly. "You had to have picked up on some of his tricks."

"That guy from earlier. He claimed he was pack." The bouncer wet his lips. "He was legit?"

We had come to the right place if Midas beat us here, but the sensual music spilling out onto the street conflicted with the earlier techno beats. This wasn't where his call dropped then. He must be elsewhere.

"Midas Kinase." I waited for recognition to dawn. "What rock have you been living under?"

Gray skin mottled his fists as he clenched them. "You got a problem with stone trolls?"

A troll able to turn his fists to stone would be just the ticket for policing rowdy supernaturals.

"You're fae." I didn't step back, but I shifted my weight onto my heels. "I thought this was a warg party."

"Blithe Danann is hosting." He adjusted his tie, which was pinned with a silver oak leaf. "This is her place."

The name meant nothing to me, aside from the obvious nod to her heritage, but Bishop set his jaw.

"We should go." He closed his hand over my arm. "Now."

"What about Midas?" I jerked free of him. "We have to warn him."

"You do not want Blithe to notice me." He ground his teeth. "Trust me. We're done here."

"All right." I did trust him, and this Blithe person was freaking him the frak out. "Let's go."

While Bishop watched the swirling crowd, waiting for it to eddy, I kept an eye on the bouncer.

"Repeat that." Plugging one ear against the ruckus, he shoved his earpiece in tighter. "Are you certain?" Adjusting his tie yet again, he shifted his gaze to Bishop with a swallow. "Ms. Danann wishes to see you."

"No," Bishop said without turning, then stepped into the flow of bodies and dragged me with him.

The laughing crowd with their bright eyes and grasping hands shoved against us, herding us backward, toward Greenleaf, as if it possessed one consciousness and one purpose.

"*Bishop.*"

The single word rang with deafening finality, despite the utter chaos around us.

"Find Midas." He shoved me through the front line into the less turbulent core. "Go."

Flinging my arm back, I cursed him as my fingers slid free of his. "I'm not—"

"You're leaving," he snarled, "or I'm calling Linus."

The threat worked its magic, and I stopped fighting the current and let it sweep me away.

"Jerk," I muttered as I navigated the streaming bodies in search of any port in the storm.

A clammy hand circled my ankle just as I broke clear, and I almost kicked it off me on reflex.

"Hadley," the slight woman crumpled at my feet rasped. "Hadley."

With the space around me as open as it was going to get, I hooked my hands under her arms and hauled her against the nearest building to give us a wall to put at our backs. Only with that scrap of reassurance did I risk crouching to examine her.

"Do I know you?" I checked the pulse at her throat and found it thready. "Hey." I patted her cheek. "Can you hear me?"

"Lis..." Her eyes rolled around without settling on me. "Lis..."

Whatever grip she had on my name had slipped as she repeated the new one over and over.

"Hang in there." I pulled out my phone. "I'm going to get help."

The sentinels had been alerted to the situation in Midtown, but this woman needed immediate medical attention.

"Lis..." The woman closed her hand over my wrist. "Lis..."

"You're okay." I eased out of her grip when her nails started to bite. "Medics are on the way."

"Lisbeth," she murmured. "Lis...beth."

Sweat popped down my spine and blended with the dampness already there. I hadn't met any members of the OPA team, aside from Bishop, and I wasn't meant to. Ever. I didn't know what to do. There were no protocols for this. This—this was like spotting a unicorn in the wild. One that might stab me with its horn to preserve its anonymity once its mind defogged from the high.

"You're Lisbeth?" I clutched her hand. "*My* Lisbeth?"

A long exhale passed her lips, and she slumped against the pavement.

"Lisbeth." I shook her shoulder, and her head sagged to one side. "Frak. Frak. Frak."

Bishop had ditched me, and I had yet to spot Midas. That left me precious few other allies to call.

No.

Not allies.

I had to stop being such a coward about labels.

Friends.

I had few *friends* to call, and the first one who popped into my head wanted space.

With that in mind, I dialed up Remy. She didn't answer, which wasn't unusual when she was on the clock at the kiosk, but her dedication to the sale had never irked me more than it did right then.

Hating myself for putting him in this situation, I called my first choice before I changed my mind.

"Ford," I blurted. "Don't hang up."

He blasted a sigh across the receiver that spoke volumes.

"I've got a team member down on Crescent Avenue Northeast one block east of Greenleaf." I trained my gaze on the raucous partygoers, praying to spot the familiar in the churning faces. "Near as I can tell, she ingested the new drug that hit the streets tonight. She needs to be evacuated immediately."

Before any sharp ears overheard us, realized who she worked for, and figured payback might be a giggle.

"A member of your..." He grew more animated. "She's OPA?"

"Yes." I trusted him with another clue that risked exposing her identity. "Her name is Lisbeth."

"Damn it, Lee." A *tick, tick, tick* filled the background. "I'm on my way."

"Thank you."

He ended the call with a muttered curse that made me feel three inches tall.

Hunkered down while I waited for backup, I sought out Ambrose through our bond and found him strolling down the center of the sidewalk, uncaring if I noticed him absorbing trickles of ambient energy from the crowd. The effort of snatching him back to my side was exacerbated by his mini power trip, but I got him locked down before he stirred up more trouble.

Crouched over Lisbeth, checking her every so often, I caught a flash of gold fur from the corner of my eye.

Midas had shifted. And so had...Ares?

This section of Midtown was heavily populated by paras, and clubs on this strip were for paras only. That didn't mean clever humans never tricked or bribed their way in, or that the club owners didn't pay them to be the entertainment for a night or two before wiping their memories.

That said, Gwyllgi had no business on four legs in this area without a frakking good reason.

The golden gwyllgi walked right up to me, his gaze sliding over me with a questioning air.

The dark gwyllgi beside him tipped its head in greeting but kept vigil on the clubgoers.

"She's one of mine," I explained, touching Lisbeth's cheek. "She's OPA."

That sparked their curiosity, and they paid the unconscious woman at my feet closer attention.

"Ares?" I checked with the dark gwyllgi to be sure, and she nodded once. "Can you wait with Lisbeth until Ford gets here?"

The hairs on the back of her neck bristled, and she stepped over Lisbeth's supine body.

Midas watched me with such intensity that I rubbed the fur of his ruff against the grain to annoy him as much as his perception irked me. Proving two could play that game, Midas licked my wrist, leaving me a bracelet of warm slobber.

"I'll remember this, mister." Gagging, I wiped my hand on my leggings. "When you're trying to stick your tongue down my throat, I'm going to remind you of this exact moment."

Ares chuffed with canine laughter until a growl from him silenced her.

"Who knows where your mouth has—" I spluttered as he stepped in and licked me from chin to hairline, "—been."

No expression leaked onto Ares's somber face, but her sides heaved with silent laughter.

Midas, quite proud of himself, lolled his tongue out one side of his mouth.

"I hate you both." I pointed a finger at him. "You're sleeping on the floor tonight."

Confident in Ares's ability to protect Lisbeth, I left a vital part of my team in the capable jaws of the pack.

FOUR

Our hasty exit to avoid Ford prickled over me like cowardice, stung like shame, and hurt like heck. Lesser of two evils? Maybe. Or maybe I was too chicken to face him less than twenty-four hours after he asked me for space, with yet another favor to beg of him. Either way, it was done. All I could do was hope Ford would forgive me. Eventually.

Done tormenting myself for the moment, I asked Midas, "Did you find the teens you were looking for?"

Ears twitching, he shook his head then barked at a man who paused beside us with wide eyes.

"That's one gnarly dog," the guy said, swaying on his feet. "What's wrong with his fur? Scabies?"

"Yes," I said solemnly. "He's got scabies, and it's highly contagious."

A splash of red magic hit the pavement beside me as Midas traded one form for another.

"Whoa." The guy poked Midas's arm. "Did that just happen?"

Poor guy must have missed the *highly contagious* part.

"No," Midas growled. "It's your imagination."

"You don't see a man?" The guy pointed at Midas. "He's right there."

"Nope." I ran my fingers through Midas's hair. "All I see is Princess Pooferella, my dog."

"This stuff warps your mind." He rubbed his eyes. "I've got to get more."

"Hey, friend." I fisted the back of his shirt before he escaped. "Where did you get it?"

"I tell you that," he whined, "and it's two more people dipping into the party favors."

"We don't want the drugs." I tightened my hold as he flailed. "We want answers."

"The Bone Lounge," he panted. "I got it from Skullduggery, okay?"

"Enjoy the rest of your night." I let him go. "Thanks for your cooperation."

Stumbling free of my grip, he disappeared within seconds.

Eager to get moving, I checked with Midas. "You can track him, right?"

"Princess Pooferella." He narrowed his eyes on me. "Your dog."

"I could hardly tell him you were my horse."

Midas glanced to one side, but I saw his lips twitch. "You're still not funny."

"And yet you're still laughing." I took his hand. "Maybe there's hope for us yet."

"Come on," he sighed, and began pursuit of our new friend, who led us on a merry chase.

Maybe he smelled us. Maybe we invited too much attention wading against the flow. Or, more likely, maybe he was that paranoid there would be nothing left for him if he led us to his stash.

"Surprise, surprise." I held Midas back as the guy dipped into line at Greenleaf. "Do you think everyone got their freebies from there?"

"Hard to tell," he admitted. "There are dozens of people on the streets, but it's only the one club."

They all couldn't have fit in there at once, but the bouncer kept the line moving at a steady clip.

"Where's the emergency exit?" I eyed an alley clogged with stumbling partiers. "Must be down there."

"What are you thinking?" He tightened his hand around mine. "You've got that look in your eyes."

"Greenleaf went through a lot of trouble to ensure this outcome." Their new product was an instant hit. "They must have been prepared with enough samples and a solution for the traffic flow problem for it to go off without a hitch."

"Let them in the front, get them high, then send them out the back?"

"Check out the people in line. They're all clear-eyed and alert. They haven't gotten theirs yet."

"The people out here..." He scanned the street. "They circled around to see if they could go again."

Proving us right, we watched as the bouncer spotted our greedy new friend attempting a double dip and told him to take a hike.

"That guy is hardcore," I said with respect. "He wouldn't let us in, and I hear he didn't let you in either."

That last part surprised him, and he smiled. "Checking up on me?"

"Your call dropped," I grumbled. "I worried."

His smile kept growing until his dimples winked at me.

"Shut up." I shoved him. "No one asked you."

"I like that you worried about me." He used our linked hands to jerk me close. "It's nice."

"Yeah, well." I leaned against his side. "You took off like a shot for the worst place to be tonight. Somebody had to worry about you."

"I brought Ares with me."

"I brought Bishop with me." I waved my hand. "And yet, we both got ditched."

Granted, Ares had stuck with Midas until I set her on Lisbeth. One could argue her absence was my fault.

"I'm a beta." Amusement crinkled the corners of his eyes. "And a gwyllgi."

"I'm a wannabe potentate, and I'm telling you, you can't risk this again until we know more."

The order was what did it, kindled crimson in his eyes and ignited a challenge in his blood.

Always ready to poke the lion, I stared him down. "Do *not* growl at me."

"Do *not* tell me what to do."

"Do *not* talk down to me."

"Do *not* stand on your tiptoes." He rested his hands on my shoulders and pressed until my heels touched the sidewalk. "It's cheating."

"Do *not* tell me what to do."

"I already said that one."

"Now look what you've done." I settled flat on my feet. "We've lost momentum."

"Don't worry." He gazed down at me. "We'll be fighting again before you know it."

"Promise?" I looped my arms around his neck. "Guess we might as well kiss and make up then."

Without giving his temper a chance to cool, I dragged his mouth down to mine and tasted every corner.

"Will it always be like this?" he rumbled near my ear. "The arguing?"

A sliver of fear wedged in my spine, but courtship was the time for full disclosure. "Probably."

"Good." He laughed softly and pressed his nose under my jaw. "You smell good when you're angry."

A beta and a future potentate were bound to bump heads. A *lot*. Gwyllgi protective instincts set my teeth on edge, but I'm sure Midas would say the same about my tendency to wade in to save others at any cost to myself.

As long as we ended our arguments with a smile and a kiss, we might actually nail this relationship thing.

Pulling back, he gazed down at me. "Are we okay?"

Scrunching up my face, I pretended to think about it. "We're not *not*-okay."

He blasted out a sigh, but I was getting better at reading him.

"You're fine." I winked. "And I mean that exactly how it sounded."

A line bisected his forehead, and he worked his jaw over words that didn't form.

"One day you'll make peace with my hilarity," I said sagely, "and embrace it openly."

"And one day you won't rush headlong into danger without checking your speed."

"It's good we both have dreams." I tapped his chin. "I read in *Cosmo* that's important in relationships."

Exasperation clear, he stared down at me. "Hadley."

How many times had Dad used that tone with my mother? Not the Whitakers, the Pritchards. How often had he spoken with a voice tinged with a wish to be anywhere other than there, with anyone other than her? They fought often, but quietly. Theirs was a disappointment left to simmer beneath the surface of every look, word, and touch. And while Dad found other outlets to express his unhappiness, I had always been hers.

The danger had passed after that kiss, I told myself, but still my shoulders tightened. Midas would never hurt me physically, but emotionally? I was in deep and sinking fast. "Yeah?"

"You're standing in urine."

That was not what I had expected to hear. "I huh?"

"That?" He pointed at the thin stream. "That's pee." He indicated a man leaning his forehead against the wall. "His, if you want to get specific."

"Oh gag." I danced back and bumped into three other people. "Why didn't you warn me?"

"You had this look…" He reached out to steady me. "What did you expect me to say?" Understanding softened his features, and he lowered his arm slowly when I kept staring at his fingers where they dug into the skin of my upper arm. "What did you expect me to do?"

Crack my heart over his knee then watch this tender feeling *drip, drip, drip* onto the sidewalk?

"I trust you." I took his hand to prove it, and mine trembled. "I know you would never hurt me like that."

Like that.

I bit my tongue, but it was too late. I had slipped up in acknowledging I had been hurt in the past, that I knew to fear the hits that hadn't landed yet more than the quick jabs of a provoked temper that struck where no one else would see.

Just me.

And my mirror.

The reminders lasted for days. Sometimes weeks. Once, a month. But she was never that careless again.

"Someone did." He cradled my cheek in his palm. "I recognize the signs."

"It was a long time ago." I shuddered out an exhale. "She can't hurt me anymore."

Midas drew me against his wide, warm chest. "The past is always looking over our shoulders, isn't it?"

The comfort seeping from him into me felt too good to push away, so I didn't even try.

Ambrose leaned against the brick wall, head angled in our direction, his attention making my skin crawl.

"Yeah," I rasped, hating that he was watching. "It's always there."

"Good thing you're not afraid of heights." Midas made a humming noise. "It will make this easier."

"Huh?" I tipped my head back to look at him. "What does that have to do with anything?"

"Up might be the only way in." He pointed to the fire escape between buildings. "It will be hard to reach, but no one has thought to use it yet."

There might be wards preventing access was my first thought, but it was worth a shot.

Much to Ambrose's delight, I sent him to inspect the fire escape while Midas and I cut a path toward it.

Ambrose made fast work of his recon then he honed himself into a bolt of pure agony he hurled through my brain. I bumped into the person next to me as I absorbed the hit of information, but I doubted Midas noticed it was my fault and not the woman swaying to unheard music.

All that pain for a simple confirmation that yes, there was an active ward in place. I could have guessed that myself without the migraine.

No chocolate for you, I thought at Ambrose. *Jerk.*

There was a fine line between Ambrose hearing my thoughts and reading my intent, and I worried one day we might cross it. Honestly? Some days I felt we already had.

The shadow bowed his head, the picture of remorse, but he was in rare form tonight and couldn't be trusted. Not that I ever did. Trust him, I mean. But I could rely on him in certain situations with the proper motivation. Truffles must not be cutting it if he wasn't even trying to behave.

Blocking out my annoying shadow, I processed what little else he had discovered about the fire escape.

A nasty ward began on the lowest portion, encompassing the ladder and continuing up onto the roof. As I had suspected. Also as I had suspected, Ambrose offered to disarm it for me in greedy gulps.

Any other time, I might have let him swallow the energy to grant us easy access, but he had been snacking on and off without asking my permission. He just...soaked up the magics whirling on the street.

Queasy with dread, I feared what it meant for me if he had learned to feed independent of my will. Without his hunger to leash him, I would lose control. Maybe not tonight, but eventually.

Midas popped his knuckles as he measured the distance. "Do you want me to go first?"

Lost in thought, I hadn't noticed the crowd pushing us until we stood directly beneath the fire escape.

"I'll do it." I knew what to expect, so it would hurt less. Sure it would. "Here goes nothing."

I jumped to reach the bottom rung on the ladder, and the second my fingers closed over the metal, pain flared through my nerve endings. I yelped as I dropped to my feet and tucked my hand against my chest.

"Are you okay?" Midas pried my fingers open. "The skin is red, but there's no wound."

We had to get into that club, and this was our best shot. I couldn't abandon it without trying, even if it meant giving Ambrose the upper hand. "That ward means business."

"Can you break it?"

Midas had witnessed me work small magics a few times now, so I wasn't surprised he would ask.

"Give me a second." I slung my hand to ease the throb. "I'll see what I can do."

Stepping back, he gave me room to work, but I only needed to hide my communication with Ambrose.

Take it down. I felt his thrill in the permission. *We need to get in there.*

Ambrose, acting as if he was the one doing me a favor and not just given permission to gorge at an all-you-can-eat buffet, slithered around the ladder and latched on with his greedy fingers.

I hit my knees with no memory of dropping, and coughed up smoke.

What the actual hell?

Sadly, I still felt my connection to Ambrose, but the shadow was gone. *Poof.* Vanished.

The ward packed a nasty punch all right, and it must be part siphon too. Anyone who touched it would get shocked back as a warning, but it would also leech enough of their energy to make them think twice about trying again.

A reserve of energy stolen from its victims must be what powered the ward. Self-sustaining workings were critical on areas of this size. Otherwise, the maintenance required made them impractical for everyday use.

Ambrose was a creature of energy, magical energy, and it had drained him to the point he retreated to recharge. Even after hours of sneaking tastes from passersby. The shadow had failed me, its hunger not up to the task, and I seesawed between the stark hit of joy I experienced whenever Ambrose was checked by an outside force and frustration my best chance at getting in had gone off to lick its metaphysical wounds.

"Leave it." Midas made it an order, and he helped me to my feet. "We'll find another way."

"There is no other way."

"The kids are the priority." He brushed the hair from my eyes. "Let's focus on finding them."

The gwyllgi teens would be the first of many victims if we didn't get this drug under control, but I couldn't do a frakking thing without Ambrose, and he wouldn't tackle that ward again tonight if I gave him an entire box of La Madeline au Truffle straight from Danish chocolatier Fritz Knipschildt's own kitchen.

The reminder of the pack's involvement did make me curious. "Who told you about Faete?"

"The pack frequents bars all over the city, and we tip well."

And in return, I imagined, the bartenders called when pack kids found trouble or trouble found them.

We linked hands, more to keep track of one another in the crowd than for the romance, but it was still nice.

An hour slipped through our fingers, but we combed every inch of Crescent Avenue Northeast with no luck. About to expand our search, I noticed a young woman standing still as others swirled around her.

"Hey." I tugged on his arm. "That girl looks familiar."

Zeroing in on the crowd, he picked the lone sober face from among the dizzying crush. "That's Krista."

"Looks like she's alone." I began weaving through the bodies, dragging him in my wake. "She can have the pleasure of ratting out her friends."

Drugs were just as illegal for para teens as human ones. Even a blip in their control could cost someone their life. These kids were getting *spanked* once Tisdale got ahold of them. Their parents wouldn't be too thrilled either.

"She smells strange." Moving into position beside her, he filled his lungs then sneezed at the smell. "Not like pack."

"Maybe that's why you and Ares couldn't find them earlier?"

"Maybe," he allowed, "but the implications are dangerous."

Aside from the obvious inability to track them, I didn't get his worry. "What do you mean?"

"The core Atlanta pack is enormous, and its satellite packs are healthy sizes too. Even I don't know all the extended members by name or face. I know them by smell, though. This drug, if that's what's causing this, has erased the one form of identity guaranteed to keep them safe."

"Are they in immediate danger?"

"No adult gwyllgi will attack a child unless the adult is sick, but older teens exist in the limbo of pack hierarchy. All it takes is one aggressive adult who thinks they've discovered a trespasser for blood to spill. It's our nature, and it's usually a death sentence for the younger gwyllgi."

The unwelcome news set a clock ticking over our heads, as if we needed more incentive.

"Krista," I called over the noise. "Hey, girl."

Whipping her head toward my voice, Krista beamed for the split second before she recognized me. Then it registered I wasn't whoever had earned that smile, and the flush drained from her cheeks. Panic bright in her eyes, she bolted around the corner.

"I've had a long day," I grumped, "but I don't smell that bad, do I?"

Midas leaned in, ran his nose along my jaw, his breath warm on my skin. "You smell like—"

"Woo later." I ducked out of his reach then broke into a jog. "Chase now."

Unable to stop the grin from spreading, I didn't fight it. The hunt was in my blood, the same as his.

Nudging me aside, he took point and followed his nose. Now that he had a lock on Krista's scent, he could track her. She must be terrified to have Midas on her trail, but she wasn't doing herself any favors by running.

"That girl should try out for the Olympics," I panted. "Are you sure she's not a gazelle shifter?"

Laughter tickling the back of his throat, he called back to me, "Our foremothers ate most of those before they migrated to Earth from Faerie."

I stumbled, but then I narrowed my eyes on his back. "You aren't serious."

Pretending not to hear me, he didn't answer, just kept shouldering through the masses.

"They were people, right?" As I hit my stride, my breathing evened out. "You ate people?"

"I've eaten people," he confessed, now that I was at his elbow. "How about you?"

"Um, no." I had devoured victims' essences but not their flesh. "I don't eat people. I *am* people."

"You live through hard enough times, and that ceases to matter."

Without knowing his age or much of his history, I was in no place to judge him for what he had done to survive.

"People are safe from me as a food group unless they start coming chocolate-covered or bacon-wrapped." I elbowed him in the ribs. "Then all bets are off."

The look he shot me gave me ideas about other things I wouldn't mind tasting covered in chocolate.

Ambrose wavered into being, a watery echo of his usual self, to protest the dirty turn of my thoughts.

That's what you get for listening in, perv.

Krista led us a good mile away from the clubs in Midtown before she stumbled and tipped into a wall. I put on a burst of speed, but she was too far ahead, and I couldn't catch her without Ambrose to loan me extra oomph.

As if coming to the same conclusion, Midas unleashed his inner beast, let it claim his skin, and used those precious seconds while Krista recovered to corner her. Carefully, he took her wrist in his jaws while he waited on me to catch up to them.

"I'm sorry." Krista went limp in his grip and sagged over his furry shoulder. "I didn't mean to do it."

Midas didn't see the hand she slipped into her pocket, but I did, and I lunged for her. I captured her wrist, twisted it, and watched a hypodermic needle full of goddess knows what hit the pavement. Faete, most likely.

"Cooperate," I warned her. "This will go easier if you do."

The girl went limp in my arms, her broken sobs heart-wrenching, but I didn't loosen my grip. I didn't trust the calculation in her eyes. Or the fact that, despite all the noise she was making, her cheeks remained free of tears. Her sniffles were dry, forced, and touching her made my skin crawl.

A quick swipe from my modified pen bound Krista's wrists behind her back with a sigil, and I checked her twice before pivoting toward Midas. Scarcely breathing, he watched the scene unfold. The blank slate in his crimson eyes had me tasting cold fear in back of my throat.

FIVE

The last few seconds flashed through Midas's mind, as brilliant as lightning, and he glued his paws to the asphalt while his brain chewed over how those few seconds had changed his life. Forever.

The seismic shift in his chest, in his perception of the world, happened so *fast* it gave him whiplash.

"Midas?"

Krista seeks comfort from him, from pack, her fingers digging in his fur.

"Did she get you?"

Hadley tackles her, binds her hands behind her back, sets her aside and away from him.

"Midas."

Krista sits on the pavement as the wrongness wells in her and sobs as if her world is ending.

And then his shifted on its axis with a groan that reverberated through the marrow in his bones.

The urge to bristle at Krista's rough treatment had stung the length of his spine, that he recalled clearly.

This is Hadley, he had reminded himself. *My mate wouldn't hurt my people.*

His...mate.

Hadley was his mate.

"Midas?" Hadley knelt beside him, her eyes wide and dark. "Did she get you?"

The weight of his revelation made him dizzy, and his stomach lurched until he tasted bile, but at least time had snapped taut again.

"Shift for me." She cupped his chin. "I can't see a frakking thing through all this fur."

Magic spilled out of his pores and splashed onto her hand where she touched him, but she didn't flinch.

"Where did she pop you?" She reached for the hem of his tee and yanked it over his head without ceremony. "There's no mark." She smoothed her trembling hands over his bare torso. *"Where is the mark?"*

"Hadley." He captured her wrists and restrained her before she stripped him naked in the alley. "She didn't inject me."

"Thank the goddess." Her eyes slid closed for a long moment. "I thought I didn't see it in time. I thought I was too late. I thought..."

"I'm okay." He drew her against him. "Thank you."

With his realization ringing in his ears, he had let his guard down, and it almost cost him dearly.

"I can't breathe." Her nails dug into his shoulder blades. "My chest hurts too much."

"Sorry." He relaxed his grip. "Am I holding you too tight?"

"No." She hauled him back, nestled her face into his chest. "It's not that."

"Adrenaline," he murmured, tightening his arms around her until the shakes quit. "It will pass."

"Not adrenaline either." Voice muffled by his chest, she braced as wild laughter punched through her. "Terror." She tipped back her head. "Unmitigated terror."

Holding Hadley was no hardship, but they had to figure out what Krista had done, where the other teens had gone. He just couldn't find it in him to let Hadley go. He might have held her all night, marveling at what he had discovered, if she hadn't rallied the strength to release him.

"All right." Her tears left his skin damp. "I'm good now."

They rose together, neither of them steady, and faced the girl who had folded her legs under her, lotus style.

"Where did I go wrong?" She leaned forward, invested in the answer. "The dry eyes, right? I've never been good at crying on demand."

Hadley's voice rang clear. "Who are you?"

"I'm Krista." Rolling her eyes, she channeled her best teenage rebellion voice. "Who else?"

Midas's gut tensed with the possibilities, and he sank power into the question. *"Who are you?"*

"I am...embarrassed to have been caught, that's who." Her jaw set. "I'll have to do better next time."

The girl shimmered, warped, and a muscular black horse sprouted where she had been sitting.

The magical restraints had either broken or had been bound to Krista's skin. Either way, they were gone.

"A púca," Midas growled and jerked Hadley aside. "Get back."

"I thought those were fluffy bunnies." She punched her hand into the night and withdrew a sword. "That is *not* a fluffy bunny."

The mare rose on its hind legs and pawed the air, walking forward to force them back, then broke into a punishing gallop that smashed the addled partygoers under its hooves.

"I have to shift." He let the magic sting his skin. "It's the only way to take it down."

"She's coven," Hadley said, the request for permission clear.

Seven hearts. That's what they owed Natisha. This might be the first.

"We honor the bargain," Midas bit out, then surrendered himself with a throat-rattling song of mourning for the girl the witchborn fae coven had killed for the use of her body.

The clopping noises gave away the púca's direction. Hadley would have had no issue tracking it alone.

Anger scorched his tongue, and he snarled his hatred for Krista's killer with every exhalation. Saliva pooled in his mouth, and he wanted nothing more than to rip out the creature's heart for what it had done to a child of the pack.

An equine scream reverberated between the buildings where the púca had fled, and Midas shot ahead of Hadley.

"This belong to you?" Bishop stood with his hand fisted in the horse's flowing mane. "You don't see too many of these on this side of Faerie, thank the old gods and the new."

"She's coven," Hadley confirmed from behind him. "She was wearing a pack member. A teen girl."

"That so." With a pulse of blistering magic, he unraveled the horse, its shape twisting and writhing until it shrank into a snarling man. "You killed a girl for her skin?"

"I've killed lots of girls for their skins," he spat. "What's one more?"

"Your job was to lure the pack teens to Greenleaf." Hadley made it a statement, not a question. "Why?"

"Why not?" The man twisted in Bishop's hold. "You're not pack. What does it matter to you?"

"Hadley is the future potentate of this city," Bishop purred next to the man's ear. "She's not as forgiving as Linus, and he's not exactly known for looking the other way while his people are preyed upon."

Midas snapped his head toward her, and the hard set of her delicate features almost convinced him Bishop was right.

"No one preys on the kids in my city." Streetlight glinted off the wicked blade in her small hand. "Tell me what I want to know, and I'll show you mercy." She stuck her empty hand into the darkness and drew her second sword. "Or I'll gut you now and figure it out for myself."

"Kill me." The man lifted his chin. "I won't betray my coven."

A kick from Bishop took out his knees, and he hit the pavement in a kneeling position.

Knuckles gone white where she gripped her blades, she clenched her hands tighter. "Where are the other gwyllgi teens?"

"As good as dead," the man spat, "if they aren't already."

"Last chance," she offered, a fine tremor in her voice Midas doubted anyone else would have noticed.

"You will die for this," he hissed. "My kind will wear your skin as—"

Hadley walked up to him, rested a blade on either side of his throat, and cut without further hesitation.

The scissorlike motion, fueled with inhuman strength, lopped off his head and left Bishop holding it by the hair.

"Goddess," she breathed and swallowed convulsively. "That bastard."

A final act of cruelty had stamped a vicious smile on the man, and death had frozen it there.

Except it wasn't his face but Krista's that gazed at them with eyes gone dull and lifeless.

The petite body collapsed in a heap, a *best friends* necklace slung free across the asphalt, and fresh blood wet the parched road while Hadley stared and stared at half of a jagged heart-shaped charm.

"We have to move fast," Bishop said softly, a reminder of their gruesome bargain. "We need the heart."

Midas traded skins in a flash of red magic and approached them.

"Give me some room." She wet her lips. "This is going to get messy."

"You don't have to do it alone." Midas didn't budge. "We're in this together."

Hadley, who was the bravest, strongest, most spirited woman he had ever met, couldn't face him.

"You're not a monster." He sank his fingers into the curls at her nape. "Tonight, you slayed one."

That earned him a slight tilt of her head, but she ignored him in favor of Bishop.

"Claim the heart like we practiced," Bishop urged her. "I can get it to the box before it stops beating."

"It's not like we practiced," she whispered, voice breaking. "I've killed in the heat of battle, to defend myself, to protect others, but this..." Her throat worked as she struggled to swallow. "Never like this."

"I know, kid." He cursed under his breath. "I know."

"Let me borrow one of your swords." Midas held out his hand. "Let me do this for you."

The offer made his gut rebel, but Krista was his, and he owed it to her to make her death count.

"You heard Linus." Hadley sheathed one but kept the other. "Natisha set the terms with me in mind."

Midas fought the growl, but he failed to throttle it. "This is not what he meant."

"We can't chance it." She sliced Krista open using a precise Y incision then set to work opening her ribs to reach the delicate organs underneath. Hands steady as a surgeon, she freed the heart, and it pulsed in her hand as she passed it off to Bishop. "There." She stared blankly at the corpse and vanished her final blade. "Go."

The shadows licked over Bishop as he walked through them, and his footsteps faded with him.

"I need to call the cleaners." Hadley's rock-steady hand shook until she dropped her phone. "Frakking hell."

"I'll do it." Midas took her phone and sent the message. "There."

Switching phones, he texted Ares with an order to round up more enforcers to finish sweeping the clubs and surrounding area for the remaining teens.

How many times had he hit the clubs in search of kids being kids? Or ducked in and out of every bar with a reputation for serving minors? Or checked cabins for squatters and found teens using them for sex? He couldn't count them. They were a monthly occurrence, the result of hormones and bad decision making.

Tonight should have gone the same way, with the row of youthful offenders lined up in front of his mom to await their punishment. Now he had to live with wondering if he had brought more enforcers if Krista would have been found in time, if the other kids would have been home already, if he could have spared Hadley the nightmares this guaranteed her.

"Thanks." Her wobbly smile didn't fool him. "One down, six to go."

Before he could think what to say, she lurched to one side and threw up everything in her stomach.

The incessant chatter of her teeth, the loose way she swayed on her palms, shot alarm through him.

"You're going into shock." He caught her and rubbed her back. "We need to get you to Abbott."

The girl had already been dead when Hadley killed her and cut out her heart, the coven saw to that, but Midas couldn't blame Hadley for struggling to process what she had done when Krista's likeness stared at them from where Bishop had set her head on the pavement.

"Abbott will fuss at me." She sucked in air, great heaving gasps. "I don't want to be fussed at tonight."

"I'll take you home then." He got his arm around her before her knees buckled. "How about that?"

"I don't want to bring this home," she said, her voice empty. "Goddess, I don't know what I want."

"I have an idea." He scooped her up then sat in the empty street. "Let me place a call first."

"Okay." She buried her face in his shirt. "Okay."

Chin on top of her head, he held her while he made arrangements for still more enforcers to meet them and claim the body. It wasn't Krista, not really, but the witchborn fae wearing her skin was all he had to give her parents.

GWYLLGI REQUIRED NO WATERPROOF TENTS, insulated sleeping bags, or crackling fires to enjoy a night beneath the stars, but they often mated other species less at home in the forest. For that reason, the pack had an unusual number of permanent campsites on their property for mates and children less suited to exposure to the elements. As of last fall, there were even three isolated one-room cabins designed to fade into the surrounding trees.

A good third of the pack had fought his mom on building the cabins, small as they might be. The permanent campsites were already an eyesore, they argued. The den was meant to be a wilderness oasis, a place to shake a long week of working downtown out of your fur. Not walk manicured trails or choke on pungent mosquito repellent.

Mom decreed the pack had to accommodate all its members, and then she bit anyone who dared oppose her vision.

There was a very good reason why Tisdale Kinase was alpha of the largest gwyllgi pack in the Southeast.

Sharp teeth were only the tip of it.

Tonight, with Hadley's mental wellbeing hanging on by a thread, he was grateful for the cabins. He carried Hadley into the closest one, woke her for a shower, then heated up chicken soup from a can in the pantry. She was asleep on the bed, bundled up in an oversized towel large enough to dry a wet gwyllgi, before the first bubble broke the surface in the pot on the stove.

Guilt churned in his gut over leaving Midtown before the teens were located, but Mom was always telling him half of being an alpha was learning when to delegate. Ares was his right hand, and the enforcers were highly trained members of elite teams. As much as it twisted him up inside, he had to believe he'd made the right call. Hadley teetered on the breaking point, and it was his duty—no, his privilege—to help her regain her balance.

After pouring the soup into a bowl for himself, he took it outside to eat on the dirt porch so as not to waste it.

"What happened?"

The fact his mother had hunted him down was about as surprising as the sun rising in the east.

"Hadley paid the first installment on our bargain with Natisha." He stirred the soup but didn't eat. "She's in a bad way right now."

"I'm sorry." She joined him on the porch, not caring if her neat mint-green pantsuit got dirty. "Do you think she'll cross the finish line?"

Break a deal with the fae, and the bargain came undone, for starters. But that was only fair. From there, they decided how much was owed to them for the betrayal and how to collect what was due.

Hadley had no choice but to cross the finish line, or Ford would die, and Natisha would get her chance to have what Linus had hinted she wanted in the first place: Hadley.

"She's stronger than she looks." He picked the carrots from the bowl and flicked them to the ground. "It will cost her, but she'll make it."

"I wish I had never summoned her," Mom muttered, meaning Natisha. "I should have let it alone."

"Ford would be dead if you had," he pointed out, for all the good it would do.

"I don't want this to break Hadley." She drew her legs to her chest then wrapped her arms around them. "I don't want you to hate me if it does."

"I could have paid a tithe of forgiveness and sent Natisha home." He started to work tossing the noodles. "I'm the one who chose to bargain with her."

"And Hadley chose to bargain for you."

Her inflection, the gentle cadence of her voice, sent his gaze seeking hers. "What do you mean?"

"She made this choice, the same as you." She dug her toes in the dirt. "Don't blame yourself."

"She saved me, and Ford." Left with only thin broth and chicken, he spooned up the salty cubes of meat. "Natisha didn't want anything I had to offer."

"Yes, she did, and she got it too." Mom leaned her head against the cabin. "There's something about Hadley."

Midas put the bowl down and gave her his full attention.

"Linus trusts her, and I trust Linus, but I get the same feeling around her as I do around him."

"They're both necromancers," he reminded her. "They're both bonded to…"

"Exactly," she murmured. "Bonded to what, exactly?"

The taunting Hadley received every now and again made him think his mother wasn't the only curious one. He didn't have to reach far back in his memory for the most recent incident.

"Why did she call you shadow child?"

"All potentates have wraiths."

"You're not Potentate yet, and that's not an answer." He spun it around on her. *"Have you bonded?"*

"Yes."

Unsure what he expected, her candor surprised him. "You have a wraith?"

"Remember when you told me there were things about your past you couldn't share with me?"

"Yes."

"Remember when I said I'm in the same boat?" She clenched her fists at her sides. "This falls under that heading."

A sudden chill raised gooseflesh down his arms, but he still argued on Hadley's and Linus's behalf. "You've met Cletus."

"I've met a few wraiths in my time, and they're nothing but smoke without orders." She pursed her lips. "Either Cletus is self-aware, or Linus is the best damn wraith pilot to ever walk the earth." She cut him a sharp look. "Have you seen Hadley's wraith?"

"No."

"You need to figure out her secret, and quick."

"It won't change anything."

"As you might recall, I was mated to your father." She patted his hand where it rested on the bowl. "I am familiar with the unbreakable bond our kind feels with their mate." The bowl fell from his hands and splashed its contents onto the dirt. "I'm your mother. Did you think you could hide it from me?"

Midas piled dirt over the mess he made. "No?"

"You're protecting her." She hummed. "It's good to see both your halves in sync again."

Because she was also his alpha, and her warning could be construed as a threat, he had to admit, "I'm not sure what I would do if you threatened her."

"Silly boy." She rose gracefully and didn't bother dusting her pants. "She's your mate. That makes her pack." She bent down and kissed his cheek. "What should worry you is what I would do if someone else threatened her."

"I love you." He dragged her into a hug. "I don't tell you often enough."

"No, you don't." She laughed in his ear. "Children never do."

"We need to talk about what happened tonight."

"Yes, we do." She started down the path toward the den. "But first, I need to speak to Krista's parents."

Rising, Midas took a hesitant step after her. "I can go with you."

"Stay with Hadley." She kept walking. "You can give Krista's parents the details when they're ready."

The dueling urges to perform his duty to his pack or to perform his duty to his mate left him jittery in his skin.

"Stay with Hadley," Mom called back. "That's an order."

The release of his obligation sagged through his shoulders, and his instincts roared for him to return to Hadley.

Entering the cabin, he placed his dishes in the sink then crawled into bed.

He fell asleep with his nose pressed into Hadley's nape, but still the nightmares found him.

SIX

Mumbling woke me from a dead sleep, and I jerked upright in a strange bed in a strange place.

No, no, no. This can't be happening. Not again.

I clutched the fabric covering my chest with a shaking hand, puzzled by its nubby texture.

A towel.

I was wearing a towel, the material damp along the edges from the shower I had taken...at a cabin.

The owner of that voice finally pierced the panic clouding my brain, and I almost sobbed with relief.

Ambrose, leaning against the wall, watched me tremble and tear up while shaking his head at my hysterics.

For reasons that eluded me, he felt I ought to trust him to look out for *our* best interests. When he was on good behavior, it was tempting. But that never lasted for long. Then he went right back to building his stores, tugging on his leash, and attempting to sever our ties through any means necessary.

And yet, he still took offense when I side-eyed his motives.

Happy to turn away from Ambrose, I pushed the damp hair off

Midas's brow. He turned his face into my palm, his distress easing, but he didn't rouse. He kept talking in that low, rich voice thick with an accent I doubted modern Gaelic speakers could parse.

He had fallen asleep curved around me, but I had to move. I couldn't bear the stillness any longer.

Untangling from him with care, I slipped off the bed and peeked out the front windows to discover forest spreading in all directions.

We were at the den.

Midas had taken me home with him.

The warmth spilling through me chilled as I recalled what I had done.

Acid rose up the back of my throat, and I padded onto the dirt porch where I dry-heaved until my eyes watered from the strain. Sure. That was why I couldn't stop crying.

This whole time, I had made Ambrose out to be the bad guy. He had committed murder. Several times. I had no issue with accepting half the blame, since I had been the power-hungry idiot who invited possession in the first place, but it had been his hands with blood on them. He had always done the actual deed.

After this, I could no longer tally myself in a different column.

I had killed in the line of duty as Linus's apprentice, and it had been justified, but this was an execution. I could have made my peace with that, the man deserved to die for what he did to Krista, but it was different killing a child on her knees and then slicing her open to harvest her innards.

Desperate to get out of my head, I checked my phone and found texts from Bishop, Remy, Ford, and Linus.

That last one broke me out in cold sweat, even though he had negotiated on Midas's behalf and was fully aware of the debt we owed for Lord's recovery. He knew what it would take to hold up our end, but what we had agreed to do struck me as wrong on so many levels I felt guilty at the prospect of confessing to him.

The phone rang in my hand, and I switched it to silent before it woke Midas. "Hello?"

"Hey." Adelaide came off as distracted. "Linus mentioned you had a recipe for horchata I might want."

"Horchata?" I rubbed my eyes to make certain I wasn't still dreaming. "When did he tell you that?"

"About an hour ago." She slammed something shut. "I've gone through every drawer in the kitchen, and I can't find mine. Gramma Dietrich swore by it, but ugh."

"I do have a recipe." I downloaded it off the *A Warg Called Wanda* blog. "It's not something I would pass on to the grandkids, but it will do in a pinch."

Wanda was helping me learn my way around my own kitchen through her online tutorials. What I loved about her was how often she set things, and herself, on fire. Which, now that I thought about it, might not be the best credentials. Her recipes always turned out, though. Maybe not great, but they were edible. As defined by wargs, anyway.

"Can you email it to me?" Adelaide begged. "Dad put in a special request, and I'd hate to let him down."

"No problem." I might link her to the blog too. She would probably get a laugh out of it. "How's life?"

The awkward segue made me flush, but Adelaide didn't make me feel lame for my rusty social skills.

"Your brother is driving me nuts. He has started and stopped four projects around the house in the last two weeks. I get his job is demanding, and I understand he works all hours, but come on. The man has serious commitment issues. He's always hopping to the next shiny thing that catches his eye."

I bit the inside of my cheek until I tasted blood to keep from agreeing with her.

Boaz did have serious commitment issues, and I wasn't convinced their engagement would be enough to hold him in check forever without a deeper investment on both their parts. But I wasn't about to suggest she put stock in him when he had been such a miser with his heart up to this point.

As much as it pained me, I had come to terms with the fact Boaz was a grown man, and his romantic problems were for him to solve. All I had ever done was make things worse when I meddled, for him and the poor girl involved. This time, that girl was my sister, and I didn't want to see her hurt.

And yes, that made their relationship sound...icky.

But, and it was a big *but*, they weren't blood related, despite the fact I was stuck in the middle with distant claims to siblingship on them both.

Frakking hell, life was complicated.

Addie chattered about her dad, her life, my brother, for a good half hour. I made appropriate noises in the right places, and we ended the call with the promise to Netflix a show together soon. Not until the call ended did I realize how much better I felt without breathing a word of my problems to her.

Just having someone with normal issues reach out to vent made mine somehow less.

A vibration had me checking my phone on reflex, which torpedoed my plausible deniability, but thankfully it was just Addie bullying me as if we were actual siblings instead of a technicality.

>> Say it.

>> Come on. Don't be shy.

Um.

>> I will call you back.

I am enough.

>> You typed that. Out loud this time.

A grin sneaked up on me, and I laughed softly.

You don't know that.

>> I'm your big sister. That gives me mystical powers to peer into the great unknown.

Fear she was superimposing me over her Hadley lingered in the back of my mind, and I didn't know how to fix it. I didn't know where I began in her mind and her real sister ended.

>> *Don't try to deny it. I'm marrying your ox of a brother, remember? We're sisters. Deal with it.*

"I am enough," I whispered to make her happy.

There. Done. Weirdo.

>> *Love you, sis.*

More tears overflowed my eyes and spilled down my cheeks. *"Love you too."*

While it was still on my mind, I linked her to the recipe and the video, and I hoped it made her smile.

"Trouble sleeping?" Midas leaned against the doorframe. "I heard you moving around out here."

Gwyllgi ears being what they were, I was willing to bet he had heard more than that.

"I couldn't sleep." I held up my phone. "Then I saw all this."

"Your sister called," he said, reading the top caller ID entry. "She's worried about you?"

"Linus must be," I huffed. "He's left me messages, but I haven't answered him yet."

"He set your sister on you?" Midas laughed softly. "That's brutal, exactly what I would expect from him."

"He's not so bad." A year ago, I might have fallen over dead imagining myself defending him, but I was a different person then. "He's done a lot for me."

"He's a good guy." Midas shoved off the doorframe. "Want to go for a walk?"

The warm night beckoned louder than the darkened cabin, even if I only wore a towel. Out here, it's not like I had to worry about running into anyone. "Why not?"

Plucking my phone out of my hand, he set it on the windowsill before we set out.

"I'm not one of those girlfriends who's always on her phone, am I?"

"You're only on your phone when you have to be." He draped an arm around my shoulders and tucked me against his side. "All things considered, I'm worse than you are with all the mediating squabbles."

"Just making sure you don't feel neglected."

The path he chose wound beneath pines whose plush needles choked the moonlight overhead.

"And if I do?" He cut me a look. "Feel neglected."

"I would probably offer to pamper you." I edged in front of him in case I needed a head start. "Trim your nails, rub your belly, Q-tip your ears. That kind of thing."

"I get the feeling you don't take me seriously."

Hand over my heart, I whirled on him. "I take you as seriously as a shampoo commercial."

"I'll count to five." Crimson splashed onto his feet. "Use your time wisely."

"What do you mean five?" I backed up a step, pulse thundering. "Midas?"

Magic pulled him under, and he reemerged with his tail swishing.

"Oh crap."

Spinning on my heel, I shot down the path as fast as my feet would carry me.

"I'm barefoot," I screamed at him. "And in a towel. In the woods. With the ticks and bugs."

A throaty baying rose behind me, and the hairs lifted down my nape.

"Frak, frak, frak."

A campsite sat to my right, but no one was there, and who would intervene between Midas and me?

No one, that's who.

Ahead, across a field, a glass house glittered under the moon, but it was far from a sanctuary. It was the alpha's house, the fancy one where guests to pack lands were welcomed to keep them out of the den. The true den. Not the façade shown to outsiders.

"I am not running to your momma to get away from you," I panted. "Forget it."

Sure, I had put off family dinner, but this was not the way to force an introduction.

Whooping laughter filled the woods to my right, and a young man bounded into view. "Go left."

The bright joy in his eyes convinced me to trust him. "Thanks."

"Make him work for it." He clapped until my ears rang. "I'll hold him off if I can."

A flash of light caught the corner of my eye, and then I heard two gwyllgi engaged in play fighting. Or so I hoped. It sounded only slightly less terrifying than real fighting, but I didn't dare slow down to check.

"Right," a girl called from a low-slung limb. "Go right."

Out of breath, I lifted my hand and did as instructed, veering off the beaten path.

A softer but ferocious growl made me think she had shifted to buy me time too.

"Left," a girl said as a young couple bounded toward me. "Then right at the fork."

A quick nod was all I had left for them, but I followed their instructions and came out in a glen with pine straw matting the ground and a rustic cabin backed up against a ravine. The only way out was the way I had come, and there were growls ringing out in that direction.

"I can't believe I listened to them." I smacked myself on the forehead. "They led me straight into a trap."

The door swung open, and a tiny blond boy peeked around the corner. "Hadwee?"

"Yes." I approached him slowly. "I'm Hadley."

"Here." He stuck out his pudgy hand in expectation. "Here."

I took it, noting its softness and dampness, and let him guide me into the cabin.

"Hadwee, come." He tugged on me. "Come."

The tiniest coconspirator yet brought me to a living room big enough for a family of twelve to enjoy one another's company without being on top of each other.

"Daddeee." He ditched me and toddled off toward a lean male perched on the arm of a sofa. "Hi."

"Good work." He lifted his son onto his hip in a smooth motion that spoke of practice. "You get a cookie."

"Cookicee." The boy clapped then planted a wet kiss on the male's cheek. "Mwah."

Out of place, I didn't know what to do with myself. "I'm not intruding, am I?"

"A beautiful woman dressed in a towel is never out of place."

A cushion flew across the room and smacked him in the head while the boy giggled and wriggled.

"Ignore my mate." A curvy woman with natural hair kissed the boy on the cheek and popped the male on the butt. "He means well." She crossed to me and looked me up and down. "Hadley Whitaker."

"That's my name." I checked to make sure my towel remained tucked. "Who are you guys?"

"I'm Kate, he's Sam, and that tiny terror is Samzilla." She shrugged. "It's catchier than Sam Jr."

"As a fan of the Godzilla franchise, I'm inclined to agree with you."

"Rawr." Samzilla hooked his tiny fingers into claws. "*Rawr.*"

"You're on bath duty." She squared off with her mate. "No bubbles in my hallway this time."

"Bubbles?" Sam pulled on an innocent face. "In the hall?"

Samzilla hid his face in his father's neck and squealed with laughter.

"That's what you've got to look forward to, if you mate into this pack. Most of the time Sam is the one who comes out soaked and Samzilla is dry as a bone."

"Not to be rude," I cut in, nervous about Midas zeroing in on me, "but why am I here?"

"Midas is hunting you." Her eyes twinkled. "You don't want to be out there where he can find you, do you?"

The answer took a moment to form, and it was too late by then.

"You don't know how happy this makes me." She took me by the hand. "How happy it makes all of us."

Better to play dumb than plant a dirty foot in my mouth. "That I'm being hunted?"

"He's courting you." Kate chuckled and hauled me into a large bedroom. "That's a big deal."

Especially for Midas.

For a second, I couldn't tell if she spoke the words, or if I only imagined hearing them.

"You're shorter and thinner than me, but I love a good maxi dress, and I have safety pins." She opened the closet. "Blue, red, or animal print?"

"I'm not picky."

"Then animal print it is. My mother-in-law keeps buying safari themes for me, and this is the best excuse I'm ever going to have for getting rid of one." She pulled out a long dress with thin straps and a high waist. "Zebra okay?"

The print was so loud, I could barely hear her over it. "Zebra is fine."

"Good." She tugged it over my head then let it cascade to my ankles before reaching into the neck of the dress. She unfastened the knot on the towel, which dropped onto my feet. "I'll get this washed and put back in the cabin."

The communal dressing area in my previous job meant I didn't mind a little public nudity among friends. "Thanks."

"Hold still, and I'll get you pinned so you don't flash anyone." She caught my eye, hers smiling. "Unless you want to, that is."

"Um, no." I kicked the towel away. "I'm good."

About the time she announced me done, I noticed her angle her head to one side.

"He's here." She took a few steps to the left then back to the right. "Where do I hide?"

The urge to pinch myself and make absolutely certain I wasn't dreaming surfaced again. "Why do you have to hide exactly?"

"Do you think I want him to know I aided and abetted you?" She scoffed. "Please." She flipped a hand at me. "Samzilla let you in. I just didn't kick you back out." She winked. "If anyone asks, this was all his fault."

"Duck into the bathroom with your family." Catching the spirit, I walked out with her. "I'll handle Midas."

Once she was hunkered down with her mate and son, I strolled to the front door.

Midas, proving gwyllgi had excellent hearing, said, "Knock, knock."

In my sweetest voice, I called out, "Who's there?"

"Midas."

"Hmm." I inched closer. "Midas who?"

"Midas well let me in. I'm not going anywhere."

"Hey!" I flung open the door. "I'm the funny one in this relationship."

"Then you only have yourself to blame for rubbing off on me."

Folding my arms over my chest, I inched closer. "So, you admit it."

"That you're a bad influence?" He tilted his head. "Yes."

Barefoot, I kicked him in the shin. "That I'm funny."

"I would say *funny looking*, like I used to tell my sister, but we both know you're beautiful."

"Aww."

Midas slid his gaze behind me. "You might as well come out, Kate."

"I'm not here," she sing-songed. "Go back to being adorable together."

Crooking his arm, he held his elbow out for me. "Can I walk you to the cabin?"

"You shifted and chased me through the woods. I'm not certain I feel safe with you alone in the dark."

A flicker of...something...pinched his features before he wiped them smooth.

Lately, he had been smiling easier, laughing quicker. I had almost forgotten how somber he could be.

"I might require an escort," I kept going, desperate to dig myself out of the hole. "Samzilla?"

True to his mother's word, he emerged from his bath dry as a bone. "Hadwee!"

Sam squished when he walked as he trailed his son, and he left wet footprints behind him.

The kid bulleted at me, naked as a jaybird, and I knew what I had to do.

I scooped him up in a practiced swing, setting him on my hip, the way I had with my little brother.

"This is my champion of choice." I checked with Kate and Sam. "As long as his parents don't mind."

"Well..." Kate slanted her eyes toward Sam. "It's not like he's had his bath, so why not?"

Leaning in, I whispered to Samzilla, "Will you protect me in the scary woods?"

"Yep." He wriggled to get down. "I big *grr*."

Reddish-pink magic swirled around his feet, and he splashed in it until it covered his head. His giggles were infectious, and I couldn't help smiling. And, okay, my heart melted with the magic when I saw my first baby gwyllgi.

About the size of a beagle, he was covered in downy gray fur like you expect to see on baby chicks.

"Oh. My. Goddess." I squealed, but I couldn't help it. "He's the most adorable thing I've ever seen."

"Gwyllgi pups *are* the most adorable thing you'll ever see," Kate agreed. "They're also nearly indestructible, thank God, because they're the sneakiest, most destructive, dare-deviling things you'll ever see too."

"Samzilla climbed one of the longleaf pines last week, testing out his claws." Sam all but glowed with pride. "He jumped from the highest limb. Just leapt into thin air. Totally fearless. I caught him, but it shaved a century off my life, if you know what I mean."

"Not fearless." Kate worked to sound scolding, but she smiled. "He knew his daddy would catch him."

The family moment washed over me, and I soaked in how life should be for all kids.

Loving parents, beautiful home, tightknit community.

What Kate said stuck with me. How Samzilla had taken a leap of faith, certain his father would always be there to catch him. How secure he must be to have that much trust so young. How confident in his parents' love for him. How bold to test his limits without fear because he hadn't learned to be afraid.

"I'll keep him out of trouble," Kate promised, and then shifted into her primal form.

Samzilla, taking his duty seriously, bounded between Midas and me the whole way back to our cabin. From there, Kate swooped in to tussle with him in the dirt then darted off with him in pursuit.

"They welcomed me into their home." I hadn't meant to say it, but it fell out of my mouth. "Why?"

"We're courting." Midas closed the gap Samzilla had kept between us. "You're as good as pack to them."

The squeaky barks grew more distant, but I could still hear the littlest gwyllgi challenging his mom.

Heart brimming from the encounter, I glowed with the aftermath of our game. "Are all pack families...?"

Loving. Happy. Nurturing.

"No." He eased behind me, slid his arms along my sides, and linked his wide hands above my navel. "Not all of them."

"Why did you chase me?" I twisted around to see his face. "I thought you were playing but..."

"The pack wanted to see you, and you needed to see them."

"You were bribing me with your pack." I elbowed him. "With Samzilla."

"I don't know why you've put off dinner with my mother, but I wanted to show you there's more to this pack than her." His shrug moved through my back. "Or me."

The pack embraced me for one reason, and one reason only: Midas.

These people loved him. That much was clear. The gwyllgi I interacted with on the regular at the Faraday were enforcers. They looked to Midas for leadership, not comfort. Not fun. They acted more like employees. This—coming to the den—was meeting the family.

And since he wanted me to see this, to experience it, he must be closing in on my vulnerable spots.

"You owe me a secret."

We had promised to exchange one every day, but we didn't always remember. Between the witchborn fae and Natisha's bargain, we had so much else on our minds it was hard not to let the small things slip.

Midas exhaled, warm across my nape. "I ate the last of the chicken wings."

"That's not a secret." I elbowed him again for good measure. "You had sauce all over your muzzle."

To hide the evidence of his crime, he had gone as far as to shift and gulp them down, bones and all.

"I also ate the last slice of tiramisu."

"The horror," I breathed. "You, sir, are a monster."

"Now tell me your secret."

"I prefer Coke to Pepsi."

"That's not a secret."

"Neither is the disappearing act my food has learned since you moved in with me."

We both tensed, and my stomach dropped into my feet.

Moved in sounded so…permanent. If he brushed it off as a sleepover, I didn't know what I would do.

"I like living with you." He pressed his lips to my throat. "I like sleeping with you."

Heat curled through my gut, and my chest went tight. "I've noticed."

Resting his forehead on my shoulder, he laughed softly. "I noticed you noticing."

Hard to resist the invitation pressing against my backside every dusk.

Very hard.

Very, very hard.

Phew, it was getting hot out here.

"Thank you for this." I leaned my cheek against the side of his head. "I needed it."

Angling his chin, he spoke against my throat. "How did you know what to do? With the heart?"

The pleasant buzz from the brush of his mouth on my skin helped me keep my nerve. "Bishop." From what I could tell, his stomach was cast iron. Mine? Not so much. "He sent me autopsy videos to watch."

I had thrown up. A lot. A *whole* lot. It was necessary, though. I couldn't afford to damage the hearts.

"I can't talk about it more right now." I swallowed the excess saliva pooling in my mouth. "That okay?"

"You don't have to ask me." He withdrew. "You know your limits."

No matter how much I wished otherwise, I blew out a sigh. "We can't hide out here forever."

"The city can wait." He guided me back into the cabin to the bed. "Just a little while longer."

SEVEN

The weight of the witchborn fae heart I had taken still pressed on mine when I woke at moonrise to Midas wrapping me in his arms like the tortilla to my burrito, but I had felt the burden shift during the day, so that Midas and I shared its load.

Mmm. Not gonna lie. A loaded burrito sounded good right about now.

Ambrose paced along the far wall and jerked his head toward me when he sensed my attention.

Last night had gone sideways, in all ways, and I wasn't sure what to do about any of it today.

Bishop owed me answers for his link to Blithe, given her connection to Greenleaf and Greenleaf's connection to Faete. We had to check in with Gayle to see how the Mendelsohn wargs were recovering. We also had to track down the missing teens, if they hadn't returned home.

The overwhelming urge to turn into Midas's warmth, bury my face in his chest, and forget the world hit with dizzying force.

Ambrose, who appeared unimpressed with the lack of people to watch in the forest, sat on the bed.

Without features, I couldn't read his expression, but I didn't need a clearer picture than what he fed me through our bond.

"We need to get moving," I murmured to him in reluctant agreement. "Break over."

Midas grumbled and turned onto his back. "All right."

"Thinking out loud." I grimaced as I shifted onto my opposite side to face him. "Sorry about that."

"I'm getting used to you waking me up at ungodly hours."

"I'm up at dusk like any respectable necromancer."

"That's the equivalent of Mom rising with the dawn." He squinted over at me. "You're both nuts."

"Goldie, you're the one who climbed into bed with me first. You invited yourself into my crazy. All I did was make room for you."

"You have soft sheets," he mumbled through a yawn, "and you smell nice."

"I could spritz my deodorant onto a set of sheets and have them dropped here for you."

"Grr."

"Did you just *say* grr?" I dug my fingers into his ribs until he laughed. "What kind of gwyllgi are you?"

"A sleepy one." He rolled off the bed to escape. "You think it's cute when Samzilla does it."

"Breathing is cute when Samzilla does it." I scooted into his spot. "I might have to save myself for him."

This time, the growl he turned on me was real. "You are *mine*."

The thrill zinging down my nerve endings would only encourage more dominant behavior, so I nipped it in the bud with reluctance. "I'm actually *mine*, but you're cute for thinking so."

The way he tugged on his hair would leave him with bald spots one day. "Hadley."

"You're jealous of a toddler. Let that sink in." I paused for effect. "He's like two. Or three. I suck guessing kids' ages." I should have let it drop, but I was having too much fun yanking Midas's tail. "Now his dad..." I chuckled evilly. "He's one hot—"

Midas pounced on me, pinned me to the bed, and I screamed until my throat burned with laughter.

A snarl revving in his throat, he delivered punishing bites to the tender skin of my neck while I kicked my legs and tickled his ribs until his chuckles interrupted his feasting. The way he smiled, so happy and light, I couldn't have resisted him if I tried. And I didn't. Not even a little.

I fused our mouths together and answered hunger for hunger. He lowered his hips into the cradle of mine, and I arched into his first thrust. The fabric of my dress, of his jeans, did nothing to hide his need. I twined my fingers in his hair and rocked against him, keeping him too busy to stop and overthink it.

"Hadley," he groaned. "I..."

"Shh." I visited stinging kisses along his jaw until I reached his favorite spot, and then I bit him until I tasted blood and sweat and his surrender. "I've got you."

Midas shuddered, his hips gone loose, and I wrapped my arms and legs around him to hold him through his release.

A long while later, when his breaths lengthened from jagged pants against my cheek, I leaned back and searched his face. "Are you okay?"

"I don't know." He attempted to withdraw, to escape, but I was stubborn, and I felt in my bones if he got away, he wouldn't come back. "I haven't..." He ducked his head. "It's been a long time since..."

"Oh, I didn't mean that." I licked the wound shaped like my teeth. "You're bleeding."

Midas touched his fingers to the side of his throat then examined the red stain.

"Oops?"

The crinkle of his forehead deepened, and then it relaxed. "You marked me."

"Yup." I didn't ease my grip, I tightened it. "What are you going to do about it?"

A gleam brightened his eyes, and he lowered his head, teeth on display, ready for payback.

Squirming beneath him, I could hardly wait for my turn.

Three punishing knocks rang through the small room as a visitor pounded on the door.

"Ignore them," I whispered, aware whoever was out there could hear. "Maybe they'll go away."

For a split second, Midas gave every sign of agreeing with me, no matter how fruitless the endeavor.

"We found the others," a miserably familiar voice called through the wood. "Can we talk?"

"I'll be right there," Midas yelled back, then kissed my forehead. "Stay put."

Threat or promise, I couldn't tell, but I was tempted enough to do as he asked. For now.

Wedging his body in the gap, Midas opened the door. "How are they?"

"They're in ICU," Ford growled. "The drug they snorted collapsed their lungs."

"Let me get dressed." Midas took a step inside the cabin. "I'll go with you to see their families."

"I have something to say." Ford pushed open the door, his gaze landing on me. "To both of you."

Just as before, Midas allowed Ford to run roughshod over him. Over us. And my stomach cramped.

The certainty Midas was about to resume his game of hot Hadley potato with Ford made me ill.

"You're my friend," Midas said, squaring off with him, "but you need to get out."

A slow inhale glided into a long exhale, and Ford glanced between us. Rather than leave, he spoke.

"I came to let you both know I'll be transferring to the Buckhead pack for the next six months." He let a shrug roll through his shoulders. "I wanted to do it in person." He shoved his hands deep into his pockets. "Your momma told me what to expect when I got out here, but I'm still having trouble."

Ford didn't specify if it was *me* trouble or Martian Roach trouble, but I could guess which bothered him.

"It's not you." He stared right at me, as if he had plucked the thought out of my head. "It's me."

The line was designed for a laugh, and I gave him one, but it hurt. "How are you feeling?"

"Not right." He lifted his tee, revealing a mass of scabbing. "I wake up scratching. There's this itch under my skin I can't get to, and it's always there." He yanked it down again. "I can ignore it during the day, but I can't help what I do when I sleep."

Ford was an easygoing guy who didn't let much rile him. Right after Natisha healed him, he came to me. He wanted a goodbye kiss, which I gave him on the cheek, and we parted on what I considered amicable terms.

In the process of avoiding him at the Faraday so as not to rub Midas's new living situation in his face, I had failed my friend. A healthy dose of ego and remorse had prevented me from seeing that until now.

The offer turned my blood to ice in my veins, but I made it. "Do you need Natisha?"

"I'm healed in here." He pointed to the center of his chest. "It's here that's giving me fits." He knocked on his forehead. "I have a few cousins in Buckhead. I'm going to room with them. See if a change of scenery helps."

"Call if you need anything." Midas stuck out his hand and shook Ford's. "We're here for you."

"I know." He yanked Midas into a manful hug then turned him loose. "I appreciate it."

Uncertain if an embrace from me would be welcome, I kept my spot on the bed. "We'll miss you."

"Maybe somewhere down the line we can Skype a movie night." He didn't approach me, and I wasn't certain if it was for his sake or Midas's that he avoided me. "Just...stay safe."

"I'll do my best," I promised him. "You too."

Without warning, Midas slugged Ford, and Ford hit the floor on his butt.

"What the actual hell?" I leapt to my feet. "Midas, what is wrong with you?"

Ford waved me off, so yeah, he didn't want to touch me. Or he wanted to avoid round two with Midas.

Goddess, gwyllgi males made my head throb with all their posturing.

"Good for you." He smiled at Midas, his lip smeared with crimson. "Guess you figured out what you want after all."

"Yeah." Midas locked gazes with me. "I did."

"I'm going to brush my teeth." I swept into the bathroom then paused to glance over my shoulder. "When I get back, I expect you both to have finished punching each other."

"Yes, ma'am." Ford got to his feet. "I'll do my best not to ruin his toothpaste-commercial smile."

"I would appreciate that." I shut the door and left the men to sort themselves out, but I pulled up short at the sink when I noticed Ambrose sitting on its edge. "What do you want?"

The shadow swung his legs and stared at me.

"I don't get it." I kept my voice soft. "What is it?"

He pointed at my chest and then at his.

"Not helping."

He pointed at my chest and then his and then the door.

"We're leaving in five minutes." I gave up on him. "Don't get ants in your pants."

An involuntary shudder rippled through me.

Ugh.

Ants.

Heaving a sigh with lungs he didn't have, Ambrose hopped down and gave me room to brush my teeth with the individually wrapped supplies I located under the sink. The vacation from reality had been nice, but it was time to get back to the city.

An incoming call from Bishop coaxed a sigh out of me, so I answered while I flossed. "Yesh?"

"Where are you?"

"Somewhere you're not."

"I get the sense you're miffed about Blithe."

"Miffed?" I cheesed for the mirror, checking my teeth. "Who says miffed anymore?"

"You're pissed I shut you out. That better?"

Just to annoy him, I made chomping noises.

"Kid, I would apologize, but I'm not sorry. Blithe is bad news, and her club is the epicenter of this mess."

"What's your deal with her?"

"I have no deal with her, and that's the problem. She wants to marry me off to her son. Forge an alliance. Seize control of the city. Crush other species under her boot. That kind of thing."

"That sounds like something you should have told me before now." I tossed the floss. "It's the coven's MO, minus the marrying-you bit." I searched the far corners of my brain but came up empty. "I didn't realize you had a thing for guys too."

More than once, he had dated women. Nothing serious. Just fun and done. Maybe guys had been in the mix too. It's not like Bishop advertised his personal life. Goddess forbid someone else be on the receiving end of the team's collective romantic wisdom.

"I had a thing for *one* guy," he corrected me. "He turned out to be a raging momma's boy, beautiful but spineless, so we broke up. End of story."

"A raging momma's boy?" I squinted at the phone. "Are you telling me Blithe's son is the guy you dated?"

"Blithe has been meaning to get around to taking over the world for the last five centuries. All she's done in that time is addict herself to Faerie-grade drugs and push out one very beautiful and very annoying son who sticks his nose where it doesn't belong and always comes running when she crooks her finger. He's her enforcer, and she trained him to be a nasty piece of work."

A nasty piece of work he had called beautiful twice in one conversation. "Um..."

"You begin to see why I don't want you anywhere near her."

"I understood, on some level, that Midas had fae blood." I washed my face but couldn't meet my eyes. "I'm still wrapping my head around the fact I had no frakking idea how much fae blood everyone else and their mommas have in this city."

"You'll get there." The jerk had the nerve to laugh. "Now where are you?"

The last several hours spent on pack land had pulled me out of a tailspin and given me a glimpse of what life might be like if Midas and I continued down this path. I didn't want to share it. No, that wasn't it. I didn't want to tarnish it.

"I'll be back in the city in two hours." I winced at my rumpled dress. "I'll change then head to HQ."

"I'll put in calls to the team, see who's available for—"

"Lisbeth." I thumped my forehead on the mirror. "I met her last night."

"That's...interesting."

"It totally slipped my mind." I bumped my head again. "What kind of person forgets something like that?"

"You really remember her?" He sounded thoughtful. "Huh."

"What does that mean? Why aren't you having a fit?"

"There's a geas on the team, similar to the one on me. You've bumped into one another any number of times, Linus did too, but you forget. All of it. It's a precautionary measure."

"I assume that was another vow I took and then promptly forgot?"

"Yup." He didn't sound sorry about it. "Try not to think about it. You'll only give yourself a headache."

"Why do I remember her then?" I thought back on what he had said. "Why do I remember this time?"

"I'm not sure."

Lisbeth recognized me enough to call for help, but that wasn't saying much. I was out in the supernatural public. The potentate had to be, therefore his apprentice did too.

"I passed her off to Ford." I exhaled. "I'll ask where he stashed her."

Her first order of business would have been to contact Bishop or me. That she hadn't made me question if she was in any shape to reach out to us. It also made me wonder why Ford hadn't mentioned her earlier. Unless...he didn't remember her either. He wasn't OPA, so why would the geas affect him?

"I'll see you soon." I ended the call then went to find the guys. "Ford, I've got a question before you go."

The two of them had gone outside to chat, and I hated that my arrival threaded tension through them both.

"Shoot." He straightened from his lean against a nearby tree. "What's up?"

"Do you remember Lisbeth, from last night?"

"Lisbeth." He shook his head. "Pretty name, but no." He sobered at my expression. "Should I?"

"A member of my team was exposed to the drug. I found her on the street and called you for backup."

"I would have taken her to Abbott, and he would have been at the Faraday. He was doing health screenings for the elders." His frown deepened. "I don't remember doing it, though."

Fingers crossed, I dialed Abbott. "Tell me you've got a patient."

"I've always got a patient, but I believe I know the one you're interested in. Ms. Lisbeth No Last Name."

"Yes." I sagged on my bones. "That's her."

"Interesting case," he murmured. "She's got a geas on her." He paused as if waiting for confirmation I might as well give him. "I remember everything I've said or done when I'm around her, but I forget it once I leave the room." He sounded thoughtful. "I assume you're immune, since you don't appear to have the same limitations as me."

"We're not sure." I had a delayed recall of her, which might be a fluke or might herald a flaw developing in the magic. "Either way, if she's good to go, I'll pick her up in two hours."

"I can release her into your care, but she'll need supervision for a few days."

"All right." I would check with Bishop for the nurse's information he used for Ford and see if we couldn't hire her for Lisbeth. "I can handle that."

We said goodbye, and I hung up with a grateful heart that Lisbeth hadn't been lost in the shuffle.

"I have to go home, change, hit HQ, then meet Abbott." I kept my distance from Midas and Ford to avoid sparking more conflict, but I was itching to go, and that meant giving Midas an out if he required one. "I can take a Swyft if you've got more to do here."

"That might be for the best." He rocked forward onto the balls of his feet then settled back onto his heels, deciding against a more personal goodbye. "I have to meet with Krista's parents, then I'm going with Mom to visit the teens. We'll need to address the events of last night with their parents too."

"I understand." I waved to them and headed down the path. "See you at home."

The pause between the words leaving my mouth and him returning them stretched throughout infinity.

"See you at home."

The resulting lightness in my chest as I picked my way to the road I blamed on eagerness to return to the city. The goofy smile was harder to explain away, so I didn't even try. I just enjoyed the feeling of belonging while it lasted.

<h1 style="text-align:center">EIGHT</h1>

A stop at home provided me with a change of clothes, a quick breakfast, and a café mocha.

I called Gayle, but she wasn't answering her phone, and I figured she must still be in quarantine with the rest of the pack. Worried as she was about Deric, she wouldn't have left him to detox alone.

The trip to HQ was, as always, convoluted, but it had decided to be at the base closest to my apartment, for which I was thankful. I wanted to brief the team on what I knew, find out what they had learned, and then get to Abbott's and reclaim Lisbeth before she slipped our collective memories again.

All the screens were lit, minus hers, when I entered HQ, and Bishop tossed me a chocolate donut with rainbow sprinkles from a box emblazoned with a familiar logo.

Ambrose swooped around the hand holding the pastry until I took pity on him and dropped it into the void while no one was looking.

Much to my amusement, my chocoholic tendencies were definitely rubbing off on him. I just hoped the reverse wasn't true of his murderous ones.

"I have the preliminary report on Faete," Reece said without preamble. "We've got a problem."

"Hit me." I stole another donut and ate it before Ambrose guilted me out of it too. "How bad is it?"

"The cleaners' database pinged on a match for the primary component."

The best thing about the cleaners had to be their expansive database. Thanks to their in with all factions, it collated historical data on every crime involving supernaturals within city limits. Bishop nicknamed her DORA, and it caught on, but I had no idea what it meant, and still no one would tell me.

Jerks.

"That's good, right?" I took a delicious bite of a third donut Bishop forced on me when he noticed my hand was empty. "That means we've come across it before."

"It's Martian Roach saliva."

The dough in my mouth soured, and I spat it into the trash can before treating Ambrose. Again. Much more reinforcement of his bad behavior and he might begin to think disobedience paid in sprinkles.

"All those people were getting high off roach drool?" A full-body shudder racked me. "That is so gross."

Martian Roaches were a magically engineered cross between the common roach, *Periplaneta americana*, and the parasitic emerald wasp, *Ampulex compressa*.

The natural order was the parasitic emerald wasp stung the common roach, laid an egg on its abdomen, walled it up in its lair, and the larvae fed on the roach. The first sting, they aimed at the roach's thorax. It contained gamma-aminobutyric acid, taurine, and beta-alanine.

Not that I knew what any of those were, but they sounded bad.

With the roach's front legs paralyzed, it was helpless to escape before the wasp stung it again, right in the brain. The neurotoxic cocktail blocked key receptors responsible for complex movements such as walking. During the process, the host showed no signs of pain or discomfort as it was eaten alive.

The twist with Martian Roaches was they skipped entombment, overtook their incapacitated hosts, and wore their skins for a period of time before the corpse started decomposing. That was the main difference between them and the witchborn fae coven. The Martian Roaches had a shelf life, but a skin hung in the coven's closet was an outfit they could wear again and again. Forever.

"What's the endgame here?" Bishop leaned back in his chair, and it squeaked. "Why dose them with that?"

"Perhaps its release was more experimental," Anca mused. "Invite a variety of species, give them carefully measured samples, ensure they're ingested with supervision, so that everyone is dosed the same amount. Then cull the specimens. Keep a few indoors to monitor as a control group then set the rest loose to do what they will while the coven watches."

"I could see that." Milo shifted in his chair. "What did we learn about how it affects different factions?"

"I can vouch that it turns wargs, even alphas, into giggling children with short tempers." I blocked out the traumatic memory of Mendelsohn tackling me in the buff. "There was also gratuitous nudity, but we were dealing with the Mendelsohns, so that's probably not a symptom."

A grimace passed over Bishop's face at the mention of our wet warg wrestling session.

Talk about your tongue twisters. I wasn't even going to try saying it out loud.

"Ford passed on word at dusk that inhaling the drug collapsed the lungs of several teens who were lured to Greenleaf by a coven member posing as one of their friends, a teenage girl named Krista." I kept a level tone when I gave them a friendly reminder. "That first part was meant for Midas's ears. It's pack intel, and we do not share it outside this room."

"Aww." Milo heaped sugar into his voice. "Hear that? She's going all momma bear on us for Midas."

"She's protecting our relationship with the OPA's single most powerful ally," Anca chided him, but she let too much amusement flavor her words. "Do we know how any other factions are affected?"

"There were others unconscious on the street and in various states of lucidity." I leaned against Bishop's chair. "We couldn't exactly stop and check species without being trampled. Crescent was a madhouse."

"Vampires got secondary highs," Bishop informed us, shocking the heck out of me. "I saw it firsthand."

Annoyance fizzled through me, but I let it splutter and die. He had called and texted. I was the one who ignored him. He might have told me all this sooner if I had been in any frame of mind to listen.

"Jemima? The bartender Gayle mentioned?" Bishop raised his brows. "I hunted her down, asked her a few questions. She clued me in then ditched the bar scene and went home early to, in her words, beat the dickheads home."

That was an item checked off my to-do list. I was grateful, if still annoyed with him, to write off one more thing. "Any clue why Krista smelled off to Midas?"

Bonnie Diaz, aka Snowball, aka Iliana hadn't raised any red flags for him, but he had known Krista. It might be as simple as that.

"Black magic." Bishop grimaced. "They had worked a spell, perhaps the one to take Krista's body, within hours of you confronting her. That's what he smelled. She was still..." he worked his jaw, "...fresh."

Annnd that's what I got wishing for simple.

"Goddess." I rubbed my forehead, but the headache kept tap dancing a single buffalo on my brain.

"The folks zoned out on the street?" He sent a picture from his phone to the screen for us all. "Mostly vampires who fed on humans who took the drug. The humans themselves appeared to be unaffected." He leaned back. "Fae appear unaffected as well."

"Any news on how the Mendelsohns are doing?"

"They were sedated as of the last update," Reece informed us. "Three females attacked the medics who separated them from their alpha." His distaste was clear when he finished his report. "Four more turned on each other when Mendelsohn fell asleep after servicing everyone but them."

"I would joke about him having inhuman stamina," Milo said, "but it's only funny because it's true."

The side quest Midas and I had volunteered for, collecting the hearts, had been withheld from the team for now, but Bishop's sharp focus on me warned we would have a long chat once this meeting ended.

One final item headed up my briefing to-do list, but Bishop must have read it on my face.

"Reece," he said, cutting me off before I got started, "keep us updated."

"I will," he mumbled, already distracted. "We'll have access to the initial test results from the first round of warg blood work within the next six to eight hours."

"Let's tie a knot in it here then." Bishop saluted the team. "Make no apologies."

"Survive," we all echoed, and the screens went dark.

Bishop gave the silence a moment to settle, and then he appraised me. "Ready to go get our girl?"

"Born ready." I scuffed the toe of my sneaker. "Why didn't you tell them about Blithe?"

"She's the dealer, not the source." He crammed the last donut into his mouth. "She's one anthill you don't want to stomp until you're ready to hose it in gasoline and drop a match on it."

An involuntary shiver prickled down my arms, but I had to admit the gas and match thing sounded good.

"That doesn't give her a free pass, Bish."

Dealing was as bad as manufacturing. Worse, maybe, since they were the ones facilitating the buys.

"You sound like him when you talk like that." He chuckled as he stood. "Linus would be proud."

A zing of pleasure that he thought so sang through my chest. "You're bribing me into a good mood."

First the donuts and now the seal of approval from the boss by proxy.

"I should have handled last night better, but I didn't realize Blithe was in town. She's owned that club for a decade or two and never stepped foot in it as far as I know. She's been content to remain on the outskirts. Someone has offered her a bigger piece of the pie, and she's hungry for it."

"The coven has too many irons in the fire." I rubbed my forehead. "Their attack is so scattered."

The release of the drug struck me as scattershot too. Everyone had been targeted, not just the gwyllgi.

"Maybe not." He led the way out into the parking deck du jour. "The drug might have been the goal the whole time. The Martian Roaches can only infect so many people, and we're onto them. They function the same as the coven, albeit as expendable henchmen, so their existence never made sense to me. Why invest the time and expense in creating something so similar to themselves? But get a dozen of the roaches mature enough to drool into vials, and you've got yourself a bottomless supply of a weaponized drug."

"They really hate gwyllgi." I called us a Swyft to the Faraday. "There's got to be more to it than this."

"There always is," he said solemnly. "No matter how good you are, there's always something you miss."

What a pleasant thought to start our night. Talk about your high notes. A great pep-talker was Bishop.

Once, Abbott had lamented to me the infirmary in the building's subbasement was as pristine as the day construction ended. Thanks to the coven kicking our butts on the regular, he didn't have that problem these days. I, for instance, might as well move a few personal items into a room as much time as I spent there.

When he wasn't patching boo-boos, he was developing a test to determine whether packmates who had fallen under suspicion of coven tampering had been killed for their identity or used as a host for Martian Roaches. I wasn't sure if he was leaning more toward the magical or scientific approach, but I had put in a call to an authority on both to give him a hand.

Doughty was a witch by birth and a forensic analyst by trade. He was brilliant, and he was expensive, but if ever we needed those two disciplines married, it was now. We had to identify any coven members who had infiltrated our ranks and capture them. We had to isolate anyone infected by Martian Roaches and pray Abbott worked out a cure and fast. And, for extra fun, now we required an antidote for Faete.

Abbott was good, but he couldn't do it all alone, and not on a timeline that would save the teens already in distress. I had loaned him Reece, but we needed results yesterday, and I was more than happy to pay to get them.

Hank stood watch at the door, and I swear I heard him groan when he spotted me.

"Hiya, friend." I skipped up to him. "Did you miss me?"

A long exhale parted his lips. "You were gone?"

"Hadley, stop harassing the man." Bishop gave me a shove toward the lobby. "Let him do his job."

Hank smiled at Bishop—actually *smiled*, like a normal person.

Or like a smug jerk who enjoyed me getting called on my shenanigans.

"To be continued," I warned Hank on my way in.

"I hope not," he muttered at my back.

"How are you going to lead these people if you pester them within an inch of their lives?" Bishop kept pace with me to the elevators. "You should work on inspiring loyalty, not annoyance."

"Leading these people is Midas's job, not mine." I mashed the button marked with a red medical symbol I had assumed, until recently, was an emergency call button if the elevator got stuck. "Why does everyone take Hank's side?"

"Hank does his job and doesn't talk smack. That's why."

After the doors shut behind us, I glared at him. "And don't think I didn't notice you hinting at me."

"Midas is courting you." Bishop's smirk gleamed on the silvery walls. "What do you think happens after courtship ends?"

"I don't get crowned High Queen Alpha of the Atlanta Gwyllgi." I glowered at my own reflection. "Wait." A shot of panic hit my bloodstream. "Do I?"

"Midas won't be alpha until Tisdale steps down, so no. But you would be co-beta for all intents and purposes."

"I'm already co-potentate." I made a round shape with my hands. "My plate, she is full."

"Either you accept him, or you rebuke him. Rebuke him, and it's done."

"Ugh." I thumped the back of my head on the wall. "I make a life-time commitment, or I lose him?"

"Pretty much."

"That sucks."

Shrugging, he repeated himself. "Pretty much."

The doors opened onto the infirmary, and we went in search of Abbott.

Meant to accommodate various species, the space was much larger than I had been expecting the first time I saw it. More advanced too. It was basically a mini hospital. How it had sat neglected for so long boggled the mind. Unless you had witnessed firsthand the gwyllgi tendency to require house calls for emergency treatment.

"Bishop, Hadley." A young woman dressed in scrubs found us first. "Abbott is waiting on you."

She led us to a large room where Lisbeth sat on the bed, chatting away with someone hidden by privacy curtains. Expecting it to be Abbott, I walked in and stumbled when I spotted Ford *and* Abbott.

"Hey." I tried for a hesitant smile. "I didn't expect to find you here."

"I wanted to try an experiment," Bishop said, gesturing Ford out of the room. "Lisbeth is an LPN. She works at a large clinic that keeps her chained to a desk, a victim of admin drudgery, but she's an excellent nurse."

The dots connected in my mind, and I said, "Oh."

"I recruited her to take care of Ford," he continued. "I was curious if he would remember her."

"Did he?" I checked with Lisbeth. "Remember you?"

"Not until he entered the room." Her brown eyes sparked with amusement. "Watch this."

Cautious about involving Ford again, I started to protest. "I don't think we should—"

"Ford," Bishop called. "Can you come here, please?"

Ford sauntered into the room, pulled up short when he spotted me, then nodded to Bishop and Abbott. A heartbeat passed before he noticed Lisbeth, and he smiled when he did, but it was only politeness.

"Ma'am." He took a step back. "I don't mean to intrude." He checked with Abbott. "Should I go or...?"

"Ford, this is Lisbeth." Abbott introduced them. "Lisbeth, Ford."

She stuck out her hand, and Ford was too much of a gentleman not to take it. The contact sparked instant recall, as best I could tell, and he laughed.

"You got me again, didn't you?" He shook his head. "That's the darnedest thing."

It was one thing to hear a geas had been laid on someone, even to experience the limits of the ones on me, but it was startling to watch one in action on someone else.

"They spent enough time together," Bishop told me, "the geas doesn't work quite right on him anymore. One touch brings it all back."

That could explain how I remembered her too. We talked every day. We may not have shared physical space often, that I recalled, but we had an emotional connection that might have anchored her in my mind during a moment of trauma.

"I guess that settles it then." I joined Ford at her bedside. "You can stay with me until you're over the hump."

"Midas is staying with you." She kept sneaking glances at Ford. "I don't want to impose."

True, my apartment was the size of a shoebox, and I already had a whole lot of gwyllgi male in mine.

"You could stay in Midas's apartment maybe?" I would have to ask first. "That way you'd be close."

"You can stay with me," Ford offered. "Or I'll stay with you."

Frowning at this change in his tune, I asked, "How long do you have before you go?"

"Long enough." He smiled at Lisbeth. "I'm not on any set timeline."

That wasn't the impression I got during his speech to Midas and me, but I wasn't about to stick my nose into his personal life. The intersection of a member of Midas's pack and a member of my team threw up a stop sign I was all too happy to obey.

"You don't have to do that." Roses blossomed in her cheeks. "I can manage on my own."

"You took good care of me." He covered her hand with his. "I don't mind paying you back."

"That's not why I do what I do," she protested. "You don't owe me."

"Hadley," he said, dragging me into their argument. "Tell the stubborn woman to accept help when it's offered."

"Stubborn woman," I parroted, "accept help when it's offered."

"Fine." Her complexion glowed as she gazed up at him. "We'll have to stay at your place or mine, though." She checked with me. "Humans aren't allowed in the Faraday, right? That's why I was under house arrest until Ford recovered?"

The shock of learning one of my team was human struck me

mute. It wasn't that I was prejudiced against them, or that I didn't see the value in them, but I hadn't expected one to step up and put their lives on the line for the paranormal community.

"The Faraday isn't safe for humans, no." I got hives thinking about her staying here without my knowing. Bishop must have put protective measures in place, but I was stunned all the same. "Stay with Ford. Gwyllgi protective instincts being what they are, he'll feel more comfortable with you in his own territory."

"All right," she said softly.

"How are we going to get around the geas?" He kept his hand on her, and she didn't budge. "Never let it be said I mind coming home to find a beautiful woman waiting for me, but I would prefer not to take her head off if she surprises me on a bad day."

The dangerous edge Ford had been skating made him a less than ideal host. Then again, recalling Lisbeth had lit a fire under him. He was smiling, laughing, *flirting*. He wasn't a fickle man, which led me to believe this wasn't a sign of him getting over me, for lack of better phrasing, so much as it was him sinking into the mindset he had with Lisbeth before he forgot her.

That was all kinds of interesting, but none of my business.

"I can grant Ford temporary immunity." Bishop frowned at Lisbeth's mooning. "If you're both sure that's what you want." He waited for her full attention. "He might not be susceptible to the geas after this. You've had too much contact as it is, and this will imprint you on his personal space. He'll scent you and wonder even after you're gone."

"I know how to keep a secret," Ford said, a growl in his voice. "I won't endanger her."

Yup.

For good or ill, those gwyllgi protective instincts were already kicking in.

Lisbeth gave Bishop an opening to work his mojo on Ford. "Can I have a minute alone with Hadley?"

"I hope you know what you're doing," I murmured to Bishop on his way past.

Lisbeth made no bones about her flaming crush on Ford, and now we were tossing them together like fried wings and hot sauce.

"Me too, kid." He frowned at her. "Me too."

The guys filed out, and I was left alone with Lisbeth. If that was her real name.

"Nice to finally meet you." She patted the mattress on her hospital-style bed. "I've seen you around, but how cool is it that you see me too?" She tapped a finger to her lips. "Well, you could always see me. You just didn't know who I was, and you forgot the second you figured it out. On the times you did, anyway."

"It's nice to meet you too." I sat and took the hand she offered me. "I'm not sure why I remember you, but I can't help but wonder if it has to do with last night."

The segue wasn't my smoothest, but she was a witness, a victim, and I had to ask her a few questions.

"You're probably wondering what I was doing at Greenleaf." She twisted the sheet around her fingertip. "Humans aren't allowed in the clubs, and we require escorts in that part of the city after dark. So..."

Waiting for the punchline, I rolled my hand. "So...?"

"Bishop got me a charm to disguise my scent." She poked one leg out from under the covers and wiggled her toes, each of them adorned with a silver ring similar to mine. "I read as a witch. Super low level. Almost human."

"Just enough magic to get into trouble."

Faete didn't affect humans, that we knew of, or witches, who likely made the charm. Either Lisbeth had gotten sick from a much higher dose based on the assumption she was a witch, or the combination of a magic charm *on* her body plus magic drug *in* her body had fried her more fragile immune system.

"This is why the team is kept anonymous." The toes stopped wiggling, and the smile faded. "We prefer to be judged for our accomplishments and not our limitations."

"You're right." I gripped the railing. "You're right."

"You're under a lot of stress, so I'm willing to cut you some slack." She poked me in the thigh. "Just because I don't want to be judged by my limitations doesn't mean I'm not aware of them." She flopped back against her pillow. "My dad was a warg. Stepdad, technically. I've known about this world since I was two."

That explained how she knew to look beyond the mundane, but it was still quite a burden she had undertaken.

"A human killed him." She must have read my expression. "He was hunting in wolf form on our land." A grim smile tipped her lips. "He was always so careful. We lived close to town, but we owned thirty acres. He had plenty of room to roam safely when the mood struck him."

Heart breaking, I waited for her to unburden herself with the rest.

"A couple was out walking through the woods after dark, got turned around I guess, and they crossed onto our property. The boyfriend had a gun on him and..." Her hands clenched and then released. "That's when I realized paras need more protection from us than we do from them."

The sentiment was one I could appreciate, but I couldn't agree with her. Not when humans were food.

"You've been an invaluable member of this team for longer than I've been here. I'm sorry for what brought you to us, but I'm glad you're here." I thought back on Bishop's warning about Ford. "What happens if I can't forget you again?"

"I trust you." Her eyes sparkled. "And this way, you can help me with Ford."

Laughter shot out of me, equal parts relief we were okay and incredulousness. "You're horrible."

"I am." She hung her head, but then she peered at me from under her bangs. "He's just so..."

"Yeah." I had to agree with her. "But I can't help you. Ford and I aren't on the greatest terms right now."

"Midas," she murmured. "How did you ever choose between

them?"

"Easy." I stood when Ford and Bishop reentered the room. "I didn't."

Lisbeth had all but forgotten me when her crush sauntered up to her, but I had one question left. "How was the drug administered?"

"Intranasal or intravenous," she reported. "From what I can tell, species determined method of administration." Her lips twisted. "I got a tip and headed downtown to snag us a sample."

A beat of hope thrummed in me until I noted her hospital gown and its obvious lack of pockets. "Do you still have it?"

Doughty could always do with more material for testing, and so could the cleaners.

"Only what shows up in my blood work." She rubbed her nose. "They let everyone in the door, invitation or not, but they wouldn't let you leave until *after* you ingested it."

"Smart." I had to admit. "That kept the drug itself contained."

Leaving Ford with his new charge, Bishop and I exited the Faraday. Most nights I patrolled solo, with him providing radio commentary, but these days it was dangerous for any one of us to get caught out alone.

We walked Crescent Avenue Northeast from end to end, but its subdued vibe made it hard to believe the manic chaos of last night. The rest of the city hummed with its usual buzz of activity, but nothing required our intervention. Eventually, there was nothing left to do but go home.

"Do you think Faete will be distributed?" I couldn't decide yet. "Or do you think Anca was right about it being a clinical trial for the coven?"

"Hard to say." He pointed us back toward the Faraday. "A bigger danger is Blithe getting her hands on it. It might be the coven has one purpose in mind, and she has another. She's got her own chem labs. Feeding others' habits is how she supports her own. She could, in theory, begin production on her own variant in time."

"She would do that, even knowing the side effects?"

"She wants money, and she wants power." He shrugged. "They're the same thing, really."

"People like that make my head hurt." I was glad for the coming dawn and my comfy futon. "If nothing else, you'd think she would see Faete will cripple her income by killing off portions of her client base."

"Gwyllgi are the only faction experiencing catastrophic side effects, as of yet," he countered. "She might be willing to take that risk."

"We don't know if the wargs will pull through," I argued. "Their brains could still melt."

"I like your optimism."

"Even Mendelsohn doesn't deserve to have what little gray matter he's got leak out his ears." A knot formed in my gut. "The pregnant females worry me more. I hope their babies won't pay for this."

"Don't borrow trouble." He walked me to the door. "We've got enough to go around."

Hank tipped his head at Bishop, shot me a warning glance, then resumed his position.

"Get some sleep." Bishop spun on his heel and tossed a wave. "You look like you could use it."

The trick almost worked enough for me to be too annoyed to notice he had walked me home, but I did. I shouldn't have been surprised, he was sneaky like that, but he would kill my rep babying me.

Even after I put that together, the niggling sense of doubt persisted. I had missed something, but what? It finally clocked me over the head as I stepped into the elevator, and I could have strangled Ambrose for not sharing with me sooner. As much crowd skimming as he had done, he must have known.

Alone in the elevator, I hissed under my breath. "What did it do to necromancers?"

The shadow, alert now that I had deigned to notice him again, drew a finger across his throat.

Fantastic. Absolutely fabulous. This night kept getting better and better.

The Society would not be thrilled to learn a designer drug was lethal to our section of the population.

I was still digesting that morsel when the elevator doors slid open onto my hall, and I spotted Midas halfway to my apartment. Hearing the booth's arrival, its distinctive *ting*, he glanced behind him.

"Hey." He waited for me to catch up to him. "How did your night go?"

"I've had worse." I let us into my apartment. "I've had better too." I searched his face. "You?"

"Two teens in critical condition. One dead. Plus Krista." He sank onto the futon and dropped his head back to stare at the ceiling. "We have to stop the coven."

"We will." I joined him, curling against his side. The tension that touch ignited in him I ignored until he relaxed into me. "They're targeting the vulnerable, and that's not okay."

"All those parents," he murmured. "They expect me to fix this."

"I understand the pack looks to you and your mom, but that's too much to put on you alone."

"I'm not alone." He almost managed a smile. "I have you, and they know it."

"I'm not sure I would classify it as you *having* me, but I am yours for the duration."

"I like the sound of that." He touched my cheek, traced his finger down my jaw. "About earlier..."

"I'm sorry I bit you," I said solemnly before he twisted himself into a pretzel explaining what required no explanation. "I'll try to control my savage urges next time."

Midas mouthed the words *thank you* and tucked me in even tighter.

You're welcome, I pressed into the skin of his throat before grunting to my feet to order us pizza for dinner.

NINE

The goblin cackles with glee and sends the giant to fetch Midas from his cage.

"You're gonna love this, me boy." He does a little dance. "I found the most gorgeous female, I did. She's fresh. Never stepped into the ring." He clapped his hands. "This will be a fight for the books."

Midas says nothing as his cage door is wrenched open and the massive fist engulfs him. Scars crisscross the giant's skin, gifts from him and others, but fighting does no good. The giant plops him down in front of the goblin whose manic glee rouses the feral half of him in wary acceptance of what's to come.

The human half of him broken, Midas allows himself to be bathed and fed. He allows them to do what they will. None of it matters. He's not here. Not really. Not since the first female's neck snapped between his teeth.

The crowd roars when he's presented as the reigning champion, and he hates himself more the louder they cheer. But then the gate opens to reveal his opponent, and his heart stops. Turns to ice in his chest.

"Lethe," he breathes, the beast in him awakening.

Midas woke drenched in cold sweat, shivering, and...with Hadley facing him, stroking his damp hair.

"Sorry," he rasped. "I didn't mean to wake you."

"I had too much in my head to rest." She kept petting him, comforting him. "You didn't bother me."

"I can go up to my apartment," he offered, dreading her answer. "Let you go back to sleep."

"Spoon, stop talking nonsense." She turned away from him and scooted back. "Do your job."

Sliding an arm under her, he yanked her flush against him and held her tight. "Spoon?"

Laughing as if delighted to be held, she glanced over her shoulder. "Do you prefer Goldie or Prince?"

"Can I choose none of the above?"

"Spoon it is." She rubbed his arms where they crossed over her stomach. "Sleep." She yawned. "We've got ass to kick tonight."

With her warm body pliant in his arms, her gentle fingers caressing old scars, he did.

"YOU HAVEN'T BROKEN up with him yet?"

"Remy," Hadley sighed from across the room. "That's mean."

"I have a knife you can sleep with under your pillow."

"Remy."

"What? He's fruit loops. Who knows when he might snap and kill you in your sleep?"

"He's not fruit loops, and he won't snap. Even if he did snap, he wouldn't kill me in my sleep."

The ringing endorsement set Midas's ears burning. "She's right."

"No one asked you," Remy snarled. "Of course you would *say* you're not going to kill her."

Only the maddest of the stark ravers killed their mates, but

Hadley didn't know that she was his, and he wasn't about to tell her. Tricking her into courtship was bad enough, but he refused to let his instincts condemn her to a life—or a relationship—she didn't want. She fought so hard for her dreams. He would rather let her go than watch her sacrifice even one on his behalf.

The final choice would be hers to make, and he...would have to live with the consequences.

"You'll want to hear this." Hadley sat on the futon near his hip and passed him a café mocha. "We've got a party to crash."

Leveraging into a seated position, Midas accepted what Hadley considered breakfast with a smile he couldn't quite catch before Remy noticed.

"Ugh." She wrinkled her nose. "He thinks he's special because you made him coffee." She scooped a mug off the table. "She made me one too."

"Hate Midas on your own time." Hadley threw a pillow at her head. "Not while you're on the clock."

Remy grumbled loud enough for him to hear but soft enough Hadley let her get away with it.

"There's a club in Buckhead, the Ivy." She slurped her drink loudly as punctuation. "Rumor has it, there's another invite-only party there tonight. Starts in a few hours. Faete is supposed to be on tap."

"One of mine got into the last party without an invite." Hadley pulled on her bottom lip. "What are the odds we can walk in off the street tonight?"

"None to none." Remy started pacing. "The original invites were super fancy to guarantee the recipients would flash them around, help build the hype." A snarl curled her lip. "This one is to establish a supply chain. No freebies. It's pay to play."

Midas stared at her over the rim of his mug as he drank. "How did you come by this information?"

"None-ya," Remy snarked. "As in none of your business."

Anticipating the hostile response, he checked with Hadley. "Do you trust her intel?"

"I do." Her expression lingered on Remy. "Go do what you do. Report back when you know more."

"Sure thing." She yanked a crumpled paper from her pocket and slapped it down on the kitchen table. "Numbers from last night."

"You're really angling for that bonus." Hadley chuckled. "Keep up the good work."

"A bonus ain't enough for what I do." Remy yanked open the door. "I want a raise."

She slammed it behind her, and Hadley just shook her head.

"She's not wrong." She glanced at the paper. "She's a whiz at sales. Who knew?"

Having visited malls in Atlanta and experienced their breed of aggressive salesmanship, he had no trouble picturing Remy snagging shoppers as they emerged from other stores, dragging them to the Peachy Keen Sheets kiosk, and bullying them into making purchases.

Given Hadley's soft spot for the murderous young woman, Midas let it go.

"How do you propose we get an invite?" He finished his drink. "Any friends who can pull strings?"

Mouth stretched thin, she glanced at her phone where it sat on the coffee table. "Maybe."

"I need fresh clothes and to make some calls." He climbed off the futon and rinsed his mug in the sink. "What time should I meet you back here?"

"Give me two hours." She flopped sideways with a groan then raised her head. "Going upstairs or out?"

"Upstairs."

"Okay." She dropped it again. "Just checking." Lifted it again. "That doesn't count as nagging, does it?"

"No?"

"You don't sound convinced." She toed off her socks and hauled the sheet up to her neck. "I'm not sure how this relationship stuff works, so let me know if I start bugging you."

"It's nice." He shrugged. "Having someone who cares."

"Right?" She glanced over at him. "I didn't think I would like it, but...it feels good coming home to someone." Her cheeks reddened. "To you anyway."

The beast in his middle propelled him across the room, and he claimed her lips. "Are you napping?"

Proof she had sat up with him through his night terrors, which could last hours, left him humbled.

"No." She tugged the sheet higher. "I'm getting comfortable to make uncomfortable calls."

"Mmm-hmm." He crossed to the door. "Two hours enough?"

"Yes," she mumbled sleepily. "Plenty."

Leaving her tightened his chest, but he exited into the hall and bumped into Ares. "Do you always lurk outside Hadley's door?"

"Usually only when you're on the other side of it." She waved him onto the elevators. "Trust me, I don't want to hear all the mushy stuff that goes on in there. I only lurk when ordered to."

He mashed the button for his floor, and they hit his apartment for fresh clothes and shoes.

"You're half moved in here." Ares whistled. "Why not cut the cord? Leave the den altogether?"

"I might, in a few weeks."

"After the courtship ends," she realized. "How's that going?"

The beast knows its mate and has claimed her. The man is a few steps behind but catching up fast. It's done, and it can't be undone. She might not feel the same, and if she leaves...I'll never mate again. It's as simple as that.

"It's going," he said to throw her off the scent. "What brought you upstairs?"

"We got word there's another party happening tonight some-where in Buckhead. No specifics this time. I milked our contacts, but that's all they've got. Though it won't be hard to narrow the search area once the drugs start flowing."

"Any updates on the teens?"

"Abbott has them stabilized, but he says he needs a sample of unaltered roach saliva for any hope of an antidote. The magic used to create the compound has corrupted it too far."

"We have to hunt." That's what she meant. "Do we have any leads on potential Martian Roaches?"

"Nope." She busied herself in the kitchen while he changed. "They up and vanished." She lowered her voice. "Probably after they heard themselves being referred to as Martian Roaches."

Midas cut her a sharp look that warned her to leave Hadley's unique naming conventions alone.

"Personally," she said, ignoring him, "I would have gone with one of the classics. *Nasties* works just fine for me. *Big nasty* as the singular."

"Hadley loves the classics, hence the name Martian Roach."

"Hadley is a flaming geek, hence the name Martian Roach."

Midas chuckled, unable to deny it. "We'll hit the party tonight, see what we can learn."

The sellers wouldn't disclose the product's origin to buyers, not only to avoid competition should anyone decide to create their own supply, but to prevent the instinctive recoil that came from learning where this newest high originated.

Hardcore users wouldn't care, but it was hard to dress up *roach spit* for the high-end clientele.

"All right." Ares followed him into the hall and then the elevator. "Do you remember things getting this screwy while Linus was holding the reins?"

A warning growl tickled the back of his throat. "What are you implying?"

"Just making conversation."

"The coven isn't Hadley's fault."

"I'm not saying it is." She drummed her fingers on the rail behind her. "The timing concerns me, is all."

"I haven't eaten breakfast yet." The drink Hadley made him was pure sugar, and it didn't count as far as his carnivorous other half was concerned. "Get to the point."

"Predators can sense a power vacuum waiting to open, and they're happy to fill it."

A shock jolted his system. "You think she can't handle the role?"

"I like Hadley. I do." She exhaled. "But she's dragging the pack deeper and deeper into her troubles, and that can be viewed as a sign of weakness. We were never called upon to aid the previous potentates, but we're at her beck and call. Any outsiders who pick up on that might consider her easy prey."

"She's not." As much as his protective instincts screamed at him to keep her safe, she was a predator, the same as him. "Anyone who tries her will learn it too."

"What about anyone who attempts to get to her through you or the pack?"

"Where is this coming from?" He mashed the button to stop the elevator between floors. "What's wrong?"

"Liz is pregnant." Her hand clenched on the bar behind her. "We've been trying for years with donors from her species and mine, and now it's happened at the absolute worst time."

"The alpha's duty is to put their pack before themselves and their own happiness."

"God." She ducked her head. "I didn't mean…"

"You want me to give up Hadley."

"I don't want Liz to get hurt in the war that's brewing. I don't want to lose this baby either." A tear rolled down her cheek. "It would kill Liz. She's five months in, just starting to show. How can I ask her to risk it?"

"I never wanted to be beta. I always thought Lethe would lead the pack when Mom stepped down." Midas straightened from his lean and hit the button. "I've never wanted this, and now I can't escape it." He exited the second the booth hit the lobby. "Don't ask me to give up the one thing I've chosen for myself."

Hadley, still in her pajamas, waited to get on with her arms loaded down with boxes. She must have been called downstairs for a delivery after he left.

"What is all that?" He noticed the label as he reached for the topmost boxes. "Inventory?"

"I got it." She sidestepped him, ignoring Ares, and got in the elevator. "Later."

"Aww hell," she mumbled. "I didn't mean for her to overhear that."

Midas didn't comfort her. He was too riled, his feral half too alert to a potential threat to his mate. Instead he led the way to brief the enforcers for the night, unsure how to smooth things over with Hadley and wishing he had time to call his sister. Just to hear her voice and remind himself she was okay, that she had survived. For the first time, it felt like maybe they both had.

TEN

"*Don't ask me to give up the one thing I've chosen for myself.*" That choice soundbite, paired with Midas decking Ford at the cabin, left me with few illusions Midas was taking our courtship seriously. As in, he was picturing a life with me. As in, he wanted that big *M* word at the end of it. As in, he wanted me to...

As in, he wanted me.

Me.

What was he thinking? Had he met me? I was a hot mess. Steaming hot. Flaming hot. Solar flare hot.

The packmates I met at the den had been kind to me, and I was now madly in love with Samzilla, but the first glimpse they got of me wasn't the same version as what Ares and the other enforcers at the Faraday saw. They had fought alongside me, patched me up, and witnessed the troubles that came with my position. They had the clearest perspective outside my team of what I brought to Atlanta, and what I cost it too.

That Ares, who I had considered a friend, provoked Midas into making that comment hurt.

A lot.

No conversation leading up to that declaration could be a good one.

The unexpected delivery had put me in the wrong place at the wrong time, and now my head wasn't where it ought to be prior to infiltrating a club full of dealers ready to poison the city for a few extra bucks. I had to shut down this self-doubt before it got me—and Midas—killed.

"This is going to be one of those nights." I let myself into my apartment and set the boxes in the entryway. "I can feel it."

Ambrose, who didn't care one whit about the Peachy Keen color of the month, circled the boxes.

"What's got your tail in a twist?" I watched him spin faster and faster. "They're just sheets."

Had I not been grinding my teeth so loudly, I might have heard the subtle *tick, tick, tick.*

I definitely heard the *boom.*

ELEVEN

The floor trembled beneath his feet, and Midas knew in his bones that his world was ending.

"What was that?" Hand over her heart, Ares scanned the ceiling. "It sounded like..."

An explosion.

Alarms screamed through the room, deafening him, but he ignored the ringing in his ears.

All Midas could see beyond the red haze of his beast rising was the stack of boxes Hadley had been carrying. He skipped the elevator and hit the stairs, running as fast as his preternatural strength allowed. Prayers he had forgotten how to shape fell from his lips, pleas for mercy, for Hadley.

The knob on the door leading to her floor scalded his hand when he grasped it, and his heart lurched. He ignored the stink of skin cooking and yanked until it fell off its hinges. A gust of smoke blasted his face, and his eyes watered from the heat.

"Hadley," he screamed over the roaring flames licking up the walls. "*Hadley.*"

Man and beast synced with a tectonic shift within him, and the two discordant halves aligned in a desperate bid to pool their resources to reach their mate.

Rushing into the hall, he pivoted toward her apartment and almost fell to his knees.

The door was gone, and shrapnel peppered the hall. Open sky nursed whirling smoke through the shattered windows, but the haze persisted as the fire burned hotter and spread faster than was natural.

"Goddamn it, Hadley." His voice broke on her name. "Answer me."

"Here." A throaty cough pinpointed her location. "I'm here."

Midas sprinted down the hall, burst into her apartment, and found her seated on a perfect circle of uncharred flooring.

"You set a circle," he breathed, and instantly regretted it. "Thank God."

With her finger, she smudged the line and lunged for him. "You're on fire."

"I'll heal." He would have carried her, but he couldn't get his hands to work. "Don't...worry...about me."

"Your hair." She hit him in the head and on the neck. "Why are you so flammable?"

Hair product, he wanted to quip, for one more of those smiles, but the edges of the hall warped and twisted as he ran out of oxygen.

Too much smoke in his lungs. Too far to run. Too late to escape.

Hands on his shoulders, she gazed into his eyes. "Tell your ego I'm sorry for this in advance."

The world tilted horizontally, and he couldn't figure out why.

"I've got you," she panted. "Think light thoughts, okay?"

Disoriented, he didn't fight the delusion of her carrying him to safety. It beat the reality, he was sure.

"Lighter," she wheezed, her voice faint. "Light as a feather, a balloon, a..." She lapsed into a coughing fit. "I love barbeque too much to go out like this."

Might as well tell the delusion the truth since the real Hadley was beyond his reach. "I love..."

Cool air kissed his face, sweet and clean, and he sucked in heaving gulps.

"Hang on, hang on, hang on," she chanted as she carried him down the stairs. "Just another minute."

Voices rang out in the stairwell, and more hands touched him until he wanted to scream from the agony.

"I'm Captain Gray," a man rumbled from the other end of a long tunnel, "from Fire Station Thirteen."

The man's name was unfamiliar, but thirteen was the unlucky station that fielded the paranormal calls.

"Aubrey," Captain Gray bellowed over the chaos. "Get upstairs and contain the fire."

"Yes, sir."

"Bring him to the infirmary," Abbott barked over the others. "Her too."

Hadley protested as Midas was wrenched from her arms, but Captain Gray didn't bend.

"I've got him, sweetheart." He called out two names, and more feet pounded the stairs. "Carry her."

The grunts and curses told Midas that didn't go over well with Hadley, and he wanted to smile with pride at how fierce she was, even with embers in her hair.

The bright scent of the blood she had drawn, fighting like a wild-cat, stained the air with the smell of crimson...and feline.

God, his senses were fried if all it took was *thinking* cat to smell one.

The next thing he knew, he was lying in a hospital bed harder than some forest floors with Hadley next to him.

"Your hair," she whispered, eyes closed. "I protected it."

Midas glanced at her hand and the fistful of scorched curls she held in a death grip.

"It will grow back," he assured her, grateful to be able to touch her, to convince himself she was alive.

"Promise?"

Smiling hurt, but he couldn't help himself. "I promise."

THE SQUEAL OF rubber wheels over laminate flooring dragged Midas up from sleep, and he woke buried under Hadley, who had climbed over him in a protective cling while he rested. It made him ache, but not enough he would ever tell her so.

"First, she faked the flu to avoid a family dinner, and now this." Mom clucked her tongue and gestured for the two packmates in the doorway to enter. "Am I such bad company that she would prefer blowing herself up to eating one meal with me?"

"I don't think she blew herself up," he rasped, his voice deeper than ever.

The nurses had wheeled a rolling tray over his bed and Hadley's, which had been pushed together, giving them a broad dining surface. His mother had a third tray placed near the guest chair. Her helpers for the day unloaded fried chicken from Ben's, mashed potatoes with gravy, biscuits, corn on the cob, and potato wedges. There were individual chocolate lava cakes too.

"I wasn't sure if you two were up to drinking more than water." Mom did her best not to hover in front of the others, but her nervous tension vibrated through the room and cowed them all the same. Noticing this, she set a hand on each of their shoulders to disperse the oppressive sensation. "Thank you for your help. I'll be home in an hour or two."

Knowing better than to argue with their alpha about shucking her guards, they left.

"Water is fine." He stroked Hadley's hair, the ends as blackened as the curls she still gripped in her fist. "The more ice, the better."

Mom ducked out to request three glasses of water from the nurses, and he used that time to wake Hadley.

"Open your eyes," he coaxed, "and I'll give you chocolate."

"Mmm." She snuggled closer. "Chocolate."

"And fried chicken. From Ben's."

The faint rumble of her stomach where it pressed against him must have tipped the scales, and she yawned deeply.

"Breakfast in bed." She went to rub her eye and got a face full of scorched hair. "What is...?"

"Hadley." He clamped his hands on her wrists as her eyes rounded. "It's okay."

"I'm holding half your scalp in my hand." She flexed her fingers. "That is not okay."

"It's only hair," he soothed. "It will grow back."

"Your skin," she cried. "Goddess, why didn't you shove me off you?"

"I didn't mind."

"You're covered in blisters." Her eyes glimmered as they traveled to his face, over his head. "And you're bald."

"They shaved my head." He twitched a shoulder. "It was easier that way."

Tears falling, she reached over him and dumped the handful of blackened hair onto his head. "There."

Midas chuckled, and then he laughed, and then he coughed until he tasted blood in his throat.

"Told you I was funny," she said softly, her eyes full of worry. "What were you thinking?"

"That I had to get to you."

"You could have been killed."

"The bomb went off in *your* apartment. *You* could have been killed."

"I, for one, am grateful you're both still alive." Mom carried in the water then began to serve them, as she would have at her own table. "The pack is still talking about how Hadley carried you to safety."

Stunned, Midas stared at Hadley. "I thought I was hallucinating."

"I did apologize to your ego before I lifted you." She slid off him to her side of the bed. "That's not going to cost you points, is it?"

"On the contrary," Mom assured her. "You're courting." She cut him a sharp look that warned he better come clean with her sooner rather than later about the mating. "The pack views your heroics as a positive sign that Midas has chosen a worthy partner." She bent and kissed Hadley's forehead. "I am inclined to agree."

"He pulled me out of the fire," she stammered. "I would have been trapped there."

"The pack saw him rush from the meeting straight to your door." A smile curved her lips. "He won't lose points on any front." She patted Hadley on the cheek then removed the clot of hair from Midas's head and tossed it in the trash. "You behaved as any mated couple should in a time of crisis."

A frown knit Hadley's brow, but she let it go. She must have taken Mom's statement as a future possibility and not a present situation. He was just thankful she didn't run screaming from the room.

"I didn't get blown up to avoid family dinner," she mumbled in the face of her heaping plate.

"No one that dedicated to my son would commit suicide to avoid his mother," she said lightly as she took her seat. "Now, Hadley." She bit into a biscuit. "Where do you see yourself in five years?"

Hadley swallowed audibly and shared a worried glance with him.

He took her hand under the table, and he didn't let go.

TWELVE

When Abbott arrived to brief us on our injuries, I tried my best to look innocent. Since he kept staring down his nose at me like I really had decided to blow myself up for funsies, I assumed it didn't work. Somewhere along the way, he had become my de facto personal physician, and he wasn't amused when he was forced to glue me back together.

"Midas has third-degree burns covering one quarter of his skin. He will heal the worst of it within the next thirty-six hours. He'll be sore, but he will fully recover. Scarring will be minimal." Abbott used his pen to knock a stubborn black curl off Midas's head onto the floor. "Hadley is healing much faster than anticipated from smoke inhalation and is otherwise unharmed."

The room had a watery quality, as if it wasn't quite real. "Why am I so loopy if I didn't get hurt?"

"You drew your sword and attempted to skewer one too many nurses. We sedated you to treat Midas."

"Oh," I said in a quiet voice. "Sorry about that."

Midas chuckled under his breath, devolving into a coughing fit that required water to sooth his parched throat.

"It's fine." Abbott spread his hands. "It happens more often than you might think."

That made me feel slightly less like a homicidal freak. Until he assured me the two firemen I had no memory whatsoever of assaulting when they took Midas from me had both been treated and sent home to recover from their injuries.

Oops.

"Bishop is here, if you're up to seeing him." Abbott paled before adding, "So is Remy."

A low growl rumbled through Midas's chest, but he rubbed his throat, too sore to fuss about her.

Poor Remy.

She wasn't all that bad once you got to know her, assuming you survived the process. On the other hand, she did have a reputation for attempted vehicular manslaughter where gwyllgi were concerned. I could see how that would make Abbott nervous given Midas had been the target, and he wasn't at his best.

"Send them in." Might as well get this over with all at once. "And thanks."

"It would have been much worse without your help." He smiled. "Thank you for saving him."

Uncomfortable with the praise, I squirmed beneath the weight of his gratitude. The tender kiss Midas pressed to my cheek was much easier to bear.

"We missed the party last night." I frowned at him. "I assume? I have no idea what day or time it is."

"Pretty safe bet," he agreed. "That means the drug has been distributed to sellers."

"Great." I drank more water to lubricate my dry mouth. "Now we'll be chopping the heads off hydras."

"We need to take out the source," Bishop said, entering the room on a cold breeze. "We're going to kill those sons of bitches." He crossed to me, yanked me into a hug that brought up the coughs I was trying to suppress, and pulled back to look me over. "I'm glad you're okay, kid."

"Me too," Remy chimed in. "I'm vague on the legalities of taking over a business after the owner dies." No one said a word, and she swallowed. "What? I'm happy you're not dead. You're the only boss I've ever had who didn't fire me within my first week."

"Your concern humbles me," I said dryly. "Truly."

"Hey, I did you a solid." She dug into the paper bag of leftovers for the container the mashed potatoes came in and scooped out the remnants with her finger. "I sent a few friends to the party, and let me tell you, the things they saw..."

When she moved on to eating the wedges the gwyllgi had only picked at, I prompted her. "What did they see?"

"The vampires, the wargs, and the fae all bought in. The necromancers and the gwyllgi passed." She crunched through the cold potato. "Here's where it gets interesting." She wiped her hands on her shirt. "The gwyllgi and necromancer representatives were from out of state, right? No one local wanted to go up against Tisdale or Linus if they got caught peddling lethal—to their species—drugs."

"Okay."

"When they passed on the buy-in, Blithe made an example of them. She had them bound, carried up front, and force-fed them Faete." Remy shivered. "The necromancer died within minutes. The gwyllgi took a lot longer." She wet her lips. "I figure its body was regenerating damaged tissue as fast as the drug destroyed it, but the drug won out in the end."

A horrible death by any metric, and it made me regret the meal I had just eaten.

Those poor teens. That must be what kept them hanging on. Their bodies refused to let them die.

"We need to get word out to everyone vulnerable to Faete." I shoved my tray aside and swung my feet over the edge of the bed. "The coven is pushing us to play defense, and that's not getting us anywhere. It's time to go on the offense."

"Are you sure you should be standing?" Bishop took my elbow before my full weight hit my feet. "You haven't been discharged."

"Midas is the injured party." I didn't wobble, and I was happy about that. "I need to change and then…"

I had no clothes. I had no apartment. I had…nothing.

I was right back to square one, like when I first moved to Atlanta with only the clothes on my back.

"About that." He mashed a button on his phone and passed it over to me. "Here."

"How are you?" Linus's cool voice filled the line. "How is Midas?"

"We're both alive." I shivered at the chill in his tone. "I'm about to head to HQ."

Everyone in the room gave me death stares, so I elected to ignore their hostilities.

"Bishop tells me your apartment is ruined."

"Yeah." I shivered from the breeze of my hospital gown parting. "I'll ask management if they've got another efficiency I can lease until mine is repaired."

Thankfully, Tisdale had passed along the news that no one else had been harmed in the blast. Their apartments on the other hand… That entire floor would require a facelift before all was said and done.

"You're moving into the potentate's suite." He made it an order. "Bishop has the keys."

The charred gwyllgi across from me raised an eyebrow, and I chewed on my bottom lip. "Midas is…"

"I'm aware." Linus warmed his voice with intent. "The suite is yours. Your guests are your business." He hesitated. "Do you need me?"

Yes, I wanted to cry, *a thousand times yes*. But he was my boss, and I couldn't afford to appear weak.

I was bruised, my hair crispy, and I wanted my big brother to swoop in and hug me until I stopped falling to pieces. But Boaz wasn't an option. Adelaide wasn't either. The coven had moved against me. In my home. To prove they could get to me anywhere. I couldn't invite family into the mix. It would put them in danger, and I would never forgive myself if I got them hurt.

"I can handle it."

With Natisha's bargain always at the forefront of my mind, I debated how much help Linus could offer. He had given her his word he wouldn't help us secure the hearts, but the bomb was a separate matter. Or was it? The vicious nature of the attack screamed coven to me, but we had no concrete evidence of their involvement yet.

We had collected one heart out of seven. They must know, or at least suspect, the game had changed to strike back this swiftly. At me, in particular. If I had kept the heart in my apartment, it would have been toast. I doubted that was a coincidence. The coven hoarded power. They wouldn't give up an ounce of it without a fight.

"I'll inform the Society, and my mother, of what you've learned."

Briefing his mom was ten times worse than facing Tisdale. "Thanks."

"Reach out if you need me."

"I will."

He ended the call before I could change my mind and beg for his help climbing out of the hole I dug for myself the day I dragged him to the den to bargain on Midas's behalf. The alternative, though, had been unthinkable. Midas would have given all he had to save Ford, and Natisha would have let him. Clearly, the man couldn't be trusted to let others gauge his worth.

Those nightmares of his were vicious, and they messed with his head. He woke from them haunted in a way I saw in the mirror a few times a week. Less now that he was a wall of warm muscle I sheltered behind when I woke from dreams, sweaty and trembling from the reminder of what I had done, what I was deep down in my soul.

Tapping the phone against my thigh, I searched for the bright side. "At least now I'll have an espresso machine."

"About that…" Bishop dug a debit card out of his pocket. "There you go."

"What is it?" I accepted the card and frowned at my name on the front. "This isn't my bank."

We all carried expense cards linked to the OPA, expenses—much like our salaries—paid by taxes on the paranormal citizens, but this logo was different from those too.

"Here's the thing." Bishop settled into a ready stance that set alarm bells clanging in my head. "When Linus moved out, he told me to get the penthouse ready for the next potentate."

"I remember." Linus offered his old suite to me that night, and I passed. "That doesn't explain this."

"He took what he wanted and told me he didn't care what I did with the rest." He paused. "Have you been up since then?"

"Without Linus there, I haven't had a reason."

"You remember all those paintings and sculptures?"

I'm sure my thoughts on them leaked onto my face. "Yes."

"Turns out his interior designer purchased them from up-and-coming local artists."

That sounded about right. The place had a classy but cold feel. It was glossy and perfect like a magazine. Linus lived there, had for years, but it was clear it wasn't his home. Just a place where he slept.

"You're the one responsible for that paras-only silent auction." Midas sat upright. "Mom bought a godawful red painting from it when she recognized the work as Leo Morgan's. He's one of our old ones. I respect that, but it's literally a solid-red canvas." He glared at Bishop. "It looks like blood spatter, smells like blood too. It cost her seventy-three thousand dollars. A dozen more paintings from other artists, and twice as many figurines and sculptures, were on the auction block that night. We're lucky she stopped with one."

"Bishop," I said calmly. "Tell me you didn't do what I think you did."

"The apartment is empty, a blank slate. You'll need funds to dress it up, make it your own." He stared at me, daring me to refuse. "You need the money to start over, and I hate to tell you this, but it might not be the last time we have this conversation. I'm going to teach you how to invest what you don't use, and we're going to set you up for life."

"You need to transfer these funds to Linus."

"He doesn't want them. He didn't want anything but his personal art. That's all he took when he left."

Those portraits had been a study in Grier, as I recalled, and it didn't surprise me he wouldn't part with them.

"I can't accept this." I pushed the card back at him. "It's too much."

"Think about your family." He held up his hands, palms out. "Addie could use the money, and so could your dad. Think what you could do for them, for your ancestral home."

The dissonance between what I expected him to say and what he said jarred me so much I almost said something stupid, like *My family doesn't need the money.*

Boaz and Macon were both still Pritchards. I was the one who had been disinherited. They had family, homes, and trust funds. I had...a cool breeze on my backside from the crack in the hospital gown. The Whitakers didn't have much more than that to their names either.

"I can't." I set it on the nearest solid surface. "I appreciate what you did, but it's not mine to spend."

"He said you'd say that."

Linus, no doubt. The man was darn near prescient.

Remy, done eating her way through our leftovers, chimed in. "That's why he bought shares in your company at a ridiculous markup."

"There are no shares. There is no company." I owned a franchise, that was all. "What did you do?"

"As your business manager—" she lifted an imperious brow, "—I took it upon myself to secure us an investor so that we might expand your brand."

The whole purpose of the mall was how easy it made collecting gossip. I couldn't afford to lose that, even with Remy's ability to split into multiples.

"In addition to opening a storefront," she kept going, "we'll be opening kiosks in every mall in the city."

The storefront would go a long way toward legitimizing my business, but goddess. The expense left me shaking in my boots. I teetered on my feet and sat on the bed before I collapsed.

The MBA I earned in my past life glittered in my mind's eye, tantalizing me. I used to have such different dreams, and this touched on one of my old ones. Entrepreneurship had sounded so fancy back then, like a ticket to the good life.

"I can't do this." I kept shaking my head. "It's not my money, fake investor or not."

"Linus is very much real," said the man himself as he entered the room carrying a diamond cut crystal vase stuffed with three or more dozen blush-pink roses.

"W-w-what are you doing here?" I yanked the sheet over my lap. "I thought you were in Savannah."

"I came to finalize some paperwork." He flicked a conspiratorial glance at Remy then back to me. "They've caught you up to speed?"

Bishop rubbed the base of his neck and stared at the overhead air vent, utterly absorbed.

"Yes." I thrust out my arm to point at the card. "You have to take back your money."

Remy growled at me, chicken stuck between her teeth, but we would talk later.

Ambrose, the jerk, deigned to make an appearance now that Linus was here for him to brownnose.

"As I understand it," Linus said, setting the flowers on my side of the bed, "Bishop was kind enough to liquidate the assets I no longer wanted, which gave me a cushion to invest in a local business run by a promising entrepreneur." He cut his eyes toward Remy. "And her savvy assistant."

There was that word. Plucked straight out of my head. Maybe he was psychic.

"That's not—" I flailed. "I mean—"

"Remy has assured me that you will repay my investment, plus interest. Her spreadsheets were quite impressive."

The mental picture of me writing my last check to Linus with skin wrinkled to the texture of a prune and zipping around in a powerchair came to me in a moment of perfect clarity.

"Five years," she said proudly. "I did the math."

Terrified to ask how much Linus had given me, I gaped at her. "Are you insane?"

Back to rooting through the bag, she found a crumb of cake and licked it off her fingers. "Do you ever look at the spreadsheets I give you?"

"I mean to," I said defensively. "I get busy."

"I had my accountant verify her numbers, if that puts your mind at ease." Linus placed a cool hand on my shoulder. "Spread your wings." The words carried a tangible weight. "You deserve the chance to see how far you can fly."

"But..." I wet my lips. "I..."

"This is a business arrangement." He squeezed lightly then dropped his arm. "Remy will fill you in on the repayment schedule."

"So..." That helped me find my voice. "This is a loan?"

"Yes," he said gently. "It's a loan."

I could process *loan* that better than *investment*. A loan, I could pay back. An investment implied an act of faith, of trust, of belief. I couldn't deal with that right now, while I was in a hospital bed and my apartment was a smoking crater in the side of the building.

I felt like a total failure, and this a handout, but it was easier to listen to that miserable voice in my head than it was to see myself, or my situation, clearly.

Not enough. Not enough. Not enough.

Mother had warped my perception of myself, I knew that. Year by year, she whittled away my self-esteem until I had to fake smiles for work, for school, for friends. I had to fake *me*. Hadley wasn't me, exactly, but she was *real*. Maybe realer than Amelie ever had been.

Midas linked our fingers, and I knew what he would say, that I was a fool if I passed on the offer.

"Do what's right for you," he advised, shocking me to my core. "Do what you can live with."

More tears threatened, but I squared my shoulders and swallowed the hard lump in my throat.

My mother was one person. One opinion. Her voice might always ring loudest in my ears, but it didn't have to be the one I heeded. This many otherwise intelligent people couldn't be wrong about me.

I am enough.

"Thank you," I whispered to Linus. "You're a good...friend."

During our long association, Linus had been many things to me. A freckle-faced annoyance when we were kids, a lovesick nerd when we were teens, and a nightmare come to startling life when we were adults. I had mocked him, laughed at him, and dismissed him. And he had forgiven all that. He had gifted me with a second chance to be someone whose gaze I could hold in the mirror. Now he was offering me the tools to complete my transformation.

The all-key tattooed on my forearm was a peculiar design, but at its center was a stylized version of the city seal of Atlanta. A phoenix, its wings spread, rising from the flames.

I had never identified with it more.

"I am your friend," he said softly, and there was sadness there. "I always will be."

The unspoken promise, that he would do what must be done no matter the cost, comforted me.

Bishop would fight for me. I understood that now. Midas... He would never let me go. Linus was the one person on whose shoulders the burden of my existence could rest. I hated that for him, and I wished I hadn't caved to sentimentality now. I didn't want to make it any harder on him than it had to be, if the worst came to pass.

Linus walked out with Bishop, and Remy began tiptoeing behind them to eavesdrop until I snapped my fingers to get her attention.

"You've done enough, Employee of the Month." I jabbed a finger at her. "Get back to building your evil empire and leave them out of it."

"You're mad now, but you'll get over it." She smiled, needlelike teeth on display. "And you'll thank me."

During the excitement, Midas had fallen asleep, his eyes twitching behind their lids.

Most of his exposed skin was bright pink with regrown flesh and pimpled with blisters. His hair had been buzzed against his scalp, and one of his eyebrows was missing. He would have died in that inferno, if he weren't gwyllgi and if Abbott wasn't such a gifted healer. And fine, if Ambrose hadn't been able to give me the strength I needed to walk out of there with him.

With few other available options, I leaned on my backstabbing employee. "Can you do me a favor?"

"Depends," she mumbled around food. "What did you have in mind?"

"Can you buy me an outfit to get me out of the infirmary without me flashing everyone between here and Target?"

"A Target run?" She took a swig of my water. "Why didn't you say so?"

"Buy to my tastes," I warned her. "Not yours."

"Sure thing." She pocketed my shiny new card and sashayed out humming Madonna's "Like a Virgin."

Well, that sounded promising. I'm sure nothing bad would come of letting her choose my wardrobe.

With that ball rolling, I cuddled Midas, pretended I had nothing better to do, and wished that were true.

THIRTEEN

Remy provided me with clothes, shoes, and basic hygiene products. If the lone outfit I had to my name included an eighties hairband tee and ripped jeans, I didn't give her the satisfaction of showing my annoyance. The fact my sneakers lit up when I walked meant I could never wear them on patrol without advertising my movements to predators, but again, I smiled and thanked her.

I wished I hadn't after I saw the jumbo spray can of Aqua Net in the plastic bag but *c'est la vie*. Or was that *que será, será*? Whatever. I was terrible with languages.

While I dressed like the groupie that time forgot, Midas dozed, and I was grateful to spare him from my ensemble. The man had suffered enough. Plus, he might be in reach of his phone, and I did not want this outfit captured for posterity.

Before slipping out the door, I wrote him a brief note and kissed his forehead. I hated leaving him alone, but the drugs kept him resting peacefully, and I didn't have time to hover with so many other lives at stake.

As the elevator chimed its arrival, Abbott noticed me attempting a prison break and broke into a sprint. The doors closed before he reached me, and I said a mental apology for the chaos I brought into his life as I dialed Lisbeth.

Since I still had to escape the Faraday lobby before I got intercepted, I walked and talked with purpose. "Do you think you can arrange a rush delivery on a few things for me?"

"Please give me a job. I beg of you." She pitched her voice low. "Ford has me propped up on the couch watching soaps. I'm bored out of my mind. I get enough drama at work, you know?"

Ignoring how her comment applied to me, I asked, "Have you maybe told him you don't enjoy soaps?"

"He was so proud to know what women want, Hadley. I couldn't break his heart on the first day."

"Okay, fine. Break the news to him tomorrow."

Laughing softly, she turned the conversation back toward me. "How can I help?"

"I need a king-size mattress delivered to the penthouse." The freedom to say *put it on my card* was heady. I could get used to this. "Talk to Remy about sheets. We get free samples. Color doesn't matter."

"King-size, huh?" Lisbeth cackled. "That's quite the upgrade."

"Hmm." I thought about it. "We've made the futon work this long. Downgrade us to a queen."

We.

Us.

Powerful words that gave me heart palpitations.

"I'm just yanking your chain." She snorted. "Midas is a *lot* of man. I get you want to keep him close, but come summer, you'll be glad you can feel a breeze between you." She waited for me to decide. "Well? King or queen?"

"Surprise me."

I couldn't dedicate this much headspace to the next logical thought, that if the courtship thing didn't pan out, I wouldn't need more than a futon. A king-size bed would be a reminder of the prince who no longer shared it with me.

"Okay." A worried note carried in her voice, but she kept her concerns to herself. "Need anything else?"

"Another outfit would be nice." I read her the numbers off my card. "I might need it after this."

"After what?"

"After I have a nice sit-down with Blithe," I confided. "That's what."

It was time to stir the pot and see what bubbled over.

GREENLEAF WAS in full swing when I arrived, and I stepped in line to wait my turn. I didn't want to draw the bouncer's eye, so I kept my head down but my ears open. As it happened, he wasn't paying much attention to the individuals waiting to get in. He got a call through his earpiece every so often, and he counted out the next five people to let through the door. It was very methodical, not at all based on how much flesh or cash got exposed. More than anything, it reminded me of an assembly line.

When my turn came, the bouncer didn't blink. Just counted heads and let us in. I was grateful to be the fifth in my group. I wouldn't have wanted to stand at the head of the line and wait right under his nose. So far, he had given no indication he recognized me. I wanted to keep it that way.

Inside the club, I breathed easier. The space was pitch black except where dark-green lights shone on walls of living plants that writhed with magic or an optical illusion. It was hard to tell, and I didn't plan on investigating.

"Dance with me," a male voice whispered in my ear, "you lovely creature."

Chills peppered my arms, and I turned slowly to find a slender man with leaves for hair and lips as bright as clovers behind me. He wore a costume straight out of a period feature film, something Jane Austenish, and I had to admire his dedication to a theme.

"I have a boyfriend." I honed my glare on him. "He eats men who dance with me for breakfast."

"Do you promise," he breathed, and I could tell he meant it. "I haven't been properly dined on in ages."

That sounded like a personal problem to me. "Have you seen Blithe?"

"Madam Danann is holding court." He offered his arm. "Shall I escort you to her?"

"Sure." I didn't accept his arm, and my defiance delighted him. I could tell by the quick shine in his eyes and the swipe of his grass-green tongue over his lips. "Were you here for the party a few days ago?"

"Madam ordered us all away," he pouted. "I heard about it, of course. Pity to have missed it."

"Yeah." I recalled the bodies sprawled on the sidewalk. "A real shame."

"I feel I must warn you, lovely, that there are those among us who keep an eager eye on you."

"I get that a lot." Gooseflesh rose down my arms at the implied threat. "Mostly from people trying to kill me."

"You helped one of us, and now I will help you."

Aware I couldn't speak Bishop's name, I didn't bother, but I did wonder if that was who he meant.

"I appreciate that." I scanned for the court he mentioned. "Where did you say Blithe was again?"

The man took me by the hand and whirled me into a quickstep that spun me out the exit onto the street behind the club.

"Don't come here again, lovely." A ripple made his outline blur, and then he was the man with long black hair from the blood whore-house where Linus had instructed me to leave Bishop after we sprung him from the cage the coven put him in. "Next time I might not be the one to spot the wolf among the sheep."

"I need to speak to Blithe," I protested, ready to push past him. "You don't understand—"

"No," he sighed. "You don't understand." He touched his fingers to my forehead. "You will."

Glittering trails fanned in all directions, entering and exiting the club, streaming down darkened streets and through alleys.

"What am I seeing?" I braced a palm on the building to anchor myself. "What did you do to me?"

"I opened your eyes a crack. Just as I did before." The curtain of black hair slid over his shoulder. "It won't last long, only until dawn. I suggest you hunt while you can."

Wrapping himself in what I now realized was glamour, he returned to his green costume and shut the door.

Ambrose hadn't moved a muscle since the fae dropped his glamour, and now he studied the air around us. He pointed in one direction and yanked on me through our bond to urge me on.

Despite the fact he had saved my life, thereby saving his, I recognized the danger in accepting help from him.

"One trail," I warned him. "We'll see where it goes, and that's it."

The shadow leapt and kicked its heels together.

Anything that put him in that good of a mood was bad business, but I didn't have any other leads. Given recent events, I did apply common sense and text Bishop an update.

Hit Greenleaf. Bumped into your BFF. He gifted me with the ability to see glowing trails leading to goddess knows what to keep me away from Blithe.

The distraction was a good one. Masterful even. He had offered me an opportunity I couldn't ignore.

*>> #@$%**

Just thought I'd let you know.

I pocketed the cell before he found his words and let me have it. Accepting gifts from the fae? Dumb. Really dumb. But the guy hadn't exactly given me a choice. If I was going to pay for it somewhere down the line, I might as well use it while I had it.

Curious about the trails, I reached out, expecting my hand to pass through the nearest one, but it was solid as twine. I gripped it, yanked on it, and experienced an odd sensation down its length. As if I had tapped someone on the shoulder, and they had turned to look at me.

"On second thought..." I dropped the trail Ambrose had chosen. "Let's try this one instead."

Whatever I had disturbed when I touched that particular thread would be on alert. I sensed that much. I didn't want to bump into it when it was expecting company, whatever it was.

The next trail I kept well away from, and we followed it with care not to tangle in the other threads crisscrossing the streets and buildings. Whatever the fae man had done to me, he had more than opened my eyes. He had altered my perception, made the intangible tangible.

As we gained on the person/thing at the end of the trail, I noticed its glow brightened, and the motes grew less defined, more scattered. As though its past were set, but its future was as yet undetermined.

"This is too weird," I told Ambrose, and for once he agreed with me.

The trail ended in an abandoned building, the motes diffuse around me, but nothing else moved.

"Well?" I risked the question out loud to Ambrose. "What do you sense?"

Hisses filled the darkened corners, and a clicking noise sent gooseflesh racing down my arms.

That was all the warning the Martian Roach gave me before launching its chitinous body at me.

Two thoughts battled for top billing in my head.

One: Frakking hell, that fae had given me the good stuff.

Two: Frakking hell, I was alone with a pissed-off Martian Roach.

Ambrose glided over to it and ran his hand down its spine.

The creature whipped its head toward him and issued an earsplitting shriek that summoned more motes, enough to turn the blackened ceiling into a starlit sky.

The roach had called for backup, lots of it, but all I had was Ambrose.

The shadow coiled around my shoulders, waiting for my play. I only had one, and we both knew it.

"Drain it." We needed the specimen, and I had to be alive to call it in. "*Don't* kill it."

I couldn't put off feeding him forever. Not after the energy he expended saving me during the explosion. That came with its own issues. I might as well get it over with, then worry about draining him to a manageable level.

Given the order, Ambrose dove into the creature, devouring its magic in chomps that filled my stomach with sympathetic pangs. Hungry as he was, he made quick work of it, and the creature went down hard. That was all well and good except its buddies were crawling out of the woodwork.

I had maxed out my friendship with Ford, and Midas was in no shape to help. Ares wasn't a fan of mine at the moment, and Lisbeth wasn't ready to report for duty. That left me with a pissed-off Bishop, and maybe Remy. If she answered her phone.

The magic saturating Ambrose swelled him like a tick and left him too dazed to be much use, except as a battery. That worked just fine for me.

I took the small jar of ink from my pocket and dipped my finger to draw a circle around the unconscious roach and myself, careful to keep Ambrose locked in too. I had to nudge him to push magic into the design until it snapped closed in a protective barrier the other roaches couldn't penetrate.

First things first, I called the local sentinel HQ. They dispatched a unit of their Elite to help me crush the roaches. That took care of the most pressing danger but left me with a roach in the circle with me. Definitely a job for Bishop.

"Can you rent a U-Haul and meet me?" I gave him the address. "We need to move fast before it wakes."

"You and I are going to have a talk," he warned. "You're getting in too deep with the fae."

"I didn't ask your friend to help, he just did it."

As if Bishop already knew the friend's identity, or could guess, he didn't ask for specifics.

"No fae ever just does anything, kid. He's marked you as a person of interest, or he wouldn't bother."

Magic tingled through my forehead where his fingers had touched my skin. "What does that mean?"

"Let him build enough debt between you, and he's going to ask you for a favor in return."

"How does him giving me this indebt me? I didn't agree to anything."

"You accepted his help. That's all the opening he needs to worm his way into your life. Trust me."

"He's your friend."

"He's not my friend. He's..." A spate of annoyed Gaelic filled my ear. "He's trouble. Stay away from him." He cursed, in English this time. "Don't let the bastard touch you again. Gods only knows what else he did to you when he gave you this *gift*."

"That sounds...bad." I was not a fan of people doing things to me without my knowledge. "Ambrose?"

The shadow picked up on the drift of my thoughts, which creeped me out to no end, but he shook his head. Whatever hooks the fae had used hadn't lodged in my skin. Ambrose would know, and he would do his best to devour the magic before I noticed what he was up to and reprimanded him for it.

"Don't move a muscle," Bishop snapped. "I'll be right there."

A glimmer caught my eye, and a figure emerged from the shadows. "He's such a whiner."

"Remy?" I started at her voice. "How did you get in here?"

"I have my ways."

"You were stalking me again, weren't you?" I squinted at her. "Are you even you?"

"Stop trying to define that which defies definition."

"That sounds like a *no*."

"I'm Six." She walked closer. "Happy?"

"I'm trapped in a circle with a giant bug in a warehouse full of giant bugs, so not really, no."

"You forgot him." She jerked her chin toward Ambrose. "Hello, beastie. Fat and happy, are we?"

Ambrose ignored her and curled into a ball on the concrete.

"He took down the roach." I shrugged. "He's digesting."

"I hear Bishop is on his way with a truck, so what do you need from me?"

"Ideally, I would like to pack up this nice, sedate Martian Roach for Abbott before the sentinels arrive to kill the rest."

"Except the building is surrounded by giant bugs, so there's no way that's happening."

"I said *ideally*."

"Realistically?"

"Can you bring all yourselves here? Between them, Bishop, and me, we should be able to load this guy into the truck after the smoke clears. I'll tell them we need the body for testing, which we do. I'll just neglect to mention it's still alive."

"That could work." She tugged on a piercing in her ear. "But I'm not out to Bishop."

There was nothing I could trade her about him in kind. The geas prevented it. His secrets were his own to share or not. But she had seen where I took him, and who had taken him in. She might suspect the truth of his nature based on that alone. I wasn't sure how aware fae were of one another. It's not like necromancers could tell species from a glance, except when it came to vampires, but that was a result of the necromantic magic used to animate them. That's what we picked up on, an active casting, basically. A long-term spell with a generous, but definite, expiration date.

"I'm not going to force you out." It wasn't my place. "What if he drops off the van, and you and me handle it?"

"How pissed are you about the Linus thing?"

The change in topic threw me. "I am both excited and terrified for the opportunity."

"So, you're not going to fire me?"

"Uh, no." I couldn't believe she would ask. "You got us into this mess. You're going to get us out of it."

A tentative smile teetered on her mouth. "You've been nicer to me than anybody has been in...a long time."

"You were down on your luck when we met." I slid my gaze toward Ambrose. "I know how it feels when you stumble and fall, but you can't get up no matter how hard you try." I frowned. "There are times in life when the only way to climb out of the hole you've dug for yourself is to have someone throw you a rope. You still have to pull yourself out, but at least you've got an anchor waiting for you at the top."

"I tried to kill your man, and I'm not saying I'm over the impulse."

"As long as you don't act on the impulse, we're good."

"I can probably restrain myself from murdering him." She cocked her head, considering. "As long as you give me a raise proportionate to my contributions to the company."

"You're asking for a partnership, aren't you?"

"Oh. Hmm. A partnership?" She tapped her chin. "I hadn't thought of that."

"Yeah." I snorted a laugh. "Seems to me, you've thought of *everything*."

The world had indeed flipped upside down when I was handing off a business on the verge of becoming. I had invested years to earn my MBA, and I was turning over my franchised empire to a fae without any qualifications aside from wit and determination.

"Think on it." She danced away a few steps. "Back in a few."

There was nothing to think about, really. I struggled to run a mall kiosk and keep my head above water on the potentate front. There was no way I could manage more than one kiosk, let alone a store. This was Remy's passion fueling an old dream of mine.

The surrealness of it struck me, that I was getting a thing I had always wanted only to discover I didn't want it anymore. My world had been so small and certain back when I thought earning a respectable degree for a Low Society woman that would guarantee me a respectable job and a respectable match would earn my parents' approval. Only after I realized that would never happen had I reached for bigger dreams that turned my life into a nightmare.

Now I had trouble picturing a life where that kind of work fulfilled me. Perhaps because it never had, but I had bought into the idea for so long I had been afraid to let it die until Ambrose helped me kill my old life.

The wail of sirens alerted me to the approach of the sentinels in their APD squad cars, the better to make this seem like a routine police raid and not a magical mutant shootout, which, now that I thought about it, would make an *awesome* movie title.

Used to the routine, I raised my hands to show they were empty and that I was not a threat. Most of them recognized me, but there was always a risk of a new hire getting trigger-happy before they determined I was one of the good guys.

And how wild was that? *One of the good guys.* That was me, all right.

Gunfire erupted all around, and insectoid screeches gave me a good idea of the formation the APD was using to infiltrate the building. Low Society necromancers rarely had any magic, and it wasn't the type of magic you could fling at someone or something anyway. It required tools and preparation. It was all but worthless in a fight. But guns with armor-piercing rounds, which I suggested after the OPA's first encounter with the Martian Roaches, worked just fine.

"Clear," a woman called, and she was answered by several other voices. "What the actual hell, Whitaker?"

A short woman in black tactical armor with a vicious-looking firearm in each hand entered the building.

"Hey, Lizzy." I lowered my arms. "Long time, no see."

Lizzy Frommel was the pack's liaison with the Atlanta Police

Department. She was a lawyer, but she was also an enforcer. Kind of like Rambo but with a degree. She represented gwyllgi in police custody and made arrangements with the undercover sentinels to ensure justice was served outside human law.

Between her, my Lisbeth, and Ares's Liz, I had a *Liz* adjacent overload in my life.

"It's been a week, tops." She kept her fingers on the triggers, and her eyes in the darkened corners. "What have you gotten yourself into this time?"

The tone recalled my insecurities about what Ares must have said to Midas to provoke the response I had overheard, but I couldn't let it get to me here or now. I couldn't go through life suspecting everyone wanted me out of the picture. I mean, that might be the case, but I couldn't let it matter.

"You heard about Faete?"

"Your office sent mine a dossier, so yeah."

"Well, here's your origin." I swept my arm out to encompass the destruction. "Don't let these things bite you."

"Their spit is a drug?" Her nose wrinkled. "Are you sure you're not the one who's high?"

"Their spit is the basis for the drug," I confirmed. "My team has been working around the clock to isolate the exact components used in the compound."

"You mean your team has been working alongside the cleaners, right?"

"Um, yes." I snapped my fingers. "That."

Lizzy crossed to me and crouched, taking in the bug behind me, which had started to twitch. "What gives?"

"Hmm?" I leaned into her field of vision. "I don't know what you're talking about."

"That thing is alive, and you put it in the circle with you." Her eyes narrowed. "You're protecting it." Her finger caressed the trigger. "The question is why? And you better have a damn good answer, or I'll have to assume you've been infected."

My brilliant plan had hinged on sentinels rushing in to save the day while Remy and I exited, stage left. I hadn't taken into consideration that Lizzy might catch wind of my call and decide to come on behalf of the pack. Normally, she wouldn't have done it. But, as Midas and I got more serious, I was starting to see myself for what I was: a liability to the pack. Lizzy had come here in case I got myself in trouble I couldn't get out of without help.

Ares had been right when she said this courtship thing had little to do with *twu wuv* and everything to do with politics. Though I might be paraphrasing that last bit, the logic still held, and it still sucked.

"We need an unadulterated sample in order for my people to start working on an antidote." I kept my voice low. "We will send samples to the cleaners for their database, so that anyone who wants to can access the information and help work on a cure." I leaned in closer to the edge. "We brought in Doughty too. Between him, Abbott, and Reece, we've got a better chance of cracking this than anyone else."

Bishop sauntered in, swinging a ring of keys around his finger, and I wanted to beat him with my shoe for being late and so blasé about it.

"Liz," he said in greeting. "Her authority outstrips yours, and you know it. Don't waste our time."

"I was handling it," I growled at him. "We were reaching an understanding."

"She's posturing," he sighed. "She's a high-level dominant, or she couldn't do what she does. She'll take tiny bites out of you until there's nothing left if you let her." He stepped right up to the circle's edge. "Her beta is courting you. You outrank her. Play nice if you want her to step all over you, but do it later."

As was often the case, Bishop was right. On multiple fronts.

"By the authority of the Office of the Potentate of Atlanta, we're seizing the body. We'll send out samples to all major factions as soon as they've been collected." I crased the line with my finger, and the circle collapsed. "We're happy to share our resources with anyone who has a better idea about how to assist people who have been victimized by this drug." Ambrose slithered across the ground, alert at last, and sniffed Lizzy's ankles. "But you won't stop us."

"Big words."

"I have big swords too, if you need me to clean out your ears."

"I heard you carried Midas out of the fire."

"He saved me first. I was repaying the favor."

"There are people who don't care much for your relationship."

"So I hear."

"You want my opinion?"

Not really, no. "Sure."

"Fuck 'em." She offered me a hand up then held on. "Bad things happen, and it sucks, but it's life. There will always be some dickhead next door who spots greener grass in your yard and has to trample it to be happy."

"That sounds perilously close to an endorsement."

"This was coming. That it's arriving now, before you officially take over, tells me the people behind it are more afraid of you than they were of Linus. They want this done before you take office and claim Atlanta. They're worried what you might do with that power boost."

"And if your pack pays for it?"

"We're gwyllgi. We fight. It's what we do. We wouldn't have held on to this territory against all comers for this long if we weren't willing and able to defend it. Anyone who tells you different is a coward."

Or they didn't want to die, which might be the same as having a reason to live.

Gwyllgi protocol gave me a headache on the best days.

"Besides, the coven hit us first. They didn't use you to get to us." She grew pensive. "They might use us to get to you, though."

That was a sobering thought, but one I'd had myself.

A sentinel called for Lizzy, and she nodded at me before prowling over to them.

"I'll take the keys." I held out my hand to Bishop. "I got this."

"You're going to lift that entire roach on your own?" He snorted. "Not happening."

"She's got backup," Remy said from behind him, and several more of her stepped out too. "Plenty of it."

Bishop's jaw dropped, but I couldn't tell if it was shock at her big reveal or horror at the thought of so many Remys running loose in the city. Either way, I patted his shoulder as I studied her. "I thought you weren't coming out to him."

"I've been hiding a long time." The Remy army crossed to me, the lead Remy acting as their collective mouthpiece. "I'm tired of it." They encircled the roach and began lifting it without her, or our, help. "You need me. I'm here."

"That's that?"

"That's that," she agreed, then grinned at Bishop. "Besides, I sold the expansion pitch to Linus based on my ability to simultaneously run all the stores in the same manner as the original kiosk. It's the only way to guarantee the sales numbers."

That went a long way toward explaining why Linus had entertained her business offer. He was the curious sort, and I bet his analytical mind had devoured the peculiarities of what made Remy's magic work. He might have agreed just for the excuse to meet with her every so often and examine her to his heart's content.

"I haven't seen one of your kind in..." Bishop shook his head. "I have no idea."

"You've seen more of us than you think." She laughed at her own joke. "You know, because there are seven of me?"

"Seven?" His gaze skipped over the gathering, counting. "Your kind divide evenly. Where's the last?"

"Midas killed her," Remy announced before I could salvage the big reveal. "I tried to kill him, but it didn't stick." She sounded cheerful as she winked at me. "Currently, I'm biding my time."

"You shouldn't go around telling people you're open to the idea of murdering a prince." He glanced at me. "Are you sure *she* didn't blow you up? Maybe she thought Midas had slept in."

"She's not that sloppy." Plus, her murderous tendencies had a specific focus, and I wasn't it. "She would have detonated the bomb in the lobby when I walked past him."

"She's right." Remy shrugged. "I would have."

"See?" I sighed in her direction. "She's as innocent as a newborn babe."

Bishop shook his head. "Let's get the roach and go."

And get the roach and go, we did.

FOURTEEN

The murmur of low voices dragged Midas up from sleep to find Hadley and Abbott discussing him at the foot of the hospital bed. Her hand curved over Midas's toes, and she didn't seem to notice the instinctual urge to touch him when in close proximity. It was a promising sign she was bonding too, and it gave him hope.

"Can I take him with me?" Her fingers tightened in a possessive hold. "We can put him in a wheelchair and hook his IV bag to that connected pole thing, right?"

"He can't be seen leaving the infirmary in a wheelchair," Abbott soothed. "He'll have to walk."

"I want to punch whoever cooked up these half-baked rules in the face."

"As a physician, I agree." He sighed. "As a gwyllgi…"

"I can walk," Midas rasped. "I'm done with the IV anyway."

"You're not the doctor." Hadley rushed to his side. "You don't get to make that call."

The longer he kept his eyes open, the clearer his vision became until he noticed the change in her.

"Your hair is shorter." He touched the soft curls. "It's nice."

"I was due for a trim anyway." She blew off the reason for the new style. "I like it shorter in summer."

"You can take him home with you if he can walk out of here," Abbott said, ending their argument. "That is the best I can do."

"Well?" She studied him. "Can you make it, or are we bunking here today?"

The easy way she said *we*, discarding her comfort for his, made it a simple choice.

"I can walk," he said again. "I'm dizzy, but I can manage."

Hadley made it clear she wasn't impressed with his struggle to pull on clothes, or his wobbling attempts to navigate the room. She shadowed him, her arms out to catch him if he fell, like he wouldn't crush her in the process. Then again, she had carried him down more than one flight of stairs. Adrenaline might have given her an edge, but he knew there was more to it.

Shadow child.

Wraith or otherwise, the creature she had bonded with fed her strength. That much was clear. The cost of its aid, and the result on her health, worried him, but he could only wait to see if she confided the terms to him.

The deeper the bond burrowed into him, the harder it became not to share everything of himself with her. He might be repeating his mistake of tricking her into a courtship by not fully informing her of who she kept company with, but he couldn't work up the nerve to make confessions that might tarnish him in her eyes. Not when she gazed down at him as if he were a good man she was proud to have by her side.

The walk out of the infirmary wasn't too bad. Abbott emptied the halls, so Midas was able to keep a hand on the wall to steady himself. The elevator ride could have been just as painless, had the car been empty. The four enforcers already packed inside hesitated when they spotted him, their nostrils flaring in an instinctive hunt for signs of weakness. They wouldn't have acted on the impulse, not with Hadley there, but they would have filed away his injuries. It was the way their minds worked, the wildness in them, and he respected that.

"How are you feeling?" Carson, a seasoned enforcer, asked quietly, his attention on Hadley.

A smile tugged up one corner of Midas's mouth. "Like I know how a match feels after its been struck."

They laughed, but it didn't reach their eyes. They worried, he knew, but he was at a loss as to how to reassure them. He wasn't much good with people, and he was too tired to fake it at the moment.

"Oh, please." Hadley waded right into the conversation and the elevator. "Are you still whining about your hair?"

"It was my one great beauty." He picked up the banter and focused on walking as if his head weren't swimming with a mixture of drugs and trauma. "Now how am I supposed to attract a mate?"

"They make wigs out of real hair these days." She ran her palm over his scalp. "Then again, synthetic might be a better option for you. Something flame retardant, maybe?"

The guys in the elevator snickered as they shuffled back to make room for them to stand together.

"Funny." He took the hint when Hadley stepped into him, wrapping her arms around him. "Very funny."

The strength that allowed her to save him helped her prop him up without the others noticing beyond their embrace.

"Never thought I would see the day I had to beg Midas Kinase to stop it with the PDA," one of the guys quipped. "You're making me jealous over here."

"Don't sweat it." The guy next to him punched him in the shoulder. "Your inflatable girlfriend will kiss it and make it better after your shift."

"At least I have an inflatable girlfriend," he countered, then frowned. "Wait. That's not what I meant."

"Give it up, Dawes." His friend laughed. "Marinate in your shame."

The guys ribbed one another about their girlfriends, inflatable or otherwise, all the way to the lobby.

When the doors slid open, they jostled past with smiles and smack talk that drew attention to them, and to Midas. A few noted his proximity to Hadley and frowned. A few more goggled at his hair. One child cried at the splotchy skin healing in pink and red patches over his body until his mother exited the lobby.

Still spinning the situation like a pro, Hadley pulled him down to her for a slow kiss that earned them applause and a few good-natured teases.

Once the doors closed and they were alone, he panted into her mouth. "Ouch."

It cost him to admit he was in pain, and the softening of her expression confirmed she knew him well enough to guess that and appreciate it.

"Just a little farther." She couldn't be too obvious about supporting him even now, with the camera recording them and the potential for stops along the way. "And here we go."

The entire uppermost floor of the Faraday was the penthouse suite, and Linus had called it home during his tenure as potentate. Now it belonged to Hadley.

Across from the door, floor-to-ceiling windows stretched tall to offer a prime view of downtown Atlanta. The blackout curtains were remote-controlled, he knew from experience, to accommodate necromancers' nocturnal sleep schedules. The wall behind them, where the door stood, had been hung with Sheetrock and painted a neutral color between gray and beige. The walls to either side of him showed exposed brick with artfully applied plaster patches that softened the overall industrial vibe. The floors were polished concrete that reflected the overhead lights.

To the right, a narrow staircase with glass panels in place of rails had been built along one wall and led up to an open loft bedroom. To maximize space, the staircase had been hollowed out and transformed into a series of bookshelves that had once overflowed with

Linus's personal library. Beneath that was a closed door, and to the left was the bathroom and kitchen.

"The bedroom is in the loft?" Midas's joints protested the idea of climbing the ladder.

"The interior designer had all kinds of weird ideas. Apparently, that was one of them." She led him straight to the office door. "This is the original master suite." She shoved open the door. "Linus used it as an art studio. There's only the one bathroom, and it's off the main space. No en suite."

"One bathroom in this entire place?"

"Nuts, right?" She shook her head. "What was that woman thinking?"

"That it would only have to suit Linus?"

"Forever?"

"He didn't have a lot of prospects until recently."

"He had his pick of the litter. He just didn't want any of them."

Once she stepped aside, he could see the interior better. "That is a big bed."

"Looks like Lisbeth opted for a king size after all." She wrapped her arms across her middle. "I hope you don't mind. Your toes won't hang off now, and you'll actually be able to turn over. With this much space, we might not even stick together anymore."

"I loved that futon."

"Liar." She chuckled. "You slept with one cheek flapping in the breeze."

"But I slept with you." He took her hand. "That made up for it."

"Sweet talker." She tugged down the sheets on his usual side. "Climb in."

He did as he was told, grateful when he sank onto the cool sheets and soft mattress.

"Are you thirsty?" She covered him up to his waist. "Hungry?"

"All I need is you." He reached for her. "Come to bed."

A happy sound escaped her, and she launched onto the mattress. Rather than bouncing, she stuck fast in the dense memory foam and frowned as she sank in. He barely felt her wiggling free from his side of the bed.

"That was more fun in my head." She inched closer to him then settled in. "It feels so weird to be here."

"In Linus's old suite?"

"It's like I'm sleeping in my parents' room while they're away. Like Linus might come home early and find me with a boy in my bed." She stared around the room. "I also feel like there are eyeballs in the walls, like Grier is watching me."

"He did have an abnormal amount of Grier-based art in here…"

"Right?" Her breath huffed across his shoulder. "The man is *obsessed.*"

"He's in love."

Hadley made a thoughtful sound. "Is there a difference?"

That she had to ask meant she hadn't experienced it yet, and he rubbed a dull ache over his heart.

"I'm not sure," he confessed softly. "Maybe."

"Stop that." She caught his hand and lowered it to his side. "You'll hurt yourself."

"You handled the situation in the elevator like a pro." He refused to let her go, so she laced their fingers. "I was impressed."

"I'm trying to walk the line between what's acceptable to the pack versus what's acceptable to me."

"Keep that up, and they might think you're serious about me."

"I can't remember being more terrified in my life than when you dropped in the hall." Her expression grew haunted. "Trust me." She shivered. "That's saying something."

The sensation of fur brushed along the underside of his skin as his feral half relaxed again, even as its curiosity prickled. "You owe me a secret."

"I thought about scooping your hair out of the trash and putting it in a plastic bag."

Midas cranked his head toward her. "Are you serious?"

"Can you imagine Ford's face if he opened a letter, and there it was?" She mimed wiping tears from her eyes. "What about you?"

"I want to know more about you."

The laughter dried in her throat, and she swallowed hard. "You might not like what you find out."

"Please." He tightened his hold. "Don't pull away from me."

"I didn't mean to, I just...have to think about this." Her gaze went distant. "I can't give you an answer tonight."

"I don't need one tonight, or tomorrow, or next year." He pinched her chin and angled her head toward him. "I had to say it." He scented her fear, regret, grief. "You can say no, and I'll still be right here. You can say yes, in five years or ten, and I'll still be right here."

"You can't promise that." Her eyes glittered. "You don't know me well enough."

"You saved my life. A couple of times. You're smart, brave, and dedicated." He exhaled. "Whatever you tell me won't change any of that, and I don't need a preview of coming attractions to make that vow."

"Movie joke," she teased. "I like it."

"I thought you might." He kissed her knuckles. "I meant to tell you Dani sent me a text reminding you to come to the gym with me first of next month."

"She's got a phone?"

"Her grandparents pay the bill." He kept in touch with her and reported to them weekly. "She could go live with them, but they're out of state, and she won't leave her mom. They showed up out of the blue one day with sentinels to force her hand, but she disappeared for a month. They haven't tried it again."

"Poor kid." Her fingers slid from his. "Tell her I'll be there." She shifted onto her back. "For my safety, and the safety of everyone else in attendance, I think I'm going to start her out with pool noodles."

"Sword Fighting 101 with Hadley Whitaker," he mused. "BYOPN."

"Evildoers tremble with fear." She turned back toward him, scooched a little closer. "I'll think about it."

He didn't have to ask what she meant. He knew she was giving him his answer.

Smile tugging on his lips, he let his eyes close and fell into a healing sleep.

FIFTEEN

Reece texted me while I was attempting to figure out how to work Linus's fancy espresso machine. It was the only countertop appliance left, proving how well Bishop knew me, and it was smarter than me. I could tell by the tone it used every time I got the button sequence wrong.

"I will end you." I slapped the top with my open palm. "Give me my coffee."

"That model is worth a few grand." Midas padded into the kitchen, skin light pink in spots but steady on his feet. "You can always sell it and use the cash to buy a machine like the one you had. *Or* you could use it to pay one of the twins to bring you coffee every morning from the shop around the corner."

"I thought they only did laundry."

Simply known as *The Twins*, sons of one of the pack enforcers, they had absconded with the rolling laundry cart Bishop *acquired* for us to smuggle Bonnie Diaz, in gwyllgi form, into the Faraday. They used it to launch their own laundry service for single, busy, or just plain lazy gwyllgi in the building.

I wasn't gwyllgi, but I was plain lazy enough to use them when I got tired of scrubbing out the stains that came with the job and wanted to dump that pleasure into someone else's lap for a change.

"They've expanded to delivering coffee and pastries."

"I'm impressed, and also hungry."

Another text reminded me I had been about to read Reece's update when the lack of caffeine sent my brain into meltdown over the absence of café mocha in this joint.

"Whoa." I leaned a hip against the counter. "Reece says Doughty has synthesized an antidote."

"Good news then." A frown pinched his forehead. "That happened fast."

"Doughty is very good at what he does, and with magic to speed things up, he delivers results fast." That's why he charged a small fortune for consultations, and this went far beyond that. "Abbott elected to stay put, thanks to recent events, but Reece says he's driving the antidote and their notes to Savannah to consult with Linus and Grier before administering it to a volunteer patient." I kept reading. "Doughty referenced the formula for creating *Atrax robustus* antivenom, and it appears to be effective in simulations." I Googled that real quick. "That would be the Sydney funnel-web spider."

"How soon do you think he can have it ready for distribution?"

"Within the week." I set my phone aside. "I'm sorry I don't have better news."

"They're making progress. That's all we can ask of them. Magic isn't a cure-all."

"Sadly not," I agreed. "What are your plans for the night?"

"I've been recalled to the den to brief Mother and the other elders on recent developments." He waited a beat then prompted me. "How about you?"

"Patrolling the streets, searching for coven members, and hoping not to run into any naked wargs."

"Bishop going with you?"

"Yes." I rolled my eyes. "He's attached at the hip until our heart quota is met. No one else can guarantee they'll reach the box before they stop beating."

He'd timed me with a potato enchanted to beat like a heart, which put me off French fries forever, give or take a week. First, I had excised the organ from a dummy, taking care not to damage it. Then I ran like heck or called a Swyft to carry me to HQ. The potato was DOA every time.

"Any new leads on that front?"

While the espresso machine mocked me, I filled him in on the fae at the club, the trail, and the visit from Lizzy. I had been too preoccupied with getting him safely into bed to brief him last night. Then he went and dropped the bomb about wanting to learn more about me, and everything else scattered.

I had worried we would come to this, and I still had no clue what to do about it.

Mortifying as it would be, I might have to ask Linus for romantic advice.

Gulp.

"Bishop is breathing down my neck now that he thinks that fae has a vested interest in me, so I can't go to him and request another dose of the sight." I turned it over in my head. "I'm not sure if he led me to the Martian Roaches because he guessed that was my more immediate need, or if he just wanted me out of his hair and figured that was the quickest way since there were so many of them."

Given the debt we had racked up with Natisha, I ought to nix the idea of incurring more with another fae, but I feared the day might come when I had no choice.

A knock on the door drew my ire away from the espresso machine, which had earned itself a one-way ticket to the new storefront's breakroom, whenever Remy got it up and running. Assuming I didn't murder it for denying me that which was rightfully mine before then.

"Listen to Bishop." Midas headed to the bathroom. "He knows what he's talking about."

Unsure if that meant Midas was aware of Bishop's fae nature, or if he just assumed that since Linus had left Bishop in charge of the final stages of my education that meant he knew what he was talking about when he warned me away from the fae in general.

Ambrose slid toward the door, announcing the arrival of a person of interest, and I could guess who.

"I'll consider it." I crossed the room, pitching my voice louder as I traveled. "I don't want to give him a big head. His barely fits through the door as it is." I opened the door and gasped. "Oh, hey, Bish."

"I brought you this." He lifted a tray with four steaming cups of what smelled too chocolatey to be anything but café mochas. "But since my head won't fit through your door, I guess I'll take them and go."

"How long were you listening in before you knocked?"

"Long enough to know that espresso machine's days are numbered."

"I apologize for my rudeness. I haven't had coffee, chocolate, or caffeine in any form today."

"Poor baby." He thrust the tray at me. "That's why I made a pit stop. I figured you would pout if I didn't leave the espresso machine, and I also figured you wouldn't believe it's a bitch to operate if you didn't try it for yourself." He glowered at it. "Do yourself a favor and buy a Mr. Coffee."

Or a hammer. Or a Mr. Coffee and a hammer. I might need to show the new machine what happens when you hold out on me.

"You got the update from Reece? Good." He breezed past me. "You did good work last night, kid."

"Thanks." I tossed back the first cup and let it burn all the way down. "Do you think we could—?"

"Ain't happening." He jabbed me on the forehead, right between the eyes, in the same spot his buddy had touched. "You think Natisha is scary?" He jabbed me harder. "She ain't got nothing on Ruel."

Ruel.

"About this money thing," I began while I filed away the name in case I needed to invoke it later.

"Not this again."

"I want half of it put into a trust for the next potentate," I blurted. "I want to pay it forward."

Bishop measured me for the span of a few seconds, and then he smiled. "Of course you do."

Halve my debt to Linus *and* put my future replacement in a position to focus solely on their sworn duty? Talk about your win/win situations. "You'll help?"

"It's your money." He shrugged. "Do with it what you like."

Remy would probably murder me in my sleep for this, but it felt right. The next person to take office might have fewer resources and less powerful friends than I did. I had grown to love Atlanta in my time here, and I wanted her left in capable hands when it was time for me to pass the baton.

A text chime brought Bishop's attention to his phone, and a feral grin spread across his face.

"We've got a lead on an ex-coven member." He snapped his fingers. "Let's go."

Taking a second cup with me, I went to get dressed for the night in the clothes Lisbeth had bought me.

By the time I had yanked the tags off my new outfit and emerged wearing it, Midas was gone.

"His mom called." Bishop didn't snicker, but it was a near thing. "He had to go."

Mouth thinned while I sipped my third coffee, I asked, "What do we know about this ex-coven member?"

"They got tagged for selling Martian Roach spermatophores as aphrodisiacs."

The mention of *sperm* paired with *aphrodisiac* sent my brain to a bad place. "You've got to be kidding me."

"For the record, it's a capsule full of roach sperm." His expression soured. "Do you think I would do the research to find out what that is, let alone imagine someone desperate enough to try it, for a laugh?"

"Your face says no, but I think deep down the answer is probably yes."

Ambrose swirled around Bishop's ankles, eager to get out on the streets, which made me suspicious.

"That never gets less creepy." He shuddered. "He's worse than the spermatophores."

"Ambrose isn't worse than roach sperm."

"You named it Ambrose, and that's what makes it worse. Names have power. You shouldn't have done that."

Ambrose came with the name, whether it had been his originally or one he adopted later, I couldn't say. I hadn't realized Bishop didn't know that choice nugget of intel. Maybe he wasn't as all-knowing about my situation as I thought.

"I know, I know." I kicked at Ambrose, not that he felt it. "He just had that *Ambrose* look about him."

"Midas hasn't seen him?"

"Midas can't see him, or he would have brought it up by now." I thought about it. "No pack member has mentioned it, not even Abbott, so I'm guessing no one can."

It happened like that sometimes, even among the supernatural set. Creatures who could practice magic, like necromancers or witches, could often see beyond the veil if they had enough power. Creatures whose magic was sewn into their bones, like wargs or Atlanta's gwyllgi hybrids, were more grounded. They might sense a presence or catch a glimpse from the corner of their eye, but they couldn't see things like Ambrose unless he manifested. And to do that, I would have to be feeding him a lot more than I ever planned on.

"That's going to make for an awkward conversation," he said on the ride down to the lobby.

"You have no idea."

Ambrose was our third wheel, but Midas had no clue our every move was catalogued by the creep. He was always around, always snooping, always interrupting our private time. I definitely needed a stronger barrier between us now that things were escalating between Midas and me in the romance department.

No one stopped us on our way out, but I got looks from several pack members. Mostly curious. None hostile. I called that a win.

"Ares was looking for you earlier." Hank held the door for us. "She's back at the den now."

News of my relocation must not have made the rounds yet then. Too bad it wouldn't stay that way.

"Thanks." I called for a Swyft, and Bishop stared at me. "What?"

"You and Ares are friendly, right?" He held the door for me. "What's with the tone?"

"I overheard the tail end of a conversation not meant for my ears, and I'm not sure where we stand."

"Ah." He gave the driver an address. "You're coming up in the world, and there will be people you pass along the way."

The situation wasn't that black-and-white, but then nothing was, really. "I get that, but it still sucks."

When the driver stopped at our destination a few minutes later, I pulled out of my head enough to gawp. "This guy is operating out of a church?"

"He's the janitor." Bishop led the way out of the car and up the stairs. "He should be on shift."

A sour taste coated the back of my throat as I wondered if I was about to collect heart number two. The analytical part of my brain that warned he was no longer coven and therefore might not count was no easier to swallow. Who had I become that these decisions fell to me? How much worse would it be once I bonded with the city? I had a feeling I wasn't ready for the answer.

A thin man with hollows under his eyes answered the door before Bishop could knock. "Yes?"

Bishop flashed the man a roll of cash. "Are you Lucas?"

"Luke," he corrected out of habit then nodded. "Who sent you?"

"Ben Franklin."

Luke cracked a smile and waved us in. "What's the problem?"

"This one is a succubus." Bishop hooked his thumb at me, wisely positioning himself out of striking range. "She keeps me wrung out, if you know what I mean."

"We don't get many of those in the city." Avarice glittered in his eyes, as if I were one more object for him to buy or sell. "I have just the thing." He swept his gaze over me. "Though there's a free solution."

The portrait of innocence, Bishop leaned in. "Oh?"

"Let her feed on multiple partners."

Ugh.

I never saw that one coming.

"She's got a taste for me, I'm afraid." Bishop rubbed at his mouth. "I heard you've got a fix for that."

"I've got a stimulant that will keep you going for days." He dialed the ick factor up to ten when he waggled his eyebrows at me. "How's that sound?"

Like he wanted me to punch in his teeth. "Great."

"Let me check my supply." He scanned the massive open room from left to right. "Give me a minute."

Once we were alone, I glared a hole through the side of Bishop's head. "A succubus?"

"He's a little blue pill dealer. I had to pitch him a plausible issue."

"You couldn't have told him you were an incubus?"

"How sad would that be? An incubus who couldn't get it up?" He shook his head. "I flattered you. Why would you want to insult me?"

The cover did fit the situation, but sheesh. All this sex talk was squicking me out. For the most part, Bishop treated me like a kid sister. Hearing the fictional state of his erection made me super uncomfortable.

And, if I was being honest, it might have also slid my thoughts in a different direction. One with blond hair, blue eyes, and a spot reserved in my bed.

Truth be told, I had trouble relaxing when his hands roamed in his sleep. It made me wonder if I could get away with blaming my subconscious for my hands wandering too.

Probably not.

"This is the last batch." Luke jogged over with a vial in hand. "You're lucky you got here in time."

That line didn't really work on people, did it? I bet he had a box full of the stuff hidden away.

"Good enough?" I checked with Bishop, who nodded. "Excellent."

I stuck out my hand to accept the vial then tossed it to Bishop. He caught it while I clamped my hand over Luke's wrist and twisted his arm behind him. I leveraged his arm higher until he squeaked and trembled, and then I got down to business.

"You're ex-coven." I gave him time to answer, but he shut his mouth. "That's what I've heard. The thing is, you're peddling roach Viagra out of a church, and that makes me curious how you came by it if you've cut ties with them."

"I left with my supply after some psycho bitch killed Iliana." He struggled against me. "I haven't had contact with them since."

"How did you come into possession of the spermatophores then?"

"Spermawhat?" He wrenched his head toward me. "What is that?"

"You're selling mutant roach sperm. Did you not get that memo?"

Pallor swept through him, and he sagged. "I didn't know."

"No one ever does," Bishop chimed in. "The *I didn't do it* disease is sweeping the nation."

"A friend gave them to me to unload," he protested. "She said they were too hot for her to move."

"She's coven, I assume."

"Yeah." His knees buckled, and I had to help him sit or let him fall. "She's still in."

"Hadley," Bishop warned, taking a step closer. "Get back."

"Where are they?" I used my modified pen to draw a restraining sigil on his wrists. "Help us, and we'll go easy on you."

"You can't..." He toppled onto his side. "I can't believe she..."

His eyes rolled back in his head, and froth dribbled from the corner of his mouth.

"No, no, no." I rushed over and checked for a pulse but found nothing. "He's dead."

"He recognized you." Bishop cursed under his breath. "He took something when he went to the back. That or he tucked a pill into his cheek just in case."

Coven members probably kept a wanted poster with my name on it stuck to their refrigerators, but he was supposed to be out, frak it all.

The heart was viable for the next few minutes, so I had to ask, "Do you think he was still active?"

"There's no way to tell." He loomed over the body. "We better err on the side of caution."

Natisha didn't strike me as the forgiving sort, so I nodded quick agreement.

"The coven must have invested a chunk of time and money into creating the Martian Roaches." He crouched and went through Luke's pockets. "Maybe they cut a dead one up into little pieces to find out what, if anything, the other bits and pieces were good for. Luke might have been placed here to peddle spare parts to parishioners. Easier to track folks, and their reactions, when you know where they're going to pop up every Sunday."

"Or his partner, if he was telling the truth about having one, might have thought it was a great way to make extra cash. The coven is focusing on the saliva for use in Faete. She might have determined what parts were worth selling then drafted him to work in the last place a coven of witches would expect him."

Given how many various eyes, fins, organs, feet, and everything in between got marketed as medicinal, I couldn't say I was surprised the coven had experimented with various other, potentially lucrative uses for the creature. But I couldn't decide if this particular sideline was officially sanctioned or not. I couldn't see it furthering their overall goal of dominion over the city. Still, I couldn't afford to make assumptions. We needed more information.

"Safe to assume he called his girlfriend, or girl friend, whoever she may be, to warn her away." I hated when that happened. "You got his cell?" Bishop held it up. "We'll hit the nearest drop box and alert Reece he's got a special delivery."

"I'll handle the data recovery." He pocketed the phone. "Reece has his hands full."

The fission of doubt that swept through me was unwelcome. I trusted Bishop. Just because he wanted to keep me as far away from Blithe and his fae friend as possible didn't mean he would tamper with evidence to do it.

Probably.

We called the cleaners to dispose of the body, and we did it from the backseat of the Swyft we took to HQ to prevent segues like *did he have a phone* or *where is his phone* or *everyone has a phone these days* or other lines of inquiry that might incriminate us.

It's not like the cleaners didn't get their turn with it, just some-times after we did. I didn't begrudge them their priorities, but they were spread thin at times. When we needed more immediate results, and we had a person who could get them, we tended to ask forgive-ness later.

With no other pressing leads, Bishop and I resigned ourselves to patrol. A crucial part of the job was maintaining a street presence, and Milo had been putting in overtime on that front as the others worked on various facets of the job, but this was one night I wished I had a target for our frustrations. And if it had antennae, so be it.

SIXTEEN

The first four hours slogged past, business as usual. I should have been grateful to catch a break, but the normalcy made me twitchy when so much tension bubbled beneath the surface of the city. I didn't trust the quiet. I knew Atlanta, and she was primed to boil over at any moment.

When the status remained quo, Bishop and I decided pizza sounded good and went to get some.

We cut our last quadrant short to hit the part of town where para-owned food trucks congregated late at night. About halfway there, I heard a *click-clack-thump* on the pavement behind us.

"Turn left." Bishop urged me toward the darkness rather than the light. "Head to Brunner's Sports Bar."

We kept our pace easy, our shoulders relaxed, and waited for our pursuer to reveal themselves.

A short yip urged us to wait, and I grasped the reason for the peculiar gait before I spotted the warg.

A female limped toward us, chunks of hide missing and blood running down her sides. She made it three more steps and collapsed in a twitching pile.

Fear she was a host locked my knees. I had seen what Martian Roaches did to those. A distant worry was she might be coven, sent to trick me into taking her back to the Faraday. The old Trojan horse bit. It was a classic for a reason.

Bishop looked to me for guidance, and duty overcame caution. I couldn't risk letting an innocent die.

"Stand back," I cautioned him. "Call for a medic."

"All right." He did as I ordered, but he wasn't happy about it. "Don't touch her if you can help it."

Circling her, I got a better look at her injuries. There was no way these were self-inflicted. Having seen a roach burst from a host, I felt confident that wasn't the situation here either. She appeared to have been mauled by a creature with fangs and claws. In a city like this one, that wasn't saying much. We had all kinds. But, given the fact she was a warg, I was willing to bet another shifter had done it to her.

Her groans and whimpers grew louder, and she began to thrash on the asphalt. Her spine bowed, and her legs kicked wildly.

"She's shifting," Bishop warned. "Don't get too close."

"Yes, Mom." I eased back slowly, so as not to provoke her when she was most vulnerable. "Will she survive?"

The change for wargs was bone-snapping agony, unlike the sanitized magical gwyllgi transformations. It took a long time, and it was a show of faith on her part that she allowed herself to be vulnerable in the presence of fellow predators. That made up my mind for me. She must know me from somewhere.

During the Bonnie Diaz debacle, I had met several pack members of the alphas I interviewed. I had passed out a lot of cards too. Their animal halves weren't inclined to trust paper, so I had a bad feeling I could guess who was about to be revealed to us.

"Gayle." I padded closer. "Can you hear me?"

Her shallow breaths weren't promising, neither was the amount of exposed bone.

"Help..." she exhaled softly, "...me."

"We've got medics on the way." I knelt beside her. "Who did this?"

"He killed...them." A sob hitched her chest. "All...of them."

"Deric?" Ice spread down my spine when she confirmed it, but I fought through the instinctive recoil. "The females in quarantine?"

"The...pack." A shudder rippled through her limbs. "Gone."

Bishop caught my eye, and he shook his head, but I refused to believe that she was beyond saving.

"You did good." I stroked her hair, aware of the comfort wargs found in touch. "You told us, and we'll go handle it. You can rest now. The medics will be here in a minute, and we'll get you help."

"Too late." Gayle lowered her eyelids, her dark lashes matted with blood. "Make the coven...pay."

The pain tightening her body released her in death, and she relaxed with an almost relieved sigh.

Grief and rage twisted through me, most of it self-directed. I had let her slip through my fingers. I called once to check in on her, and when she didn't answer, I let it go. Forgot about it. Forgot about her.

I should have remembered. I should have tried harder. I should have...been enough for her.

But I wasn't, and the mental voice that sounded so much like my mother promised I never would be.

The medics arrived and called her time of death.

Who to call? Who to notify? Who was left?

The cleaners were en route to pick up the body, they told me, but they had other calls on the board.

They left Gayle alone and growing cold on the pavement, and so I stayed with her.

I might have held vigil there all night if a familiar presence hadn't enveloped me.

Midas held me where I stood, and his scent brought me back to myself. I'm not sure how long I was gone, but I must have spaced out if Bishop had time to call in backup before I broke out of my haze.

"Deric did this," I told Midas. "That's what she said." I leaned into him. "She had a crush on him, and he killed her."

Tension ran through Midas where his body pressed against mine, and he rested his chin on top of my head.

"Either he bought more Faete," he murmured, "or there were delayed side effects from his first hit."

"I can't keep shutting down like this." I forced myself to let him go. "I have to prove—"

"—you can do your job?"

"Yes," I snarled. "Linus would—"

"—mourn in private. That you show your grief isn't a weakness."

"Are you going to let me complete a sentence?"

He waited, eyebrows raised, but I was out of steam. I hated when people turned my favorite tricks around on me.

"We need to confirm Gayle's story first." Bishop sat and took Gayle's limp hand. "I'll wait with her."

Vision liquid, I bent and hugged him around the neck. "Thanks."

"Midas is right." He patted my hand. "Linus showed no emotion, and it worked for him. Your passion is what draws people to you. It's what makes people trust you. Don't smother that spark. It's got to light your way for a long time to come."

Wiping my face with my hands, I left him with Gayle and arranged for a ride to Mendelsohn territory.

Having been out there more than a few times, I knew it for a long trip. Impossibly long for someone in Gayle's condition. Yet she had done it. Somehow, against all odds, she had reached me.

"I'm coming with you," Midas said, and I didn't have the heart to fight him.

Neither of us spoke the whole way. There was too much hurt for me to open my mouth without hateful words falling out when this had nothing to do with Midas. The pain had dug in so deep, I had to examine it before it got the better of me. That was another thing Linus had taught me—not to go off half-cocked.

Call me if you need me.

How often did I toss those words at people? I might as well punctuate sentences with it. Mostly people didn't hear, or they didn't expect me to be good for it. Gayle had called me when she was out of options, and I had gone to help her. I had done what no one else would or could do for her. It wasn't pretty, but it was necessary. And tonight, when she had run out of choices again, she had hunted me down and honored me with her final trust.

The car rolled to a stop, and Midas and I exited the vehicle on different sides. I worried that said something about our states of mind, but I couldn't give our courtship headspace right now.

We walked down to the wooded area where the Mendelsohn pack had made their camp, and I didn't require Midas's senses to tell Gayle was right.

The bodies of men and women littered the ground. No children, but the lack didn't comfort me. The bonfire at the center of it all made shadows dance where there was no other life, the effect eerie.

The wind shifted, and I caught a whiff of burning flesh. Given my recent experience with fire, I knew it was an agonizing way to go. I wouldn't wish it on anyone. Not even the alpha who sat on the woodpile, flames licking over him, as his skin bubbled and burst.

"Mendelsohn." I kept a safe distance, but I wanted to make sure he could hear. "Deric."

"They're dead."

How his voice carried, I have no idea. The fire roared around him, screaming with hunger and rage.

"Come out, and we can talk about this."

Gayle's final plea made a lot more sense. She had come to me, not to tell me what happened, but to beg me to save him.

"I was their alpha." He stared at his hands. "I should have protected them. Even from myself."

The mass murder of his pack had lent him clarity. This was the most coherent he had ever sounded. He had never struck me as a particularly good or wise or kind alpha, but his people had loved him. That counted for something.

"Midas." I took in the scene, debated our options. "How do we get him out?"

Midas didn't answer, and I found him staring at a female's corpse near the edge of the ring of light. A shudder rippled through him, and magic splashed over his ankles. He traded one skin for another, and his eyes were empty when they met mine. The humor, the intelligence, the fundamental elements that made him who he was had vanished from his expression.

The beast watched the alpha burn a moment longer, but Mendelsohn couldn't hold his gaze.

Ambrose was content to bask near the fire, happy to watch as Mendelsohn burned. There was no magic to consume worth stirring for, so he joined the other shadows in their chaotic dance. He would be no help.

That left me to figure a way to get Mendelsohn out of there without going up in flames. Again.

There was no running water, so I couldn't douse him. The bucket or two of drinking water I spotted wouldn't be enough to kill the fire either. He had built it up high, and the stink of accelerant told me he planned to go out with his pack as penance for his crimes.

Tugging my shirt over my head, I dunked the fabric in the nearest bucket then pulled it on. I poured water over my hair to wet it and had the front of my pants soaked before I heard the roar of challenge.

Midas, who was still burnt, even in this form, had leapt into the fire to haul out Mendelsohn.

I couldn't breathe, couldn't think, couldn't move.

Finally, I unlocked my knees and rushed back and forth around the ditch meant to contain the blaze. There was no good way to insert myself into their fight. It was vicious. Mendelsohn was hurt, but Midas wasn't at his best either. Mendelsohn had determination on his side, a total disregard for his life, and he was winning.

"Screw it." I leapt into the fire, but Midas knocked me aside before the first bead of sweat fell. "No."

Mendelsohn took the opportunity to impale himself with a metal skewer that appeared to belong to a rotisserie set meant for roasting game.

I fought against Midas, but he held me down with a paw to my sternum.

The cold light in his eyes chilled me, and I froze when his claws flexed dangerously close to my heart.

"I'm not afraid of you." I glared up at him. "You won't hurt me."

An inquisitive rumble in the back of his throat all but begged me to test him.

"I will kick your bald and scabby ass from here to New York if you don't let me up now."

The beast didn't want to, that much was obvious, but a familiar alertness flooded his gaze, and he backed away from me.

Once I scrabbled onto my feet, I dumped the remaining water over my head and went for Mendelsohn. He was dead before he cleared the flames. I told myself he would have died anyway, but I was pissed at Midas for interfering. A few seconds either way could have made all the difference.

I whirled on him, ready to give him a piece of my mind, but he sat with a vacant stare that chilled me to the bone. He had shifted while my back was turned, and he kept staring at his hands...the same as Mendelsohn had done.

That spark of righteous anger snuffed out to cold embers when his haunted gaze met mine.

A lilt flavored his words, but he didn't seem to notice. "I almost..."

"You almost got your ass kicked." I sat beside him. "I was playing being nice because I like you."

"You couldn't stop me." He curled his abused fingers. "Not if I wanted it bad enough."

"Try me," I dared him, proud my voice didn't tremble. "I'm tougher than I look."

"I could kill you," he said softly. "So easily."

This was about more than Mendelsohn. This was about the nightmares that woke him, the past that haunted him. I could back down, let him brood, and hope it passed. Or I could prove to him, to both of us, that I could take him. It would alleviate his fears, smash the walls between us, or kill me in the process.

Ambrose perked at the idea of pitting our strength against Midas, and I hated the thrill he fed into my blood.

"I'm done with this." I got to my feet. "I'm over it."

Midas nodded, his shoulders relaxing, as if he had always known it would come to this.

This, in his mind, clearly meant goodbye.

The ease with which he gave up on us earned him a punch to his stupid square jaw. The obvious relief at it being over between us got him a kick to the side of his stupid handsome face. The fact he let me beat on him, welcomed it, made me think I was negotiating with the wrong half of him.

"Change," I ordered him.

"No." He dug his fingers into the ground, his muscles trembling. "Hadley, *no*."

"*Change.*"

"You don't understand." His tormented gaze found mine as magic puddled underneath him. "*Run.*"

"I'm tired of running." I meant it, with every fiber of my being. "We're settling this tonight."

The change took him, swept him up, and left him in a quivering mass of rage shaped as his gwyllgi.

"Midas is *mine*." I sank power into my voice. "That means you're mine too." His lips quivered, teeth peeking through. "You hear me?" I took a firm step closer. "Knock it off." And another. "Right now." And another. "You think you can take me?" I stood toe to paw with him. "If you think...uh..."

The beast lowered his head, lay on the ground, then rolled over to expose his vulnerable belly.

Submission from a future alpha was a big deal. This wasn't Midas the man, this was Midas the beast. They were the same, but they weren't the same. Midas employed higher reasoning. The beast was a creature of instinct. Where the man might be swayed by his emotions, the beast responded to strength.

He believed I was stronger than him, and that was sobering.

Sure, I figured Ambrose and I could take him in a no-holds-barred fight. Mostly because Ambrose played dirty, and I counted on Midas not to want to hurt me.

Basically, I expected to hold my own. This...was not that.

The beast thumped his tail once, an invitation to rub his stomach, and I did. With Ambrose on standby.

Uncomfortable was a good word for seeing one's boyfriend belly up with his tongue lolling.

Relieved was another.

I got the distinct feeling the beast I had been interacting with up until now was a watered-down version Midas had deemed fit for my consumption. One with his wildness leashed, tamed by my hand. Or so he would have me believe. This guy was the real deal. Blood, fang, and claw guided him. He was a creature of instinct, and his must be roaring at him.

"Okay." I flexed my cramping fingers. "Are we done here?"

The beast whined in its throat but let the magic wash it away to reveal the man.

"You want to explain what just happened?" I waited for him to speak, but he kept silent. "You've got Jekyll and Hyde syndrome." Still nothing. "I've read about it in wargs. Most who suffer from the condition end up that way through trauma."

"I obeyed you."

Relieved he was talking again, I shrugged it off with a smile. "I'm good at yelling until people do what I say."

"I shifted when you commanded me to, Hadley. I *obeyed* you."

"Are you sure?" Yes, I felt stupid the second I asked, but oh well. Nothing new there.

"You magically forced my body to listen to you." He stared at me. "I had no will of my own."

Recoiling from him, I tasted bile in the back of my throat. "I didn't mean to do that."

No wonder he hated the power that came along with his mantle if a sharp word bent people's wills to his.

"I'm not mad." He reached for me before I escaped him. "I'm just...surprised."

"The courtship thing must be messing with us." I wished I had wiped the dampness from my palms before they slid against his. "That must be it." I searched his face. "Right?"

The cry of sirens snapped his jaw shut on whatever answer he had been about to give.

"We need to move." He stood and pulled me up with him. "The sentinels and the cleaners will be here soon. If we want answers, we need to search Mendelsohn's tent before they arrive." He yanked me after him. "Whatever happened tonight, the answers must be here."

I wasn't fooled by his sudden sense of urgency, but he had a point. We had to act fast.

"You check his." I took a moment to orient myself. "I'll search Gayle's."

We split up, and Ambrose decided I had become the more interesting one, so he shadowed me.

Most of the camp appeared abandoned, but Gayle's corner of it had been destroyed. Her thin mattress had been shredded, and so had her pillow. All her clothes and personal belongings had been scattered and smashed in a fit of rage.

What remained of her grandfather didn't amount to much, but he had died with his back to a large box.

"There's nothing here." I checked with Ambrose. "Whoever flipped this place must have found whatever Gayle was hiding."

The shadow gave a negligent shrug, bored again, but he did spare the box a second glance. It made me look at it harder too.

"W-w-who's there?" a tiny voice whispered. "H-h-hello?"

"I'm Hadley Whitaker," I announced myself. "I'm with the Office of the Potentate of Atlanta."

"You bought me ch-ch-chicken nuggets."

"Lyssa?"

"Where's Mom? Aunt Gayle?" She cried brokenly. "Great-gramps?"

"Hold tight, sweetie." I moved her grandfather's corpse and covered it in a sheet before examining the box. "Who put you in there?"

"Aunt Gayle." She sniffled. "The release latch is in here."

"Can you pull it?" I gentled my voice. "I'm right here. I promise I'll keep you safe."

"O-o-okay."

Metal grated against metal, and a pop released a breath of stale air as the box opened a crack.

"Come on out." I took her hands and helped her unfold. "There you go."

The girl tottered into me and wrapped her arms around my neck, sobbing against my throat.

From the gleam of the hinges and the exposed framing, I could tell the box was made of silver bars. A wooden exterior and interior made it possible for wargs to lift it, or shelter in it, without it burning them. It would hurt like a mother if they ripped through the thin plywood to the metal beneath, though.

Lyssa was too big to be carried, but that didn't stop me.

"Midas," I called. "I found a survivor."

The kid had seen too much already. I wasn't going to walk her into the center of camp to see what her alpha had done to himself, or the others. I stood with her on my hip, bouncing her as I would a small child, and let the nearest tent shield her from the rest.

Midas jogged to us, his expression grim, and patted his pocket once for my benefit. I nodded that I understood he had found a clue, and then the three of us waited for the medics to arrive while Lyssa sobbed into my neck and told us where to find the other kids.

I could only pray we found them alive.

SEVENTEEN

The ice in Midas's veins had nothing to do with the carnage surrounding them and everything to do with what Hadley had done. She had commanded him, and he had obeyed. That power over him ought to set the animal within him pacing, but it had sprawled in a dark corner of his mind to nap.

The two halves of his nature had called a truce, but the reprieve left him jittery with unspent energy.

With the beast ascendant, and his mind fraying, he could have killed Hadley.

A snap of his teeth, and her delicate neck would have broken in his jaws.

He had done it before, so many times, to so many other females.

Only their mate bond had saved her, and she had no idea of the power she held over him. Until she had wielded it against him, *he* had no idea of the power she held over him.

"Abbott is on the way." Hadley nudged him toward the road. "He's going to treat us and cut us loose."

The cleaners had arrived to catalog the carnage, and sentinels had extricated the traumatized children.

Ayla Clairmont, tipped off by one of her spies, had already contacted the paranormal branch of social services about adopting the pups who had lost their entire families. Wargs required pack to thrive, to learn control and how to hunt, and her alpha instincts would have demanded she assume the duty of their education.

Noticing the way Hadley used her elbows, he worried for her. "How are your hands?"

"Crisp." Her palms were mottled black, red, and white. "Hurts like a mother."

"I'm sorry we couldn't save Mendelsohn."

Midas was certain that even if they had arrived sooner, they wouldn't have stopped him from self-harm. Good alphas prided themselves on defending their pack, and Mendelsohn had destroyed his in a fit of drug-fueled mania. His bacchanalian leadership style lent itself toward his pack having a higher than usual number of females, and they had been no match for their alpha on a tear.

"We have to shut this coven down." Pain tightened her features, but she didn't complain. "They're going to pick us off, faction by faction, until they've created a power vacuum. Then they're going to waltz in and claim the territory as their own."

"We won't let it come to that." Midas ached head to toe, but he blocked out the worst of it. "We're going to hunt them, and we're going to end this."

"They're always three steps ahead." Her exhale ended on a cough. "We can't even find them."

"Faete, the club, was glamoured to conceal it from prying eyes," he reminded her. "The coven could be holed up right under our noses, and we just can't see them."

A calculating stillness swept through her body, and her lips parted. "Bishop was right."

The resignation in her tone set his skin prickling. "About what?"

"His friend gave me a gift to help me find a Martian Roach, but he gave me one before that too."

Warning sang along Midas's nerves, a premonition of danger. "What gift?"

"Sight." She tapped the center of her forehead, indicating a third eye, then brushed her fingertips over her eyelids. "*The* sight."

The moisture dried from his mouth as his thoughts caught up to hers, but she wasn't done yet.

"He gave me a preview when I dropped Bishop off with him, then he arranged for a private viewing."

"You're not making any sense." He eased closer to her. "What do you mean?"

"*You see, but you don't see yet.*" The approaching lights bathed her face in reds and blues. "That's what he told me." She frowned. "He claimed he opened my eyes a crack." She looked to him. "He knew I would need that gift to find what we're searching for, and he let me test-drive it."

"The second gift revealed a trail to the roaches. What did the first do?"

"It allowed me to see past the glamour on his home to what was really there." She flagged down Abbott. "With that gift, I could walk the streets in a grid until I found them. They couldn't hide from me."

"Think of the cost," he warned.

"I am." Her gaze drifted back to the Mendelsohn pack. "I can't afford not to pay it."

The healer and his retinue arrived with grim countenances. They saw to Hadley, and then to Midas, but Abbott didn't waste his breath asking them to be more careful. The mechanical way he treated them made it clear he had other things on his mind. That, or he had shut down his emotions to prepare for what awaited him.

Once they got the green light, Hadley lingered a moment with Midas. "I have to find him."

"All right." She hadn't let him bargain alone, and he would return the favor. "Let's go."

She salved his pride by not asking if he could handle the trip. Neither of them was in prime condition, but the coven was pounding the city on all fronts. They couldn't afford not to hit back. Even if it cost them.

"I have to call the other packs." She booked them a ride first. "Clairmont and Garou should be put on alert."

The Clairmont warg pack lived in the city, in downtown. They were small, urbane, and insular. He doubted they trolled the streets for drugs, but if the coven had thought to dress it up, make it cost, the pack might have been tempted to give it a whirl.

The Loup Garou were thugs. Odds were, they had been first in line to try Faete and decided, against common sense, to invest. They peddled whatever sold, and there would be paras willing to pay for a high that lasted hours instead of minutes. No doubt the old man would create addicts among his own people, but Midas doubted Garou lost sleep over it.

Midas gave her room to warn the other alphas while he sent a text of his own.

"That's our ride." She pulled up an address from a conversation with Linus. "This should be fun."

The way she squared her shoulders, ready for a fight, belied her bravado.

The address Hadley read to the driver was unfamiliar, but Midas recognized the gentrified neighborhood by its reputation. High-end brothels catering to every kink imaginable operated in this area. His pack had more than a few members who spent their weekends, and their paychecks, behind these closed doors. He figured it was their business, so long as they made it to work on time come Monday.

The hotel that drew Hadley's eye had an artfully weathered blue door. Haint blue, if he wasn't mistaken. He learned about the color during his time in Savannah. It was an old Gullah tradition to paint the ceilings of porches to keep away ghosts. He hadn't realized it was practiced this far north in the state.

"Ears perked and eyes open." Hadley started up the steps. "I don't know what to expect."

The door opened as she raised her fist to knock, and she cocked a hip and planted that same fist on it.

The man, who wore only black leather pants slung low on his lean hips, was aware he was beautiful in a way that mortals envied, and knew how to use his appearance to his benefit. Otherwise, he wouldn't leave so much skin on display as a carnal enticement to invite visitors to look their fill then wonder how much it cost to touch.

Dark eyes, luminous and curious, appraised them both. The tips of his ears, which he took no pains to disguise or hide behind a curtain of midnight hair, were dagger sharp in the way of high fae.

"Hadley," he said warmly. "What an unexpected surprise."

"I doubt it." She locked gazes with him. "You baited your trap." She honed her glare. "Consider it sprung."

"You aren't much like your master, are you, little shadow?" He chuckled under his breath. "He loves the game." He looked her up and down, and he took his time about it. "You're more straightforward."

More than one person had mentioned Hadley's lack of tolerance for dancing around subjects. Midas appreciated that frankness about her, but it did set her apart from Linus's leadership model.

"I don't have time to play." She tightened her hands into fists at her sides. "I prefer to speak plainly."

"So eager to prove yourself," he murmured. "So eager to matter." A smile tugged up one corner of his mouth. "You'll slow down, in time."

"As much as I love cryptic remarks, I'm sure you can guess why I'm here."

"Come in." He stepped aside. "You too, beautiful one."

Midas glowered at him as he crossed the threshold, and the twin scents of blood and sex filled his head.

"I won't hurt her," the male promised. "That costs extra."

Based on the slender whip hung from a loop on his pants, he meant it.

"The parlor is empty this time of day." He guided them into a lush room with a roaring fire that put off no heat but added ambiance. "Have a seat, please."

Several ornate chairs and one chaise framed the center of the room in a conversational grouping. Midas sat in a chair that put his back to a wall and gave him a view of the door. He sighed with relief when Hadley sat on the spindly arm of his chair rather than accept the unspoken invitation to join the man on the chaise.

"There's a witchborn fae coven killing my people," Hadley started, "and I need your help to stop them."

"Necromancers, you mean?" He flicked a glance at her shadow. "Or do I misunderstand?"

Midas frowned at the darkened outline stretching across the floor, but it was just that—a shadow.

"The people of Atlanta," she ground out between her teeth. "*All* the people of Atlanta."

"Fae are immune to Faete," he countered her. "Witches too. The coven wanted to be certain it couldn't be turned against them."

"You're telling me since it can't hurt you, it's not your problem." Hadley vibrated with rage. "How nice it must be to sit on your nice chair in your nice house and know you're safe."

"It is rather nice, now that you mention it." He toyed with the curling ends on the whip. "I could make it nice for you too. Help you forget your worries." He smiled, and it was cruel. "Help you forget yourself, your past."

"The past is what brought me here. It's what shaped me. I'm not giving up a minute of it."

Leaning forward, he purred, "Are you that afraid of what you might become otherwise?"

"I made mistakes, and I paid for them. I don't need those erased to be aware of what I'm capable of and how dangerous that makes me. I've always known. The potential for evil has always been in me, and you can't change that. Only I can."

"Hmm." A frown creased his brow. "You keep your sins close as a reminder, as a punishment."

"We're done here." She glanced back at Midas, a warning in her eyes, then back to their host. "Thanks for wasting our time, *Ruel*."

The use of his name did it. Froze the smirk on his mocking lips, darkened his laughing eyes into pits that yawned full of terrible endings.

"What did you call me?" The tips of his fingers lengthened into talons. "Who told you my name?"

His *Name*, whispered once into his ear as a child and then forgotten, the one that held power over him.

Midas let his magic hum beneath the surface of his skin, let it burn in his eyes.

"Ruel," she said again. "That is your name, isn't it, *Ruel*?"

Possession of his name was dangerous enough. To use it three times was binding.

"You will regret this inhospitality." His glamour rippled, distorted. "You were an amusement, but now I see I was wrong." The bottom half of his body shivered, exposing birdlike legs and claws. "You're an annoyance."

"You forced my hand." Hadley sounded tired. "All I wanted was your help."

"Command it of me," he growled. "Then be gone."

The promise of violence saturated the air, a vow that vengeance would be his for this insult.

"I used your name to get your attention." She strained toward him. "I don't want to force you to comply. I want you to cut the crap and bargain with me so I can get back to the people who need me."

Silence lapsed while Ruel considered her, and then he crossed his taloned legs.

"I will give you the sight," he said slyly. "I will give it to your mate as well."

"Leave Midas out of this," she warned. "This bargain is between you and me."

"Give me back my name, let me erase it from your mind, and I will open your eyes."

Midas had to admit, as far as bargains went, this was a straightforward one. On the surface. But fae were masters of exploitation.

"The bargain is struck," she said before Midas could warn her to slow down, to think his phrasing through.

Rising with sinuous grace, Ruel approached them. He knelt at Hadley's feet in a mockery of subjugation.

"This won't hurt." He raked his fingers through her hair, his claws scratching her temples. "There we go." He smiled at Midas. "I'll just take what's owed."

Black motes glittered on his fingertips when he lowered his hand, and he blew them across the room with a long breath, scattering them like seeds from a dandelion, his name lost on the wind.

"But this will." Ruel chuckled as he stabbed her between the eyes with his fingernail. "Awaken, little shadow. See the world as it truly is and be seen as you truly are."

The scent of her blood raised Midas's hackles, but Ruel impaled him in the next instant with the same claw.

"Awaken." His cold eyes laughed at Midas. "See the beast you've claimed for your own."

The fae rose and prowled from the room with delight sharpening his cruel beauty.

Neither he nor Hadley so much as breathed while the lush room transformed around them. The sight, gift or curse or both, burrowed into their minds, fading the lies and revealing the truths. But the décor wasn't the only shocking change.

"Hadley?" Midas gripped her arm. "What's happened?"

"I got what I wanted." She heaved a sigh. "But then, I always do."

Midas shot to his feet and circled around to find another woman in Hadley's place.

And at her shoulder lurked a shadow that no longer bothered to mimic her shape but fashioned itself into a tall man that stared at him openly with its blank face.

Her build was almost identical to Hadley's, but their features set them apart enough they might have been distant cousins rather than sisters. Her eyes were a startling blue, and her hair was a luminous gold. A key-shaped tattoo dominated her left forearm, and hints of more ink peeked out from her clothing.

"Amelie Pritchard." He leaned in, filled his lungs, but smelled only Hadley. "I don't understand."

She had been Grier Woolworth's best friend since they were kids. He recognized her from Savannah. She had been under house arrest in Grier's carriage house for the crimes she had committed, the murders. As a dybbuk. A creature of darkness that fed on energy, on magic, on innocent people.

"This might help." She removed a silver ring from her finger. "Now do you get it?"

A different scent filled his head, darker and richer. More potent. It made his stomach tighten, with want or sickness, he couldn't tell. The stronger her essence grew, the fainter Hadley's became, until it vanished beneath the tide of misery and grief this woman carried in her.

The fae had tricked them. That must be it. But how he twisted the vow to produce this, Midas couldn't guess.

"Let's get out of here." She refused to look at him. "We can talk outside."

All of a sudden, he regretted asking to know more about her. He should have been content with what he had, what they had, instead of pushing her. This fae bargain wasn't his idea, but it still felt like his fault.

EIGHTEEN

A lump in my throat made swallowing hard and speech impossible. Midas followed me out onto the sidewalk, and I was tempted to keep walking. I couldn't outrun my past, but I could prevent it from catching up to me for a few more seconds.

That was cowardice talking, though. I had known this moment was coming, and I should have done more to prepare for it. Truthfully? I hadn't wanted to waste the time I had with Midas on imagining our end. It had been rocketing toward me since I agreed to the courtship, and I knew that. I *knew* that. So why did it hurt so frakking much?

Midas pivoted on the top step and cast a frown back at the building. "It changed."

"The sight shows things as they truly are," I reminded him. "This address exists under a glamour."

The switch between perceptions had freaked me out the first time I had my eyes opened too.

The boutique hotel was gone, and in its place sat a cottage missing from a fairy tale. In my role as village idiot, I had wandered into the forest teeming with monsters and begged one for a favor.

Then I had the nerve to be shocked when, wrathful and petty, it bit the hand I extended toward it.

Cautious, Midas prowled up to me. "Who are you?"

The pain behind my ribs swelled until my heart no longer fit in my chest, until I wished the worthless organ would burst and spare me from the next few minutes.

"You got it in one." I started walking. I couldn't help myself. The urge to flee was too strong. "I'm Amelie Pritchard."

"That's not possible." Midas whipped his head toward the cottage. "What did he do to you?"

"Nothing."

"*This* is not nothing." A growl twitched his upper lip. "Explain this to me."

Not enough, not enough, not enough.

The balance was tipping away from me, and I couldn't hold tight enough to stop the seesaw of his emotions, let alone mine. I tried to answer him. I did. I opened my mouth and everything. But nothing happened. I couldn't do it. I couldn't wreck this unexpected and beautiful thing between us. I might have to bear the fallout, but I refused to pick up the sledgehammer and smash through it on my own.

Midas palmed his phone and punched in a number I didn't have to see to anticipate.

"Linus," he snarled into his cell after he mashed the speaker button. "Explain this to me."

"You'll have to elaborate."

"Amelie Pritchard."

The two words hit with the force of a hurricane and swept away all my silly hopes and dreams. I really ought to know by now not to pin my happiness on anyone other than myself.

A long pause lapsed before Linus asked, "Can I speak to Hadley, please?"

"Hadley doesn't exist." Midas squeezed the phone until its case cracked. "What have you done?"

"Hadley will want to tell you herself." His voice went soft. "Harm her, Midas, and I won't be forgiving."

Shock zinged through me that Linus thought Midas would hurt me, but it fused my lips together instead of loosening them in Midas's defense. I had betrayed him. I hadn't meant to hurt him, but I had known it was going to happen eventually. Only I was too selfish to carve him out of my life before I got cut too.

Ending the call, Midas stared at me until the weight of his scrutiny forced me to sit on the sidewalk.

Unable to stomach looking at him, to see the hurt I had etched onto his features, I stared at the cars whooshing past.

Midas didn't say another word, just turned and walked away from me.

Not enough, not enough, not enough.

I hated when my mother was right.

NINETEEN

No matter how fast he ran, Midas couldn't escape the truth.

Amelie Pritchard was his mate.

Not Hadley Whitaker.

The implications terrified him for myriad reasons, starting with the first time he set eyes on her.

"Your friend smells wrong." Nostrils flared, he drew in Amelie's scent. "The beast is tempted by her."

"The beast?" Grier looked back at him. "Your beast? You? When you shift?"

"Yes," he said slowly. "It's in our nature to put down injured or sick prey."

Prior to Hadley, he hadn't let himself be alone with females of any species. He hadn't known how far to trust his instincts. He'd let his guard down with her, she'd earned it, and he'd begun to believe she was safe with him.

But that was Hadley.

And Hadley didn't exist.

The scent of Amelie filled his head, and he searched every scarred corner of his soul for signs the beast had marked her as prey.

He found nothing, but he didn't believe himself now that he knew the truth.

Shadow child.

Finally, he understood what others meant when they referenced her shadow. She was a dybbuk, a creature her own kind hunted and executed for good reason. They were killers. Every single one of them, and she was no exception.

Midas hadn't been in Savannah when Amelie Pritchard went to trial for the murders of several vampires. He hadn't been there when she was stripped of her family name, inheritance, and personal assets. He hadn't been there when she was left Amelie Madison, her middle name promoted to surname, and she lost everything. But he had heard about it. The scandal rocked the Society, and it was all anyone talked about for months.

Talk was too polite for what they had done, picking her apart thread by thread until Amelie unraveled.

They fashioned her into a monster, but there had to be more to the story. Grier would have stood for her childhood friend no matter the personal cost, but Linus? He was more brains than heart with anyone but Grier. He wouldn't have vouched for Amelie, taken her under his wing, if he hadn't believed in her ability to change for the better and learn control of the thing she had willingly become through one of her kind's darkest rites.

The beast in him had wanted to hunt Amelie then, and given his violent history, he didn't trust its silence on the matter. Until he was certain he wouldn't harm her, in either form, in *any* form, he couldn't be near her.

That same inner predator rebelled at the notion he could hurt her, but Midas knew himself better.

He needed to think, and to think, he had to get away from her.

Already he could tell he was making the biggest mistake of his life in walking away, but it was worth it to protect her. She might never forgive him, might hate him forever, but she would be alive, and he would have one less black mark on his soul.

TWENTY

"I warned you, kid." Bishop sat next to me on the curb. "I told you to stay away from him."

The fae was who he meant, not Midas. I couldn't put my finger on his name, my thoughts slid away from recalling it, but I had known because I had invoked it. Too bad I couldn't sweet-talk what's his name into erasing, say, the last hour of my life too.

Shards of my broken heart scraped against each other while I breathed, and the relentless hurt reminded me that a magical lobotomy wasn't the solution. It would only delay the inevitable, and I couldn't live through this again.

"You also told me his name." I kept staring at the same reflector in the asphalt, waiting, waiting, waiting, but Midas didn't circle back. Even to yell at me some more. "You knew I would use it."

"I'll pay for it too, but I can afford it." He wrapped a brotherly arm around my shoulders. "It will be worth it, if you find the coven." He let me rest my head against him. "I'm sorry about Midas."

"I didn't expect us to last the whole six weeks." I shut my eyes to hold in tears. "This is easier."

"A clean break might be for the best." He rubbed his cheek against my hair. "I'm still sorry."

"Yeah." I barely recognized my voice. "Me too."

Most of me had gone numb, but enough common sense remained for me to worry how Bishop might appear through my newly opened eyes. Thankfully, when I worked up the nerve to check, he was as always. Unchanged. My hindbrain grasped that didn't mean I was seeing him for what he was, only that he was powerful enough to keep up appearances.

That wasn't terrifying at all, really. I didn't need to change my pants after that revelation. Nope. Not me.

"We've got a few hours left until dawn." He stood and helped me up too. "Might as well get started."

Grateful to have anything but Midas to think about, I didn't argue. "We can use the standard grid pattern."

We used it to locate missing persons mostly, and it covered the entire city as well as the nearest suburbs, should we have to push out our search area.

"The fae," I said as we walked to our starting point. "He's Blithe's son, isn't he?"

"Yeah." Bishop massaged his nape, but he only made the reddening splotches worse. "I'm the reason you got into this mess, and I still can't tell you the half of it. Suffice it to say, he wouldn't have acted on his impulse to meddle in your affairs if he hadn't spotted us together."

"Does he think we're an item?"

"You're beautiful, powerful, and deadly." Bish chuckled under his breath. "You're definitely my type." He let his hand drop. "He would have picked up on that when you dropped me off on his doorstep."

Happy for a chance to shine the spotlight on someone else's private life, I plowed ahead with a frown. "You've never made googly eyes at me."

"Firstly, I'm not a *googly eyes* kind of guy." He elbowed me for insulting his technique. "Secondly, even if I had been interested, I could see what this job meant to you, and what it meant to Linus for you to succeed. That decided it for me before my hormones entered the equation. I made a mental note you were hot when we met, but then I got to know you, and I set it on fire then scattered the ashes."

"I'm glad you did."

Smoothing his hair back, he struck a pose. "Is it because I'm not blond?"

Platinum was a shade of blond, but I didn't correct him. He was being ridiculous for me, and I loved it.

"No." I threaded my arm through his. "It's because I really needed a friend, and you're a good one."

"Back at you." He patted my hand. "I didn't know how much."

The first grid gave us nothing. The second and third was more of the same. We knocked out the fourth and the fifth as the sun rose, and Bishop ordered me to stop and get some rest. He walked me back to the Faraday, but I couldn't bear to face Hank or the others. I wasn't sure if it would be worse if they all hated me on sight or if they acted like nothing was wrong, when absolutely nothing was right.

Turning instead down the familiar alley, I used the fire escape to climb up to my old apartment. The glass was still missing in the windows, and much of the floor was questionable, but the bathroom was in okay shape.

I climbed into the tub with a towel for a pillow and wished harder than ever I would wake to find my life was nothing but a bad dream.

<h1 style="text-align:center">TWENTY-ONE</h1>

"It's been five days," Lisbeth said, tucked behind her monitor once again, her true identity safe with me. "We've hit the grids hard, repeatedly, but we're not making any headway."

Five days since Midas walked away from me.

"They must be shifting locations nightly," Anca murmured. "How else are they avoiding detection?"

Five days since he saw my true face and couldn't stomach the truth.

"We'll have to scan the hot zones again." Milo rubbed his jaw. "You've marked four or five?"

Five days since I discovered I only thought I had hit rock bottom.

"Six," Reece corrected absently, flicking new reports onto our screens for review. "As of last night."

Five days since I no longer saw my new life as a second chance but as yet another mistake in a long line of them I suspected began with my birth.

"A day off wouldn't hurt," Bishop said, his nose an inch from mine. "You could use a break."

Blinking him and the room into focus, I struggled to replay the last five minutes of conversation. I had been following along, honest. But I couldn't have told you a single point we hit up until he called me out.

"Milo's right." I worried the silver ring on my finger, a habit I thought I had kicked. "We need to hit the glamoured storefronts again, see if we can shake something loose."

The Clairmont pack hadn't lost a single member thanks to their absolute loyalty to Ayla Clairmont and her ban until further notice on recreational activities outside their high-rise den.

The Loup Garous were down five members, that Garou would admit to, which meant there were more.

Three necromancers were dead.

Four gwyllgi were dead, all of them exposed after the drugs hit the streets. As if the teens hooked on life support weren't enough of a cautionary tale.

The fae were fine, and so were the witches, and so were the humans.

Two vampires were dead because they got high off their food sources, and the frantic humans, who had been taken without their consent, killed the vampires when they came around and found they had been gnawed on like chew toys.

There were other deaths, other hospitalizations, but the coven had yet to swoop in for their coup d'état. Coupé de ville? I seriously ought to sign up for Duolingo.

All in all, it felt like I had torpedoed my new life for absolutely nothing.

Midas left the city the night we gained the sight, and I had yet to spot him at the Faraday since. The pack hadn't gone out of their way to interact with me, which told me they knew we had broken up, and it was ugly, but their indifference also helped me continue avoiding them.

Linus called a few times, but I had stopped answering. Addie called too. Usually after I missed a call from Linus. I was starting to think the sheer volume of recipes my sister was in dire need of at my new all-time low meant Linus had clued her in to my breakup if nothing else.

Even Midas had texted me. Once. I erased it without reading it and blocked his number. I wasn't strong enough to hear his voice yet, let alone his reasons for breaking every promise he ever made to me.

I knew them all. All my flaws. All my mistakes. All my shortcomings.

One wrong word from him might tip the balance between Ambrose and me, and that could be far more deadly than a broken heart.

"I'm going with you." Bishop rose from his squeaky chair. "You shouldn't be out there alone."

After he killed the monitors with a frustrated slap of his palm, I confronted the elephant in the room.

"You're worried—" I couldn't say his name. "You think he'll expose me."

Had he any choice in the matter, he would keep my secret. I truly believed that. He was a good man, and he would do that much for me. But he also had a duty to his people, and he'd just learned what manner of monster ruled the city after the moon rose.

"I bet he ran straight home to his mommy and cried into her skirts." His jaw flexed as he fought to hold back other comments on Midas. "She's going to show up at some point, butt hurt her son couldn't handle a woman with a past—like he's got room to talk—and if she comes armed, I don't want you facing her alone."

"You warned me." I was force-feeding him the argument I would have had with my mother—how right he had been, how stupid I was, how I should have listened to him—but I couldn't put down the damn spoon. "I have no one to blame but myself."

As usual.

That line ought to be my theme song. All I had to do was set it to music.

"You did what you thought was right to save the lives in your charge." Bishop jabbed me in the shoulder with his pointer. "The rest, as much as I hate to say it, goes with the territory. Sacrifice for the greater good sucks. That's why there's not exactly a waitlist to fill Linus's shoes."

"I lied to Midas about who I am."

"No, you lied to him about your name." He kept poking until he got me out the door. "You watch too many B movies to be a great actress."

"They're *classics*."

"They're just old." He locked up behind us. "Black-and-white doesn't equal quality."

The brutal assault on the one thing holding me together struck me mute.

"Besides, no one getting paid as little as you do would do what you do to maintain a cover." He shepherded me onto the sidewalk. "You've got your own reasons for doing this, but so did everyone else who ever held the title."

"I don't mind getting outed." Karma had circled back around for me again, and I had to live with that. "I do mind my family getting dragged through the mud for it."

The Pritchards had disowned me, so they didn't have to worry about me bringing shame to the family. I did, however, worry about the Whitakers. Addie wasn't immune from gossip, and her reputation would take a serious hit if my cover got blown.

The Ambrose-fueled killing spree I went on in Savannah, as Amelie, was the whole reason she wound up engaged to Boaz in the first place. He needed her last name to wash his clean. Now here I was, splashing mud on the Whitakers and endangering Addie's best shot for an advantageous marriage.

"We'll shield them as best we can," he promised. "You've got the funds now to take care of yourself and your family, if it comes to that."

The click in my head as the pieces fit together left me wary. "Do you think Linus knew?"

"That you and Midas would split?" Bishop watched me to see

how I took the hit, but I let it slide off me. "I doubt his actions have much to do with that possibility. It's not how he's wired. He's more logical than emotional, which is not to say he doesn't care. He just thinks linearly for the most part." He shoved his hands into his pockets. "More than likely he anticipated your identity would leak one day, and he wanted to protect you as best he could from the fallout."

I was being paranoid. Probably because I wasn't sleeping. The king-size mattress was propped in the hallway, free to anyone who wanted it, but the new futon I had hauled up into the loft smelled like plastic and made weird crinkling noises when I shifted my weight. The tub in my old place was more comfortable.

And there I went again, letting my thoughts circle the drain. I really ought to invest in a stopper.

"You want even or odds?" We no longer hit streets in order. "I have a good feeling about evens."

The hot spots, as Milo called them, were businesses or apartments that weren't what they appeared to be. Not all of them were sinister, as I found out after charging in the first few with swords blazing. But others left me with an overwhelming sense of darkness, and those were the ones we labeled and patrolled. Not that it had done us much good so far.

"Evens it is then."

Bishop and I hit spots two and four without any luck. Two got marked off the list when we bumped into the Unseelie fae couple who lived there. I'm not sure which shocked them more—that I could see their true faces or that I could tell their home from the brick wall it pretended to be.

Ambrose got antsy near our last stop, and his stomach grumbled. Daring to hope we were finally making progress, I dipped a hand into his core for a sword, just in case, and as I drew it, he glanced over my shoulder.

"Hadley."

Heart thundering in my ears, I whipped my head toward the voice. "Ares."

Mouth tight, she stepped into the streetlight. "Can we talk?"

"Kind of busy here." I indicated the sword. "Can this wait?"

"You've been avoiding my calls, and you don't use the lobby at the Faraday."

"I'll watch your back," Bishop offered to me then warned her, "Talk fast."

He drifted away, not that it made a lick of difference given his sharp hearing, but it did the trick.

"This is all my fault. I'm the one who put the idea in Midas's head that he had to choose." She yanked a tired hand through her hair. "I warned him you were bad for the pack. I convinced him giving you up was the best thing for us all. It came from a selfish place, and I'm sorry."

This unburdening went a long way toward explaining that day in the lobby, and his comment.

As much as it hurt to hear her say those things, I couldn't let her keep thinking she was to blame.

"Our breakup wasn't your fault," I assured her. "It was mine."

Ares wasn't listening. Neither of us were. We were too busy shouting over one another to be heard.

"Liz is pregnant. We've tried for years, *years*, and it finally happened." She wiped her eyes. "I got protective, *over*protective, and I let my fear get the better of me." Her eyes pleaded with me. "I'm— I'm sorry. *So* sorry. Please, give him another chance."

"Congratulations," I said, and I meant it. "You're wrong, though. Trust me. I screwed this up all on my own. Midas doesn't need another chance. He needs to forget he ever met me."

Bishop cleared his throat, and Ares deflated on the spot.

"I have to go." I backed away from her. "I really am happy for you."

Turning away from her, from that chapter of my past, I rejoined Bishop, and we plodded on toward our last stop.

"Do you feel better knowing?" He angled his head toward me. "It was bothering you."

"Her opinion of me doesn't matter anymore."

This gave me closure in the arena of our friendship, but that was about it. It didn't help, and it didn't hurt. Information in one ear and out the other, only passing through.

"I haven't had my heart broken in a good long while." He kept a step ahead of me. "I had forgotten how utterly miserable love makes you."

I didn't love him.

That's what I wanted to say, but I couldn't speak through the tightness in my throat.

I didn't know him that well.

Just enough I could see the hazy outline of a future together.

He didn't know me at all.

Only better than anyone.

A long shadow peeled from the darkness ahead and planted its feet wide across the mouth of the alley.

Not to be outdone, Ambrose mimicked it. Mocked it, more like. Swelling himself to its size.

The short man who walked up behind it wearing a lab coat and thick glasses squinted at us.

"What do you want?" he demanded. "You've got the stink of fae and witchcraft on you."

Thanks to the sight, and the charms I used to conceal my identity, he wasn't wrong.

"Who are you?" I reached into Ambrose for my second blade. "Are you coven?"

"Are *you* coven?" He pointed what I realized was a pen at me. "Have you come to steal from me too?"

"I'm Hadley Whitaker." I lowered my weapons. "The coven stole from you?"

"The new potentate," he said thoughtfully. "Prove you are who you say you are, and we can talk."

Aside from my debit card, I didn't carry much in the way of ID. "What proof will you accept?"

"Your word."

"I'm a necromancer," I reminded him. "You get that my word isn't magically binding, right?"

"Oh." His nose quivered. "Fair point." He eyed Bishop. "How about yours?"

"You have my oath that we mean you and yours no harm so long as you claim the same," he said without hesitation, and magic saturated the vow. "My word is given."

"Best we do this inside." He jabbed the shadow in the knee. "Eustice, come along." He glanced back. "I'm Dr. Ronald Smythe, by the way."

The towering giant shriveled to the size of a large dog and loped beside the peculiar man.

Ambrose, not to be outdone, reduced himself into a cat that pranced over to strop my ankles.

Since he had been a good boy and leapt to defend us, more or less, I tossed him a salted caramel square.

"We're safe enough." Bishop allowed me to take the lead. "He's a minor fae."

"What's that thing with him?"

"No clue."

Ambrose, in a plea to get more chocolate, volunteered that the shadow and the man tasted the same.

"All right then." Like a sucker, I dropped another chocolate into the void. "Let's be alert, shall we?"

Hurrying to catch up to the man, we met him at the entrance I had detected just yesterday.

"You'll have to forgive the mess." He flushed. "I don't often get visitors."

"You're fine," I assured him. "You should see my place. It looks like a bomb went off in there."

Bishop shut his eyes, as if my sense of humor caused him physical pain, then shook his head.

Laughter was a great coping mechanism. It was also a great

defense mechanism. I tended to joke, a lot, with varying degrees of success.

The doorway I'd discovered opened smoothly once our host found the right key, and he ushered us inside then sealed us in. He had been right to warn us. His place looked worse than my apartment, and that was saying something. Since, you know, the bomb thing had been literal.

A living area occupied the left side of the space, and it was tidy in the way of unused rooms. A lab cluttered the right side, and it was utter chaos. Potions bubbled in honest-to-goddess caldrons suspended over the hearth. Vials of liquids oozed vapor onto the aged-wood countertops. Aquariums teeming with all manner of creatures lined the back wall, most of them insectoid or amphibian.

"I expect you're here about the *periplaneta compressa*. That's what the coven stole from me." He indicated a tufted couch and claimed a chair across from it. "Poor darlings." He clucked his tongue. "They're so misunderstood."

"We're here about giant cockroaches that infect live hosts, control them while they mature, and then explode out of them to start the cycle over again."

"Miraculous creatures." Reverence seeped into his voice. "The mechanics of it all..."

"Did you hear the *live host* part?" I pressed. "Or do you just not care?"

"They feed on insects," he said slowly, his eyes shining. "Oh! Are you a fellow entomologist then?"

"Hold on." I raised my hand. "You're saying these things you created preyed on fellow insects?"

"That was the whole point, my dear, yes." He grew animated. "A hybrid of predator and prey. One might call it the ultimate hunting machine." He laced his fingers. "I hypothesized that, using modified radio waves, I could control the minds of the infected hosts. Can you imagine?"

Roaches that listened to this guy? No. Not really. "How does that work if they don't have ears?"

"Well, that is to say, I..." He flushed. "To ensure the success of the project, you understand, I made a few slight modifications." He shoved his glasses up his nose. "The alpha hybrids' reactions to radio waves weren't quite as promising as I had hoped, so I modified them. I gave the beta hybrids the superior ears of the katydid, *Copiphora gorgonensis*, which are almost mammalian in their complexity."

I had known the Martian Roaches could hear, but I hadn't been sure how much of that was based on their current host's faculties, and, honestly, it was all so gross I skimmed a lot of my reading material.

"Initial testing proved the beta hybrids were viable," he continued, "their hearing flawless, but then there was the break-in."

"How did they find your..." I wavered on what to call this place, "...facility?"

"I haven't the foggiest." He patted his thigh, and his shadow dog padded over to flop its head onto his lap. "Eustice and I don't get much company. The occasional investor, naturally, comes to check on the progress of their order." He rubbed the creature's ears. "The corporation behind the hybrids was furious when I reported that my notes and the specimens themselves had been stolen."

"You got paid for Frankensteining the hybrids?"

"I am, sadly, forced to work. I must earn money to fund my less glamourous projects."

Nothing came to mind less glamourous than breeding roaches, so I kept my mouth shut.

"I hate to tell you this, but the people who stole your hybrids mutated them with magic and set them loose on the citizens of Atlanta."

Eustice whined and leaned against his master's leg. "What sort of monster would do that?"

"A witchborn fae coven out to seize control of the city by wiping out anyone who opposes them," Bishop told him. "And it gets better."

Poor thing, he actually brightened with hope. "Better?"

"He was being sarcastic," I apologized. "They've also synthesized its saliva as the base for a street drug they're calling Faete." Might as well get it all out there. "We've also been made aware they're selling their parts for various medicinal purposes."

The man slumped against the back of his chair, and his eyes filled with unshed tears. "The poor dears."

"You said the beta hybrids were flawless." I leaned forward to get his attention. "Do you think you can do your Pied Piper thing on them?"

"I'm not sure." He stared at the ceiling. "What a corruption of all things good in this world."

Again, I bit my lip. I had smushed too many roaches in my day to fully appreciate his grief.

"We've got a live one," Bishop tempted him. "Would you like to see it? Test your control, maybe?"

"Yes." He shot upright, and Eustice yelped. "Oh, yes." He stroked his pet. "Please."

Trusting Bishop to know what he was doing, I let him bait his trap.

This guy was valuable. He could be the cure to both the roach and the drug problem. Finally, we were getting somewhere.

It wasn't enough to make up for losing Midas, yet, but it put me one step closer to making peace with the trade.

TWENTY-TWO

As luck would have it, Reece had finished his sample-taking and observation period earlier in the week. I just hadn't crawled out of my misery long enough to notice. He had surrendered the Martian Roach to the cleaners, so my worries about revealing HQ to a total stranger proved unfounded. We crashed the cleaners' lab instead, using Reece's friend as our in.

Siobhan was tall, a redhead, and in possession of a faint accent. She was also dead serious about her job.

"I can give you twenty minutes." She led us through the compound. "More than that, and I'll get fired."

"Hear that, Smythe?" I eyed his arsenal. "Twenty minutes."

Bishop, proving he was the smart one, set a timer on his phone.

"I'll have to pinpoint the proper frequency and then test a variety of sequences," Smythe pleaded his case. "It's a delicate process that requires finesse."

"Finesse it all you like," Bishop said, "as long as you don't take more than twenty minutes."

Smythe grumbled under his breath about the integrity of science, but he nodded.

The room Siobhan led us to was filled with cages for an assortment of creatures. The one occupied by our friend the Martian Roach was enormous. It hissed at our approach, and Smythe rushed to its side. Had I not rushed a bit faster and caught his hand, he would have lost it to the roach's scissoring pinchers.

"It wouldn't have hurt me," he protested. "It was merely curious."

"Yeah," I agreed. "If you taste like chicken."

"Look at that face. What a beauty." Unshed tears turned his eyes glassy. "I wonder if it remembers me."

"I'm sure it does," I lied flatly. "Look how its antennae quiver when you're around."

Spirits buoyed, Smythe unpacked his laptop, brought up his synthesizer program, and began testing harmonies.

Siobhan, Bishop, and I withdrew after extracting a promise from Smythe to keep his hands to himself.

"This creature will save a lot of lives," Siobhan said. "Thank you for allowing us to run our tests."

Unlike most cleaners, who preferred their own company to that of anyone else's, Siobhan had a soft spot for Reece. Their working relationship, or whatever it was, had benefited us time and time again.

"The local packs have lost enough." I tried not to dwell on what the news had dubbed The Mendelsohn Massacre and failed. "They're the ones being targeted hardest by the coven." I tried not to dwell on the Atlanta gwyllgi pack and failed even harder. "The OPA is happy to share our resources with anyone willing to help us secure an antidote."

"I heard the gwyllgi have teenagers on life support." She rubbed her arms. "Is that true?"

"It was the last I heard." I killed that line of inquiry. "Have you made any progress?"

"Anything we have, we put in DORA." She exhaled. "We're not holding back. We're just at a loss."

Reece and Doughty were still in Savannah with the antidote, but

I wasn't sure if information flowed both ways between her and Reece. I figured it was safer if I kept my reassurances that the best people in the state were on the problem to myself. For now.

"Yes," Smythe shouted, triumphant. "I've done it."

We all turned to find the man doing what might be loosely interpreted as a dance in some circles. That wasn't the interesting thing, well, except in the way of train wrecks you can't look away from. No, what sparked his booty-shaking fit of euphoria was the roach balancing on its hind legs with its forelimbs over its head in a mockery of fifth position in ballet.

"I can do it." Smythe whirled toward us. *"I can do it."*

The guy's enthusiasm was catching, I had to admit. "Can you help us lure them all out of the city?"

"I know just the place." He snapped his fingers. "It can be a sanctuary."

Bishop stepped on my foot before I made the colossal mistake of telling Smythe we couldn't allow them to live.

"We'll arrange for a contingent of sentinels to help us herd them," Bishop told him. "Give me the coordinates for the area you have in mind, and we'll make it happen."

"Time," Siobhan called. "You'll have to finish your scheming via text or video chat."

Extricating Smythe from his new true love proved difficult, but he got with the program after I hooked my arm through his and dragged him from the room. Unimpressed with me, but unwilling to pick a fight, the shadow dog trotted at his master's side.

"I know it's the height of rudeness to ask," I started, "but what is Eustice?"

As the not so proud owner of my own animate shadow, I was curious how a fae ended up with one.

"Questions are always welcome." He beamed. "It's fascinating, really. I was attempting to cure multiple personality disorder in a friend's carpenter bee when I mixed up the enzyme for its treatment with that of another project and accidentally ingested the formula."

"Mmm-hmm." I already regretted asking him. "Yes, fascinating."

"I haven't told you the best part." He patted Eustice fondly. "The enzyme reacted to a spell an associate cast on me later in the day to remove boils and *voila*. My shadow split from me into its own sentient being. Totally harmless of course, but great company and excellent at spooking the riffraff."

"That is fascinating," I said again and meant it this time. "Do you think you could duplicate the results?"

"I tried, for the friend I mentioned in fact, but no such luck." He deflated a bit. "I suspect there to be a species component to it. He was a witch, and his shadow remained firmly stuck to him. Who is to say it wouldn't work on another witch or another faction? I haven't tried again. No time and no funding. And, to be honest, it's not my area of expertise."

A dybbuk wasn't the same as a simple shadow, not even close, so it was ridiculous to get my hopes up for a miracle cure.

Once we tucked our scientist friend safely behind his wards with his promise to be ready for a full-on roach assault at dusk, um, I mean, our eco-friendly and totally humane roach relocation program, Bishop and I called it a night.

"Don't even try it," Bishop warned. "I'm walking you home."

I don't have a home almost popped out, but I kept a tight lid on the pity party.

With my apartment a smoking crater and my personal life a disaster movie, I had trouble remembering why it was so important to keep on keeping on. This was the sequel, after all. I had lost my home, my friends, my family once before.

"Suit yourself."

I hadn't decided yet if he was worried that I might keep walking one night, right out of the city. Just walk until I got tired and start a new life wherever the blisters on my heels burst. More than likely, he feared I might get cornered by citizens who'd learned my identity and wanted a piece of me. Dybbuks exist outside Society laws. We're the product of a broken rule. Therefore, they don't much care what happens to me.

Halfway to the Faraday, I got tired of the silence and engaged. "You're not going to let the man have his roach sanctuary, are you?"

"Do I look crazy to you?" He pointed a finger at me. "Don't answer that."

"I wouldn't dream of it, but yes."

"I have plans." He rubbed his hands together. "Big plans."

Oh goddess. "Make sure you clear those with Linus."

"*You* are the boss." He cackled. "What Linus doesn't know won't hurt me."

"I have been considering a lengthy vacation, somewhere tropical, without roaches."

Or friends who got that certain glimmer in their eyes when the opportunity for mass destruction arose.

Flamethrowers were the tip of the iceberg as far as his official arsenal went, and they had been a wish list item. Most of what he owned was just neat crap he had amassed over the years without real purpose. Given an actual goal, I couldn't begin to imagine the ideas whirling through his head.

"Keep telling yourself that." The edges of his amusement frayed. "Do you regret any of it?"

"You mean the bargain that brought me here?" The Faraday loomed, and I cut between buildings to avoid the front entrance. "Ford is a good man. He deserved a second chance more than I did." I suspected he meant the Midas situation too, but I played dumb. It wasn't hard. "The coven has to be taken out, so I'm good with that too. Hunting them down would have landed on my plate eventually." I shrugged. "I don't see how I could have done anything differently and been able to live with myself."

The matter of the hearts, however, worried me. There had to be a workaround that didn't involve giving Natisha access to so much power, but I could afford to let that be Future Hadley's problem. Right now, I had one heart to my name. Until I had the other six, I had time to figure out how I was going to pay the debt without dooming the city to a worse fate down the line.

"Night, kid."

I waved him off and climbed the fire escape up to my old apartment. I didn't feel like going in, so I sat on the metal grate, propped my elbows on the railing, placed my chin in my hands, and swung my legs.

The Faraday had hired an all-witch construction crew to make the place habitable again, but it took time to gut even a small box. Plus, the hall was wrecked, and my closest neighbors' apartments had been emptied for the foreseeable future. I didn't mind giving their spaces preferential treatment over mine since I was the bomb's target, not them, but that also extended to dibs on the vacant apartments.

I had nowhere to go but up—to the penthouse—but it reflected Linus's tastes, not mine. That was easily rectified, I knew, but I wasn't in the mood. Besides, I was more comfortable down here. Moving on felt too much like giving up, and I had to hold on to something real, something Hadley, even if it was a charred shoebox of an apartment.

The clang of footsteps on the ladder below me was an unwelcome announcement company was coming for a visit. I could guess who it was and what she wanted from me, and the necessity of it made me tired down to my bones. It was getting harder and harder to frame answers in a way that didn't come out sounding like I was blowing her off every night. I didn't care about building a new empire when I was sitting in the smoking ashes of the old one.

That whole range of emotion had been erased from my hard drive, and I wasn't sure how to reboot or if I even wanted to, honestly.

"Can we do this another time?" I was awful for treating her like a virulent plague to avoid at all costs, but I was fresh out of motivation. For pretty much everything. "I can pretend I listened to your spiel, and you can leave with a sense of accomplishment as you go about your night."

"You don't want to hear what I have to say?"

Every muscle in my body locked down tighter than Fort Knox.

Had I moved, or even breathed, I might have broken bones. "I thought you were someone else."

"Remy," Midas guessed. "I've noticed you holding meetings out here."

"The bathtub is too small for two people, and I'm guessing bathing with your employee is frowned upon in any case." I kept watch on the horizon. That's how I knew I hadn't curled into a ball and started sobbing or crumpled into a boneless heap that sobbed or flung myself over the edge while sobbing. I was definitely picking up on a theme here, a wet one. "Are you here to tell me to stay off the fire escape?"

The first conversation we had alone happened up the alley, and it involved him warning me off using the fire escape as my own private entrance. How very *circle of life* that he was here again to issue the same warning in what might be our last.

"No."

"Oh."

The horizon didn't budge, and I felt good about that. I was holding steady, and that was a relief.

"I have a problem."

The response popped out of my mouth without consulting my brain. "I'll help however I can."

Damn it.

That was not what I meant to say. I was acting like a puppy who enjoyed being kicked so much I painted a bull's-eye over my heart then gifted him with a pair of steel-toed boots.

"You're not going to ask what the problem is first?"

"I owe you." I sensed a slight tilt and corrected my posture. "What do you need?"

"You can look at me," he said, a growl deepening his naturally raspy voice.

"I don't have to see you to hear you." I swallowed hard. "Say what you came to say."

"You're my mate, and I abandoned you."

Mate?

Forget my best intentions, no force on earth could have stopped me from gawking at him in shock.

Mate?

"What I did was unforgiveable." He sat on a step out of my reach. "I have no excuse."

Except he didn't need one. I got it. Without prompting. "You didn't know who you mated."

"I mated you." Resolve firmed his mouth. "I love...you."

The horizon was no longer in danger of tilting, but it blurred as I returned my chin to my hand. "No."

"No? I don't love you, or I don't know who I mated?"

"Both." I kicked my legs. "Most days I don't know who I am. It's hard keeping my past and my present straight. It was stupid to think a relationship could work with those kinds of barriers."

"I went to Savannah."

The twist in my gut made me nauseous. "Back to the scene of the crime."

There was nothing about Amelie Pritchard he couldn't unearth if he dug deep enough in Savannah soil. Except where she went after her debt to the Society was considered paid. But he already knew the end of my sad tale.

"I went to visit Lethe for a few days."

That was almost worse. No. That was definitely worse. Lethe knew all there was to know about Amelie's dark side, and what she didn't remember, she could ask Grier. The trip would shine a light on all corners of my former life.

"Oh" seemed easiest, so I prepared to repeat it again and again until he left.

"I talked to Linus and Grier while I was there."

"Ah."

How's that for variety?

"Do you know what I learned?"

"No."

Tremble before the might of my vocabulary.

"I haven't been honest with you about who I am either."

"Okay?"

"I can't hold your past against you without giving you the chance to do the same to me."

Screwing up my courage, I put thought into words and hoped he would accept it and go.

"You don't owe me anything. We didn't make those promises to each other. We agreed to try, and we agreed to do it with blinders on. The secret idea was good, but we didn't take it seriously. We weren't ready to commit or able to commit or whatever it means when two people love each other but it's not enough."

"You love me."

Frak. Frak. Frak.

I hadn't meant to say that part out loud. Ever. It was the kind of thing that couldn't be unheard.

"I can't do this." I squinted against the rising sun. "We're just going to keep hurting each other."

"Not if we agree to tell each other the truth."

"You went to Savannah." I laughed bitterly. "You know everything about me."

"Grier loves you, and Linus admires you. Lethe envies you. Mom respects you. That's what I know."

The tears flowed over my cheeks and dripped off my chin. "What if they're wrong?"

"Then it doesn't matter." He moved a step closer. "I love you."

The strain in my throat made denials impossible, but I shook my head anyway.

"You're my mate." He claimed another step higher. "There's no going back. Not for me."

"The courtship is null and void." Goddess, it hurt to admit it. "There's no going back, period."

"The bond snapped into place before the period ended." He

inched closer. "I should have told you, but I wanted you to make the choice for yourself." He hesitated. "I hoped you had felt it too."

Ambrose, who didn't care one whit about my personal life, took the opportunity to rub it in my face that he had tried to tell me that night at the den when he pointed at my chest and then the door. Except now I understood he'd meant the man on the other side of it.

"It doesn't matter." I blew my nose on my sleeve. "We're done, Midas."

I understood why he walked away, and I would have done the same in his shoes. Maybe. I don't know. I hadn't loved anyone before. I wasn't sure how far the emotion stretched before it broke. But he had proven he *could* walk away, and that terrified me. I couldn't afford to invest in this, in *us*, again. It hurt too much.

"I'm not letting you go," he said calmly. "I don't care if it takes every day of the rest of my life to prove to you that I'm all-in, I will put in the time." He took the last step, putting us close enough to touch, but he respected my space. "I'm not going anywhere. I said it before, and I meant it." He brushed his fingers across the metal. "I broke that promise when you needed me the most, and I will never forgive myself for hurting you like that. Let me prove to you I can be trusted, that I'm done running. From my past and yours."

"This has bad idea written all over it."

"I fed into your insecurities, and I'm sorry." He hung his head. "I didn't know."

"That's the whole point." I exploded, rage and hurt and relief swirling through me. "You don't know me." I climbed to my feet. "*I* barely know me. I've got no business rushing into a relationship."

Bonus points to him for not mentioning the ignored text, which might have told me some of this, or the fact I had blocked his number. He accepted full responsibility for his actions, and I respected that he didn't try to shift even a speck of blame onto me. Even if a good fifty percent lay with me.

"Take all the time you need." He made himself comfortable. "I'll wait." He gazed up at me. "You're worth it."

Madder than a wet hen, I kicked his boots. "Are you going to stay out here all day?"

"Yes." He tipped his head back against the bricks and shut his eyes. "See you at dusk."

"I can't believe I'm doing this. I am the biggest idiot in the world." I fisted the front of his shirt and pulled him to his feet, and then I got in his face. "You're not sleeping outside."

With the coven on the street, it was too dangerous. He made too tempting a target.

Snarling under my breath the whole time, I hauled him through the window, out my old apartment door, through the staircase, and up to the penthouse. I hadn't been there in days, but someone had put the mattress to good use. The paw print on the cover told me where Midas had slept last night.

"I was ready to have this talk yesterday," he explained, "but you didn't come home."

"This isn't home." I shoved him down onto the mattress. "I'm tired, I have a busy night ahead of me, and I need to think."

"All right." He stretched out and crossed his legs at the ankles. "Rest well."

Striding past him, I let myself into the suite and slammed the door behind me.

Then I walked into the bathroom, cranked on the sink and the tub, and cried with relief.

TWENTY-THREE

Midas sat on the mattress with his back against the wall and pretended not to hear Hadley cry. And she was Hadley. Amelie Pritchard, legally Amelie *Madison*, had been too broken from her ordeals to recover. But Hadley was unbreakable. Fierce, proud, determined. She was the strongest person he had ever met.

And he'd made her cry.

The incoming call from Linus wasn't unexpected, but he wished he didn't have to answer. "Yes?"

Cold, flat, merciless, the voice of the potentate, not his friend, asked, "How is she?"

"She's in the penthouse."

The other details were none of his business.

"I didn't ask where she was," he said stiffly. "I asked *how* she was."

"I broke her heart, and I broke her trust." He stared at the door, each of her sobs a lash, a punishment he deserved. "I'm not sure I can fix it."

Linus exhaled slowly, and he came back with less frosty advice.

Midas could tell that it cost him. He hadn't been close to Amelie, even before her ordeal, but he had a soft spot for Hadley. That made two of them.

"I lied to Grier. Many times." He let a silence linger. "To protect her, to protect others, to protect myself. Out of fear, out of necessity, out of kindness." He exhaled. "We couldn't have gone on that way. It never would have worked. There was a breaking point."

"We're there now." Hadley had made that much clear. "How did you fix things with Grier?"

"I told her the truth, and I promised to always tell her the truth." He hesitated. "I'm not unlike you in that my job as potentate carried certain restrictions. The whole truth isn't something I'm capable of, and neither are you. Grier accepts it, because she knows I would tell her if I could, and she knows why I can't."

"Honesty."

"Transparency," he countered. "There's a difference."

"She left me in the hall," he confessed. "I want to go to her, but should I?"

"If I were you," he said at last, "I would respect the boundaries she set."

"And if she were Grier?"

A soft laugh escaped him, the ice breaking in a way it hadn't since Midas called him demanding answers about Hadley.

"I wouldn't give her too much time to think about what I'd done," he said. "I would be too busy showing her I would never do it again."

Permission granted, Midas ended the call and shot to his feet. Pulse thundering in his ears, he knocked on the door until the crying stopped and the water cut off. Her hesitant footsteps might as well have been punching him in the heart. The door opened a crack, but she used it as a shield. He deserved that.

"I was fearless when I was young," he told her. "Part of that was knowing my mother was the alpha, and part of that was knowing my big sister would never let anyone hurt me. I knew my whole life that Lethe would be alpha one day, and it made me feel invincible."

"You don't have to tell me this," she said, but she didn't slam the door in his face.

"We grew up hearing stories about Faerie, about how our family was descended from fae. Lethe wanted to see a *real* gwyllgi, and she wanted to do it in Faerie." He leaned against the doorframe. "Whatever she wanted, I wanted, but Mom told us no. She forbade us to go, but Lethe was a young alpha personality. Mom never commanded her not to do anything when she was little. She didn't want to break her wild spirit."

Hadley remained quiet, but the gap didn't shrink, so he kept going.

"The pack didn't take in old ones back then, but our healer was a full-blooded gwyllgi, and he had the fae sense of mischief about him."

"He helped you cross," she said softly.

"He took us there, and he left us. I was ten and Lethe was thirteen. He thought it was a grand joke." He shifted his weight. "For a while, Lethe did too. We found a pack, eventually, but they smelled the human in us. They chased us out of their territory."

The next part was harder to tell, but he wanted no secrets between them.

"One of them stalked us over the next several days. He had his eye on Lethe." Midas balled his fists at the memory. "He ambushed us before we reached the Halls of Summer, the least vicious of the fae courts. We planned to barter for the Summer Prince's help to get home, but Lethe was attacked before we arrived. I had no choice but to kill the gwyllgi responsible or let him kill me. Afterward, we fled to the Summer court."

The door opened another inch.

"The Summer Prince agreed on a price, and he began preparations for one of his underlings to cross a tether to Earth with us and deliver us to our mother to collect the payment due."

Midas recalled standing next to his bloodied sister, a world away from his alpha and mother, as the exact moment he understood his own insignificance. As big and bad as he had felt all his life, there were bigger and badder than either of them. And Mom was too far away to help.

"The gwyllgi alpha arrived the morning of our departure, and he demanded an audience with the Summer Prince. He told him we had killed one of his people, and a debt was owed to him. The Summer Prince was not amused to learn we had killed on his lands and caused conflict among his people. So, he offered us a choice."

"A life for a life."

"Yes," he answered her, not surprised she had guessed. "A life for a life." He scratched his thumbnail against the paint on the door-frame. "The alpha wasn't satisfied with the ruling and claimed that his pack would suffer the loss for decades. The male I killed had a mate and offspring, and they were left unprotected."

Hadley made a noncommittal noise that spurred him on.

"The point that he had been stalking Lethe with an eye to mate with her was glossed over entirely. We had human blood in our lineage. We were less than nothing. Worthless. Only the favor the Summer Prince wished to ask of our mother gave us any value in his eyes."

A neat row appeared above her brows. "What favor?"

"The gwyllgi pack, he explained, had been a thorn in his side for quite some time. They had a tendency to cut their elders loose to roam Summer lands. They were often feral, wild beyond their alpha's control. Other denizens of Summer put them down in self-defense, which gave the alpha means to demand recompense from the prince. To solve the problem, the Summer Prince decided he would rather deport the old ones to Earth to live out their lives, or not, under the control of a powerful alpha."

"Your mother."

"Basically," he attempted to joke, "he wanted the violent gwyllgi pack ruining his fun off his meticulously landscaped lawn, and he had grown tired of shaking his fist and yelling at them to behave."

"He exploited a loophole, very fae of him, but you were a *child*."

"I was guilty."

A curse slipped out under her breath, and he took heart that she found it in herself to care for that lost boy. It gave the man he had become hope.

"The Summer Prince decreed that if repayment for suffering was the issue, he would give the alpha one of us to punish however he saw fit. But, to prove he was a male of his word, he would honor the bargain to send the one of us home."

"You sent Lethe."

"I killed the male. It was my fault. I thought they would kill me, and I was prepared for that."

Gwyllgi are violent and territorial. Packmates die in combat, in dominance challenges, while securing mates. Death was a part of pack life he had understood, and accepted, even as a child. Mom hadn't shielded them from the realities of their natures. She had bled, fought, and killed in front of them to prepare them for what their beasts would demand as they matured. She wanted them to understand that if they were afraid to embrace their natures, they would die.

"What did the pack do to you?"

The question he had avoided answering all this time loomed between them, a gulf he could either swim across or drown in. The familiar blackness swirled around his feet, welcoming and cold enough to numb the pain, but Hadley was the lighthouse beacon that drew him over and over again.

"They beat me within an inch of my life, and I think they would have killed me if my beast hadn't been so strong. It gave the alpha the idea he could sell me to give the widow funds to care for herself and her children."

"You were enslaved?"

"I was sold to a goblin who owned a coliseum where he hosted various fights between supernatural creatures. Nothing was taboo. There were no rules. Except one." He dropped his gaze to the floor. "No matter how many went into the ring, only one came out."

Hadley peered around the door at him, but he couldn't bear to see her eyes swollen and red.

"I never lost." He gritted his jaw. "The goblin kept me for decades, and I never lost. Not once." He extended his arm. "I kept a tally, but I never counted them. It was enough to see the damage I had done written into my skin."

More of her body appeared around the door. "You fought for your survival."

"I killed for my survival."

"How did you escape?"

"Lethe came for me. She was the only one left who thought I was alive after all that time. She waited until she was grown, until she was strong, and she came for me herself. We teamed up, fought our way through the guards." A breath shuddered out of him. "She entered the ring, as an opponent. That's how she got in. That's how she found me." He tasted bile. "I could have killed her. My own sister."

"But you didn't."

"The fighting broke me." He expected she would have heard the rumors. "The beast and the man split into two personalities. I was the beast in the ring, and the man in my cell at night." He glanced up then. "That's what caused the Jekyll and Hyde syndrome."

"How does Natisha figure in?"

"Mom summoned her from Faerie to fix me. She didn't realize it was Natisha's pack we had stumbled across. I didn't either, since they didn't offer me a healer before selling me. Natisha told me later, after Mom bargained with her. She had known we were kin, in Faerie, and she never breathed a word." He rubbed his knuckles. "No one would have stood against a healer of her renown. Her word could have saved Lethe and me both, but she let us suffer."

"I wish you had told me before we struck a deal with her. Facing her again must have been painful for you."

"There was no other choice. No one else can do what she does."

"How can a healer be so cruel? That type of abuse ought to be anathema to her."

"What she did, it didn't heal me. It allowed me to recall those years through a filter. I didn't have to feel what I had done. The grief, the rage, the anger. It all went away. For a while. It gave me time to adjust to being back here, to having a normal life."

"Can I ask what made you dedicate yourself to teaching women self-defense?"

Hadley was too perceptive to let that detail slip, and he was here to tell her everything, to bare his soul as hers had been peeled back for him.

"Gwyllgi males are bred to care for females and those weaker than themselves, and I had a particularly chivalrous streak. Thanks to Lethe and Mom, I looked up to females as role models. It was part of the fabric of my personality."

"And this goblin twisted it?"

"He pitted me against females of all species, but mostly my own. It guaranteed the bouts lasted longer, and it made them bloodier. My beast didn't fight back until it had no choice, but it refused to lose. To die. It kept me locked out of its head while it fought, and then it left me to deal with the aftermath."

Grief-filled screams as he thrashed on the floor of his cell in the throes of his nightmares, hating himself, hating the goblin, hating Faerie and everyone in it, had ruined his voice beyond repair. But no matter how loudly he yelled, no one heard him. No one came to help. No one until Lethe.

"You've been atoning. All this time." She opened the door all the way, and the heartbreak on her face twisted his stomach until he worried he might get sick in her hall. "You've been paying for your survival."

He didn't dare move. "So have you."

"I brought this on myself. I made the choices that brought me here."

"So did I."

"It's not the same, Midas, and you know it."

"I was young and foolish," he said, "and I made a mistake that cost people their lives."

Her mouth worked, but she fumbled her argument.

"Lethe believed in me, that I could get better, and I refused to let her down. That's all that's kept me going. I wanted my family to finally be happy. I wanted them to think I was okay. I didn't realize how miserable I had become until I met you."

"I can't tell if that's a compliment."

"I pretended for so long, I couldn't tell what was real anymore." He glanced up then. "You're the first real thing in my life since I came back. I don't have to act when I'm with you."

"I've been lying to you since the moment we met. How can I be your one real thing when I'm fake?"

A hesitant smile twitched on the edge of his mouth. "A rose by any other name would smell as sweet."

"You're breaking out the big guns." Blushing, she wiped her face dry with the hem of her shirt. "Next thing I know, you'll be quoting full-on poetry at me."

"Go sleep." He shoved off the frame, embarrassed he wanted to be romantic for her. "I'll be here."

The way she lingered in the doorway telegraphed her fear she would wake to find him gone, and it gutted him all over again. He had known she was different. Hadn't his mother warned him to find out sooner rather than later why she set their fur on end at times? He had been so certain he could handle it, but he let his past, his fears, rule him.

"There's one more thing." He waited until she held out her hand then dropped a wide leather bracelet onto it. The heft of it made it clear it was meant for a man. For him. "The sight is permanent, for both of us. Only the fae who gave it to us can take it back, and I'm done bargaining."

"What is this?" She rubbed her thumb across the etched surface. "What does it do?"

"It's a charm that's spelled to blind me to the sight."

"Why offer it to me?"

"You deserve to choose how I see you." He folded her hand over it. "Amelie or Hadley, the decision is yours."

"Thank you." She clenched her fingers until they turned white. "Do I have to pick now?"

"No." He shook his head. "Take all the time you need."

"Okay." She cleared her throat. "I'll think it over then, if that's all right with you."

"You can always change your mind," he reminded her. "The bracelet can be removed later."

"Do you...?" She swept out her empty hand, inviting him in. "I have a new futon."

"I haven't earned that privilege yet, but I will." He risked a kiss on her cheek. "Good night, Hadley."

He shut the door, afraid if she offered a second time, that he would follow her. If she invited him to share her bed again, he wanted her to do it with clear eyes, not red-rimmed ones. He needed her to believe he was here, and there was no place he would rather be.

TWENTY-FOUR

Smythe had two hours left on his deadline, and I had a decision to make before Bishop arrived to walk me to work. For what I had planned, I could use all the backup I could beg, borrow, or bribe. But I wasn't sure if I wanted to drag Midas into my scheme. I didn't want his standing in the pack to erode further, and then there was the issue of our relationship. I couldn't risk being seen as the prop holding up the future alpha any more than he could afford to be viewed as the crutch for the future potentate.

Then there was the whole mate thing.

He kept saying it. *Mate.* Over and over. Not as in a hypothetical future but as in an incontrovertible truth. Like I had a clue what it meant when our courtship had sunk. We hadn't crossed the finish line. No vows exchanged, no questions asked, no promises made. And yet...

Mate.

The kind of bond that would tie another person to me, through the good times and bad, gave me heart palpitations. I had weathered more bad times than good, and I wasn't certain I wanted my escape route cut.

Like Mother's.

Might as well say it. I was thinking it.

If she had been free to choose a man she loved instead of falling prey to an arranged marriage, would she have been happier? Kinder? Better? If she had been free to leave when she realized Dad wasn't a man she could love, would it have made a difference? If she had been able to pursue her own happiness, without consequence, would she have loved me?

No matter the situation, the fact remained that no parent had any right, regardless of their own misery, to inflict suffering upon their child.

Midas wasn't my father, though. And I prayed to the goddess I wasn't my mother. We hadn't been forced together. Quite the opposite. We had done our best to avoid one another, to ignore our mutual attraction, and then to figure out why we couldn't quit the other so we could use what we learned to do that very thing.

And yet...

Despite how wrong we were for each other, how much we complicated each other's lives, I couldn't stop thinking about him. Based on the night he spent outside my door, I was guessing the feeling was mutual. We made no sense. None. The timing? It couldn't be worse. There was no good reason for us to keep fighting against the forces pushing us apart except...

To believe in fate was to accept my life was a set of predetermined choices I had yet to make. I wasn't in a *fated mates* frame of mind. Midas could call me Empress of the Universe, but that didn't make it true. I wanted a choice, and I wanted him to have a choice. Both halves of him. I didn't want one to choose and the other to settle. I didn't want to be a cause for more inner turmoil for him.

But I didn't want to let him go either.

Ambrose had confirmed a bond between Midas and me, and it terrified me that it might grant Ambrose access to him. And, okay, it also freaked me out that I hadn't signed off on it or even realized what it was for it to take root in me.

Breathe in, breathe out.

I would talk to Midas. I would get to the bottom of our situation. Then I would focus my panic where it would do the most good. Or maybe eat chocolate until I fell into a sugar coma after drafting a sternly worded DNR on a wrapper. I'm sure that would be legally binding.

"You ready or what?"

I whirled toward the voice to find Remy sitting on the counter in the kitchen with her legs swinging.

"What are you doing here?" I rubbed my temples. "Did we have a meeting scheduled I forgot?"

Asking how she got in would be a waste of breath. She was my spymaster for a reason.

"I heard you could use some extra hands." She spread hers. "I have a few to spare."

Six other Remys slid out of her to lean against the counter while the original drummed her heels.

"This isn't like you." I cocked my head. "Are you sure you want in?"

Remy tended to cause trouble, not snap on gloves to clean up the mess left in its wake.

"I'll handle surveillance from the rooftops." She gestured to the mini Remy army. "We'll make sure no stragglers escape." She chuckled amongst her selves. "How many times in life can you say you watched a giant roach stampede through downtown Atlanta?"

A knock on the door kicked my pulse up a notch, and Remy rolled her eyes as if she could tell.

Expecting Midas, I raked my fingers through my sleep-flattened hair then opened the door. "Oh. Um. Hey."

Hat. Plaid shirt. Jeans. Chaps. Boots.

Ford couldn't be more cowboy chic if he rode up on a horse.

"What's with the getup?" I swept my gaze over him. "Or should that be *giddy-up*?"

"Heard you could use some help." He pulled a lasso from behind his back. "So here I am."

Arms folded over my middle, I reminded him of what he had once told me. "It's rude to assume that all Texans are cowboys."

"Yeah, well." He tipped his hat. "I wanted to see you smile."

"You asked for time." I tried for the smile he requested. "You're over me that fast?"

"You were never mine to lose, and you were always upfront with me about how you felt." He tapped the lasso against his thigh. "You handled the situation better than me start to finish. The whole time I should have been listening better to what you were saying instead of to how I was feeling."

"I don't want to hurt you," I said softly. "I want us to be friends, when you're ready."

"I want that too." He flung the lasso onto the empty mattress I was pretending not to notice because I had the worst feeling in the pit of my stomach last night had been a dream. "This was like stubbing a toe, darlin'."

"You just compared me to one of life's most painful experiences."

"It was a flash of blinding pain," he elaborated, "and then it was over."

Obviously gwyllgi healing abilities meant he had no proper respect for stubbed toes.

"In that case, welcome to the rodeo, partner."

"There's one more greenhorn who'd like a ticket to the show." He gestured to someone in the hall. "It'd mean a lot to her if you gave her a second chance."

Ares eased into view holding a candy bar bouquet stuck in a vase. Even the leaves were edible paper.

"I was wrong to pin my fears on you." She thrust it at me. "I knew the kind of world I was bringing a child into when Liz and I started this. I got overwhelmed, and you were an easy target. I can't promise I won't freak out again because the whole impending-motherhood thing terrifies me, but you've got my word I won't turn it around on you."

"I can't say no to chocolate." I accepted her offering then sobered. "I don't have many friends." I toyed with a curling ribbon I was pretty sure I couldn't eat and made a mental note not to try later. "I'm glad to have you back."

"You've got seven friends right here," Remy called. "And none of us abandoned you."

"You're not pack." Ares shook her head. "You wouldn't understand."

"I understand Hadley needs me to watch her back." Remy reabsorbed her other selves. "She can't trust you two not to dip when it hits the fan. Same with Golden Boy." She curled her lip. "Bunch of traitors."

Crossing to her, I slung my arm around her shoulders. "You're a good friend, but they're my friends too."

Mollified by the attention, she sniffed. "They're not one-seventh as cool as me."

"No one is," I assured her. "But maybe cut them some slack."

"Like she did for you," Bishop said from the hall, nudging Ford and Ares out of his way. "You're a murderous little fiend," he told Remy, "and yet Hadley made you her full business partner."

"To be fair," she allowed, "I didn't give her much choice."

"Best decision I never made." I set my candy arrangement on the counter. "You ready for this, Bish?"

"Have you ever noticed how that nickname makes it sounds like you're calling me a—"

"I am hurt and offended." I put a hand over my heart. "That has never crossed my mind. Not once."

"Mmm-hmm." He passed me a café mocha and a bag with a chocolate croissant. "I see you've called in old favors." He handed Remy her own bag. "I trust everyone here can play nice for one night?"

"They're here of their own volition," I said between bites. "I didn't coerce them."

Given how most of us had parted, I didn't have the nerve to call in those kinds of markers.

"The hall smells like Midas," he said casually. "Are you guys okay?"

After everything that had happened, I was miles from okay, but I was getting there. "Yeah."

"That didn't sound very convincing." He glowered. "Linus gave me explicit instructions."

Cold dread wormed through me. "What kind of instructions?"

"Let's just say he was considering a new rug for in front of the fireplace at Woolworth House."

Since I didn't have a father figure in my life, or regular contact with my older brother, it was nice to hear someone else cared enough to threaten their fellow man if he hurt me. Forget shotguns. Linus was a nuclear option. It gave me a warm, fuzzy feeling.

"Where is the belly-crawler?" Bishop angled himself to see up into the loft. "Gone again?"

"Okay, okay." I shoved him. "Knock it off."

Bishop understood better than most why Midas had flipped out on me, and we hadn't gotten into the gory details of my past. Then again, Midas went to Savannah. He could learn anything and every-thing about Amelie there. No conversation with me required.

The window rattled, and then it thumped. No. Someone was knocking on it. I had to hunt for the remote that operated the blackout curtains, and it took a minute to figure out which button to push, but I got them raised in time to spot Midas putting the finishing touches on what promised to be my new favorite place. Maybe in the world.

"Let them get it out of their systems," Midas said through the glass. "I deserve to walk the gauntlet."

"How did you do all this?" Fumbling the latch, I pushed the window open onto the fire escape. "I didn't hear a thing."

"Lisbeth loaned me a charm." He finished twisting fairy lights on the railing. "What do you think?"

A bright weatherproof rug covered the metal grating underfoot, and a pair of blue wicker chairs huddled in one corner with a matching table between them. Lush plants I hoped he would remember to water, because I never would, sat in colored pots at the other end. Wooden poles had been mounted to the side of the building to support an awning of coordinating fabric, and more lights wrapped its frame before spreading across the railing to where Midas stood beside an outdoor bean bag large enough for me to nap on, or for a gwyllgi on four legs to flop on if he chose.

I got the feeling Lisbeth had loaned him more than the charm. Probably her sense of style too.

"This is amazing." I touched the poles. "How did you get permission from management?"

"Half of the Faraday's prestige is wrapped up in having the potentate in residence these days. It's been a huge selling point since Linus moved in, and that trend shows no signs of slowing down soon. I reminded the owners of that and suggested a few minor changes to make your new space homier might convince you to stay in residence after a security breach almost cost you your life."

Until the Faraday became famous among the paranormal set for housing the current potentate, it had been legendary for its security. The gwyllgi on staff were hardly to blame for the coven's ability to blend. They wore people's identities that we had known, trusted, and they were hard to catch in the act. It cost the security team points, though. Publicly. I regretted that, but I also couldn't spread word on the street about the coven without risking them burrowing in even deeper.

"That's sneaky." I climbed out to join him. "I approve."

"We spend so much time avoiding preferential treatment, I thought it made for a nice change to instead apply it where it would do the most good."

"And that's my fire escape?"

"You like the freedom of coming and going without announcing your movements to everyone in the building." He kicked the bag chair. "I figured it might be smart to pad my own doghouse for the next time I do something monumentally stupid while I was at it."

"You sound certain it's going to happen."

"Other than the girl I promised to mate when I was five, I've never been in a relationship."

"Same." I blew out a long sigh. "Minus the mated-at-five thing. Even then, I was wary of commitment."

I was two years old when my mother struck me for the first time. I don't remember it, exactly, but I do know that was the year my daycare teachers reported me crying whenever it was time for our parents to pick us up from class. They laughed it off as me wanting to stay and play with friends, but it got to the point they became concerned. That's when Mother started sending Boaz for me. I couldn't say no to him, though he always took me to the one place I wanted to go least: home.

"You don't have to make one until you're ready." He plugged in the lights, and the twinkle cast us in a warm glow. "You're not gwyllgi. Our rules are our rules, not yours. You don't have to follow them. I never should have put that pressure on you."

The flickering lights illuminated all the faces pressed against the glass watching our private moment.

"We'll, uh, finish this later." I pecked him on the cheek then unplugged the lights. "We've got to move out. Smythe is waiting."

Midas lingered against the railing. "Am I invited?"

The tension I already caused between him and the pack worried me. "I didn't want to assume..."

"I have another present for you." He passed me a crisp paper embossed with an official seal. "This might help."

The top sheet of what I now saw was a thin packet blocked out a route leading from Centennial Olympic Park out of the city. The bottom was a copy of a permit for a parade. A frakking *parade.*

"How did you push this through so fast?" I goggled at him. "It's legit?"

A nighttime parade, okay, plausible, but no crowds allowed? How did he expect to manage that?

"Mom pulled a few strings." He sobered. "She wants the Martian Roaches exterminated too."

"Police escort?" Bishop asked from over my shoulder. "That complicates things."

"They're sentinels," he explained. "Lizzy arranged it."

"Smart." I passed the paper to Bishop so he would stop breathing down my neck. "I'm impressed."

"They're going to maintain a perimeter for us," Midas continued, earning bonus points. "I asked the pack for volunteers to herd the roaches. If Smythe can get them out into the open and keep them sedate, we can take it from there." He shrugged. "I've got the cleaners on standby too. They'll handle any witnesses and collateral damage."

"Who spilled the beans to you?" I surveyed the room, the guilty faces. "I didn't tell anyone but Bishop."

"I updated the team, but that's it." Bishop got it a beat before I did, and we said together, "Lisbeth."

Ford shifted his weight and kept his head down. "She might have mentioned it."

Aside from leaking privileged information, I had other worries. "You're still talking?"

"A little." He cleared his throat. "She won't get into trouble, will she?"

Lisbeth had hunted down each of my closest allies and brought them here to help me. I couldn't work up a good mad over that. But I would have to sit her down and read her the riot act if she planned on Ford becoming a fixture in her life.

"Not this time," I promised him. "We'll have to have a talk about boundaries, though."

Unlucky for me, I had recent experience in that area. Lucky for her, I hadn't managed it well either.

Guess it would be a learning curve for us both.

"Let's move out." I made a twirling gesture with my hand. "We don't have long."

The others got moving, but I had trouble convincing my feet to get with the program. Plain and simple, I didn't want to turn my back on Midas. I was afraid he might disappear.

"I'm not going anywhere."

"Then you're not going to be much use herding roaches."

"Okay," he amended. "I am leaving, but I'm also coming back."

After a quick check to make sure we were finally alone, I had to ask, "Are you sure?"

"I'm here, aren't I?"

"What you heard in Savannah…" I wet my lips. "It's all true."

"No one told me a thing."

That shocked me enough I stumbled back. "What?"

"I didn't ask them, and they didn't volunteer information."

"You visited Linus and Grier." I clenched my hand on the rail. "I thought that was why."

"I thought that was why too, but I couldn't bring myself to violate your privacy that way."

"Why didn't you tell me this last night?"

"I wasn't sure you would believe me. I hoped you would open up to me if I shared my past with you."

"I thought you knew." A pit formed in the middle of my stomach. "I thought you made peace with it and that's why you came back."

"I was there when most of it happened," he admitted. "I had already formed my opinion of Amelie, but I want to hear Hadley's version of the story." He toyed with the lights. "I want to understand, and you're the only person I trust to get the details right."

During the darkest time in my life, he had been in Savannah with his sister's pack. He might have stayed there if Tisdale hadn't put her foot down and demanded her heir return to Atlanta. As he had in Faerie, Midas sacrificed himself for his sister. He let her stay in a city she had grown to love, with her new friends, free of her mother's shadow, and come back to drape the mantle of beta around his shoulders.

"You guys will have to finish this later." Bishop snapped his fingers out the window. "Let's roll out."

"He's right." I had no trouble climbing through the window with the fear of my past chasing me. "We should go." I glanced back at Midas. "You're coming?"

"I meant what I said." Midas caught me by the hand. "I'm not going anywhere." He shrugged. "Except to the roach parade."

Now I couldn't decide which made me more nervous. The upcoming spectacle or coming clean with Midas on my own terms. Either way, I was glad he would be there for both.

TWENTY-FIVE

Eustice greeted us at the mouth of the alley in his dog form, wagged his tail, and invited us to follow him to the entrance. I could see through the glamour, so I led the others right to Smythe's door. He greeted us with a backpack strapped on, a headset around his neck, and a duffle in each hand vomiting speakers.

"You're late." He shuffled out the door. "I can't feel my hands."

"Let me help." I took one bag, and Midas the other. "Better?"

"Ah, no." Smythe flexed his fingers. "I still can't feel a thing, though it might be the excitement."

"I'm sure that's it," I comforted him. "We're all on edge."

"The refuge is prepared?" He smiled up at me. "They'll be safe there?"

As gross as I found roaches, I hated lying to the guy. "Everything is in order."

I didn't know the details, and I didn't want to know them. I was leaving the ugly bits up to Bishop.

Bishop couldn't lie. He was fae. That didn't mean he couldn't tap dance around the truth like Gene Kelly.

"The roaches will get the sendoff they deserve," he said, a gleam in his eye. "Trust me."

Smythe babbled about the wonders of roachkind until I tuned him out in favor of strategizing with Bishop. It was that or throw up my breakfast.

Midas hung back with the other gwyllgi, but his stare itched between my shoulder blades.

Remy was gone, up to the rooftops, but she had her cell with her. The OPA was on surveillance duty, and she was coordinating with them to ensure the gwyllgi rounded up any roaches that broke from the herd.

The streets were eerily quiet as we walked the predetermined route to check it for obstacles or gawkers. Police radios crackled in the distance, and voices reached us every so often, but the sentinels were doing an A-plus job of keeping any curious citizens at a safe distance.

"We'll set up here," Smythe announced. "This area is perfect."

The spot on the lawn he had chosen in Olympic Centennial Park looked the same as all the others to me, but he would know best.

A tinkling lullaby grew louder and closer, and I reeled in Ambrose as I spotted an ice cream truck rolling into view. "How did that get past the sentinels?"

"Oh." Bishop glanced over. "That's our ride."

A Remy hopped out, jogged over, and tossed Bishop the keys. She kept right on going without a word.

"You rented an ice cream truck?" I ignored the rumble in my stomach. "Why?"

"Normal roaches can run up to three miles per hour. Who knows what top speed is for these guys?" He jingled the keys in his palm. "We need a way to keep up with them that won't put us at a disadvantage."

"And snacks?"

Not that I was complaining about that part, mind you.

"The sound system, kid." He shook his head. "Think about it."

I was too busy wondering if they had cleaned out the coolers full of ice cream to focus on technical details. I loved those chocolate taco things. I hadn't had one in years.

A high-pitched noise, almost violinlike, rent the night air, and Smythe began cackling like a mad scientist.

"Here we go." I clasped Bishop on the back. "Do we need his speakers too or...?"

The plan would fail if we kept piping in music here too. We had to centralize it, and, I guess, mobilize it.

"Good call." He jogged over to Smythe. "Time to take your show on the road."

"We'll have to hurry." He stared off into the shadows. "They're coming."

A shudder rocked me head to toe. Martian Roaches were hard to kill, but I had seen Smythe control one. I had to believe this idea would work to scale, and that we could perform one mass extermination.

What could possibly go wrong, right?

Together we shoved his equipment into the back of the ice cream truck and ran the audio through the built-in speakers. As we loaded Smythe into the passenger seat, the first roach scuttled into view, antennae bouncing in time to the music.

"That's our cue." Bishop cranked up and strapped in. "How long will it take the others to arrive?"

A second and third roach rocked out beside the first, and all three of them boogied our way.

I breathed a sigh of relief when the first pair of red eyes winked into existence.

"W-w-what is that?" Smythe clutched the dash. "I don't understand."

"Hadley's boyfriend is a gwyllgi." Bishop kept it low-key. "The pack offered to help us herd the roaches."

"Oh." Smythe nodded. "That's all right then."

A rustling, whispery noise assailed my ears, and now it was my turn to ask, "What is that?"

"They're coming." He bounced on his seat. "They're…glorious."

"Took the words right out of my mouth." Bishop failed to hide his cringe. "That is a lot of roach."

Two dozen by my count, and the weird sounds kept coming.

"Am I imagining things," I asked Bishop, "or do those four have numbers painted on their backs?"

"Technically," Smythe said, "you mean their carapaces."

Ignoring him, I counted up six with numbers ranging up to twenty-five. "That's not good."

Remy pounded her fist on Bishop's half door, and I leaned around him. "What's up?"

"See those painted pests?"

Smythe choked on his indignation, but I was getting better at blocking him out. "Yeah."

"I spotted one and got curious, tracked it back to its source." Her eyes brightened. "I think I found the coven's home base. These guys? They broke out of a holding pen. They must be the dairy cows for Faete."

"That is fantastic news."

"Except four coven members were home at the time, and they lost their shit when the bugs escaped."

"That is less than fantastic news."

We already had our hands full, and we didn't need more trouble.

"Hey." I caught her before she left. "Why not call with updates?"

"We only have one phone." She shrugged. "Sometimes it's quicker to run to you than to One."

The way she replicated herself, copying her clothes and hairstyle with each self, I hadn't stopped to think it wouldn't extend to technology. I would have to find a workaround for that. Maybe walkietalkies. A fix that wouldn't end up with me paying six more phone bills on the company dime.

"Let us know when the coven mobilizes." I waved her off then faced Bishop. "This complicates things."

A line bisected his brow. "We need those—"

Hearts.

That's what he was thinking. I was too. I didn't like it, but it was going through my head.

"Yes, we do." I cut my eyes toward Smythe. "But we're going to have our hands full."

Coven members held the advantage from the get-go. Fighting multiples at once? That was a recipe for disaster. Considering they must have had some measure of control over the roaches or they couldn't have used them against us, I had no illusions this wasn't about to go south on us. Fast.

"Enough are gathered to leave a rich chemical trail." Smythe fiddled with the controls in his lap. "We can lead them out. The rest will follow."

With the coven on our heels, I didn't have time to second-guess him. We might not get them all, but we could strike a blow to their Faete supply, not to mention save the lives of future hosts.

"You heard the man." I gripped the back of Bishop's seat and held on for the ride. "Roll out."

The truck puttered forward as Bishop tested the roaches' speed and the distance at which they heard the music, for Smythe's sake. We got up to a comfortable forty-five miles per hour, and I could only imagine how our procession must have looked from the outside.

An ice cream truck that had seen better days, blasting a noise that fell between a cat fight and the death of a stringed instrument, while dozens of man-sized roaches scurried in our wake.

I was going to have nightmares about this for years.

Since Bishop had things under control, I checked in with the sentinels and then with the cleaners. Anca had drawn surveillance duty on the OPA side of things while Lisbeth and Milo kept an eye on the city for me. They didn't have full control of the cameras, like Bishop did from his command center, but they could make do. Especially with Remys on the ground.

Please don't let this blow up in my face.

I really did not want to have to explain to Linus how I let this happen if it all went sideways. Don't get me wrong. *The Giant Martian Roach Parade that Swarmed Atlanta* would make a fantastic creature feature. I would totally hit a matinee for that. But I would prefer making Linus proud to making him wonder if I had been inhaling bug spray to dream up this cockamamie idea.

Baying rang out all around us, the pack at work keeping the roaches on the straight and narrow. I caught glimpses of Midas here and there. He was keeping an eye on me, and yeah, it made me all warm and gooey inside like caramel brownies fresh from the oven to know he was there if I needed him, but I tried not to read more into it than that.

No more surprise visits from Remys let me hope that meant the coven situation was under control. They might require more time to mobilize than we first thought. Or maybe they were too confused by the bug parade to figure out how to counter it before we nuked their supply chain. A girl can hope, right?

We made it two-thirds through our route without incident, and I started feeling, dare I say it, confident.

Big mistake.

Huge.

That tiny spurt of optimism was all the encouragement required for doom to settle across the land.

As we exited the city, bound for the "refuge," a yelp set my heart pounding.

"How much farther?" I leaned over Bishop's shoulder. "Can we go any faster?"

"About three miles." He coaxed a blip of speed out of the truck. "This is all I got."

"Any faster," Smythe worried, "and we'll lose some."

Another outcry caused my sweaty palms to slip off the seat. "We've got company moving in fast."

No Remy magically appeared with an update, and One wasn't answering her phone.

That couldn't be good.

"There," Bishop announced. "That's where we're headed."

I'm not sure how I expected a roach sanctuary to look, let alone a fake one, but this was a gaping hole in the earth. Literally. It was a pit with a thick reddish-brown ring crusting the upper edge.

"What is that for?" Smythe wondered. "It's rather large to be left open like that."

"Time to unload." Bishop slammed on the brakes. "Smythe, take your gear to the far side of the hole."

I helped load him up, and he trotted off with Eustice at his heels. Bishop waited until the music picked up on Smythe's end to kill the sound in the truck. I plopped down into the passenger seat and waited for Bishop's grand plan to unfurl while Ambrose went to investigate the ring around the pit.

"Smythe lures them to him, they fall in the hole, and then we trap them in a circle and blow it sky high."

As Bishop spelled it out, Ambrose relayed his surprise over discovering crystalized necromancer blood.

Linus was forever tinkering, as the modified pen burning a hole in my pocket attested to, but this was next level genius if it worked. Dangerous as hell if it fell into the wrong hands, depending on the power of the necromancer who donated the blood—in this case, likely him—but still an extremely cool example of the inner workings of his mind.

The crystals could prove invaluable for setting quick and dirty circles when relying on the modified pen or a brush and pot of ink would take too long. Dry granules would also work on uneven surfaces better than a wet medium. Assuming the desiccated form held as much power as the liquid.

"How do we get them in the hole?" I rubbed my forehead. "There's nothing to stop them from just walking around the edge."

"Hmm." He drummed his fingers on the wheel. "I hadn't gotten that far."

"This was your whole plan?"

"Yes, this is my *hole* plan, and it's a great plan," he protested. "It's not like I had long to improvise."

We climbed out as the first roach rustled past, and I threw up in my mouth a little. The way they ignored us, and the truck, inspired me to attempt what might save or damn Bishop's half-cocked idea.

"Smythe," I called. "Throw your speakers into the pit."

The little man blustered and clutched them to his chest, but he got with the program when a golden gwyllgi padded out of the woods with a snarl on his lips. Eustice took great offense to Midas, but he cowered once Ford and Ares flanked their beta.

"There." He threw the equipment into the pit. "Are you satisfied?"

The music stuttered and then stopped, and so did my heart. The fall had not been kind to the speakers. I had no clue how deep the pit was, but Bishop didn't do things by half. I should have thought of that, but I was squicked out and panicking.

About to suggest we fire up the truck and push it into the pit too, I sagged with relief when thin strains of music filtered into the night air, ensnaring the roaches.

"Get ready." Bishop pointed me toward the circle. "You're going to power that beauty."

Ambrose, who couldn't care less about our roach rodeo, shook his head firmly.

"You don't get a vote," I warned him under my breath. "We need you."

The shadow was not impressed, but he didn't push back, and I saw why soon enough.

A blonde with crimson highlights and lipstick to match picked her way across the rough terrain.

Even without a heads-up from Remy, I pegged her as coven.

Ambrose all but licked his lips, game to be helpful all of a sudden.

He must think I was an idiot. Granted, I had summoned him and bonded to him, so he had good reason to question my mental faculties, but come on. He wanted to spend every last drop of magic in him so he could replenish himself off her. That alone told me she wasn't a person I wanted to tangle with if I could avoid it.

"That's the last roach." Bishop shoved me. "Go set the circle."

The gwyllgi were closing in, one loner caught between them, but it leapt into the pit as I watched.

"I'll hold off the witchborn as long as I can." He shoved me again. "Move it."

I broke into a run and yanked on Ambrose's mental leash until he awarded me his full attention.

"Salivate later." I held my hand over the circle. "Power up now."

Crystalized blood wasn't a medium I had ever worked with, but I assumed if Bishop had signed off on it, he had every confidence it would work.

"Any time now," I growled at Ambrose. "We need these bugs contained."

With great reluctance, he pushed magic into the circle. It snapped closed around the bugs, trapping them under a dome. I really hoped Bishop had thought to line the sides and bottom, or they could dig out before we got to the raging-inferno portion of his plan.

Wobbling as I stood, I shook my head to clear it. Ambrose hadn't been playing. He supercharged the circle, which was good for us, given the coven situation, but I tingled with the effects of his magical offload.

Midas bounded up to me and leaned his bulk against my thigh. I scratched his ears while my balance returned. I was no good to anyone if I fell over and had to be rescued. Or worse, if I gave the coven a hostage.

Bishop stood three feet from the blonde, and her eyes said she could have eaten him up with a spoon.

"I owe you a boon." She wet her lips. "Lucas was skimming, and the coven frowns upon that. We had eyes on his partner, but we couldn't locate him. He was too careful. You solved that problem for us. Let us solve this problem for you."

"Problem?" He squinted at her. "Are you offering to solve yourself?"

I had caught the tail end of their conversation, and it sounded like more recruitment garbage. They must not know Bishop at all if they thought they could sway him to the dark side so easily. Screw cookies. Weapons of mass destruction were his delight.

"You're wasting your talent," she chided. "Why pretend you're less when you're so much more?"

"Lady, you can take a flying leap into whatever hole you crawled from, or you can use ours. I'm not picky."

Eyes downcast, she pushed regret into her tone. "Have it your way."

Magic sizzled through the air, and she morphed into a massive bird of prey the size of a frakking giraffe. I had two brothers. I knew my dinosaurs. This resembled a Quetzalcoatlus. A storklike avian dinosaur with a thirty-something-foot wingspan that weighed over five hundred pounds. Except that wasn't terrifying enough. The reddish-orange scales striped down its front shimmered with heat, and sparks dripped from its feathered tail. This was more a prehistoric phoenix than mere dinosaur, and why not? I had already been exploded and hauled Mendelsohn from a bonfire. Why not roast my goose flying lizard style too?

Smythe, despite having aquariums full of lizards at his facility, fainted dead away. I couldn't tell if he was that overcome, or if he'd had a stroke. I was just glad he had climbed back into the ice cream truck first.

A rumble of interest came from the gwyllgi, and a few licked their chops. I hadn't seen them clearly until now, but there must be close to three dozen in all. Midas threw back his head and sang a hunting song. The others lifted his voice, and more furry shapes emerged from the woods in the opposite direction.

Wargs.

They traveled in two distinct groups, one much larger than the other. A female led the smaller pack, and a male with silver in his fur kept the rest in line.

"The Clairmonts and the Loups?" I wondered out loud. "They're the only packs in the area."

Their numbers made it unlikely they were hosts, but then again, we hadn't known there were so many roaches infesting the city. With the wargs shifted, we had no way to communicate. The change would take too long, and it would leave the alphas vulnerable. They would never allow that, certainly not on a battlefield, and that's exactly what they had walked onto.

All we could do was wait and see which side they fell in on when the action started.

And pray.

That was probably as good an idea as any.

"I hate to say this," Bishop exhaled. "They've got us pinned between a pit and a hot place."

The Quetz was alone, and the coven traveled in pairs from what I had seen. There must be one more out here, but the wargs' appearance worried me more. The size of the coven had yet to be determined. For all I knew, they were all hosts of one kind or another. We couldn't put our backs to them until we knew, and we had run out of time to second-guess ourselves.

The Quetz shot into the air, its wings igniting. It flew circles around the clearing, gliding lower and lower, until its sparks ignited the trees. They caught fire in a rush, and soon we were trapped in a ring of fire that spread too quickly and burned too hot to be anything but pure magic.

Suddenly, I had an inkling of where they got the inspiration for the bomb they sent me.

"What is with all the fire lately?" I flexed my newly healed fingers. "I'm not a fan."

"This might not be the best time to mention it," Bishop hedged, "but dybbuks are vulnerable to fire."

"*What?*"

"The exact reason is too complicated to get into right now, but it boils down to banishing shadow with light. Purification of evil through cleansing flame."

Unable to formulate a response, I spewed incoherent noises at him.

"I researched it, after the bomb. The attack was so random. There had to be a reason for them to use an incendiary spell. They couldn't have honestly believed you were stupid enough to keep the heart with you. And then Mendelsohn. He was crazed enough to dismember his pack but sat calmly in the fire until you pulled him out. The coven was controlling him through a charm or maybe the drug itself, so I get the how, but the why bugged me." He flicked a glance at the pit. "No pun intended."

"This would have been great to know yesterday."

Granted, there wasn't much accurate information on dybbuks. Since they had the nasty habit of going on killing sprees, they were put down as soon as they were identified. I ranked among the longest-lived ones, and it was all thanks to powerful friends sticking their necks out for me, believing that I would beat the odds.

I had done nothing to deserve a second chance. That's why I worked so hard to earn it.

"Elemental fire can't harm you." He rubbed the base of his neck. "It has to be—"

"—magical."

"Primal," he corrected. "Say, from a prehistoric lizard bird of undetermined mythological origin."

"This ought to be fun then."

Without Ambrose, I was a plain Jane Low Society necromancer without a drop of power to my name. He was the jet fuel rocketing me toward the position of potentate, which I never could have held on my own. I wasn't sure I could beat one coven member without him, let alone the others. This bird needed to go dredge itself in flour then jump into a hot fryer before we discovered if it meant true death for my shadow and me.

If I killed the woman wearing the feathers now, the same creature could pop up in another coven member later. That's how their magic worked. They were, for the most part, skinwalkers. Except all coven members could borrow from the same closet of victims. This look had to get yanked off the rack permanently.

There would be no handy circle to protect me if I failed to escape the Quetz's fire. That was a sobering thought. Worse was the realization I couldn't protect my friends, or Midas, from what was coming.

"I've got your back. So does the pack. We got this." Bishop clamped his hands on my shoulders. "We got you."

The gwyllgi angled into a hunting formation, but they were at a disadvantage with the Quetz in the sky. All it had to do was wait, and the fire would take us out for it. It wouldn't have to lose a single feather to end us.

As I was thinking that, a smallish lizard with winglike flaps of membranous skin in mottled shades of orange and brown attached to either of its sides glided over the fire and landed before us. It expanded in a prickling wave of magic into the twisted form of an elderly man.

And like magic, the second coven member appeared to us.

"Give us the girl," he warbled, "and we'll let you live."

"I assume by girl," Bishop clarified, "you mean Hadley."

"Just so." He leaned heavily on a walking stick that materialized from thin air. "You all need not die." He smiled at me, kind and grandfatherly. "You are far more powerful than we ever imagined, a true rarity of your kind. Your sacrifice for those you love will be remembered."

A meteor rocketed to the Earth and smashed into my skull. Okay, so it didn't, but that's how the dawning horror of my realization struck me. "You want my skin so you can rule Atlanta legitimately."

And they had brought the one thing guaranteed to annihilate me as their Plan B.

"A near-bloodless coup," he agreed, inclining his head. "Your cooperation would save many."

Near-bloodless coup, as if they hadn't slaughtered dozens of Atlantans to reach this point.

"Linus would know." They could take my skin and my powers, but they couldn't take Ambrose. Linus would know in a heartbeat I was not myself. "And he would not be happy."

The old man considered this. "Reparations could be made."

"You can't afford to let all these people live knowing I've been hung in the coven's coat closet."

"I could wipe their minds," he offered casually. "They wouldn't have to remember a thing."

"You think we're going to let you in our heads?" Bishop barked out a laugh. "You could crush our minds with that kind of access." He slashed a hand through the air. "Forget it."

The old man turned the walking stick in his hands. "You would prefer certain death?"

"That's all you've offered so far," Bishop said. "You'll have to do better."

"Her life is worth so much to you?" A line bisected his brow. "She's a creature of darkness."

"We all have our dark sides," Bishop countered. "She's a good person."

"Good is subjective." He sought my gaze. "You would let them die in your stead?"

I had kept my mouth shut up to this point in the hopes Bishop could wiggle out of this with the others. Right now, it wasn't sounding likely. The coven were a bunch of liars and murderers. We couldn't trust them.

"I would give my life for theirs in a heartbeat," I said, and I meant it.

"You were the right choice." The old man nodded approval. "Your selflessness unifies others to your cause." He stabbed his staff into the ground. "Your facsimile will rally them to ours nicely."

A calculating expression took hold on Bishop's face, and his cunning shone through in chilling clarity. I had no idea what he had just realized, but it was vital to put that sparkle in his eyes.

"Facsimile," I echoed. "That's classier than calling it what it is for sure."

"You've made your choice." He bowed to me. "May your end come on swift wings."

Dark magic burned my sinuses, and he shifted to his winged lizard form. Lashing his tail, he leapt into the sky and flew to safety.

That must have been the signal. The Quetz hadn't attacked since spewing its initial flame, but now that peace talks had ground to a halt, it was back.

A ballooning sense of dread trickled into me from Ambrose. "How do we knock it out of the sky?"

"No clue." Bishop's lips hitched up on one side. "I'm flying by the seat of my pants here."

"Spoiler alert," I interrupted him. "Your pants are on fire."

Midas strode into view, on two legs, his eyes on the sky. "What's our play?"

"I thought it was your turn to pack the plan. Don't tell me you left it at home."

A smile touched his mouth, but it didn't stick.

"The Clairmont and Loup packs are here," he said, "but I don't know how much good they'll do us."

"Can you tell if they're clean?" I eyed them warily. "I didn't tip them off, but that's not saying much."

The phone tree had been activated in order to bring this many of my allies together. I couldn't bank on the wargs until I knew if they were simply late to the party or if they were crashing via coven invitation.

"They're keeping downwind." He watched them too. "I wouldn't turn my back on them yet."

The Quetz swooped, opened its massive beak, and regurgitated flames that caught the brush on fire and blinded in their intensity. The line of smoldering heat bisected the pit, and all our worries about the pack's allegiance got chucked out the window. They were now on the wrong side to help us either way.

Reaching into Ambrose, I claimed both my swords. They were all but useless, we were sitting ducks waiting to get roasted, but I felt better with them in my hands.

"Do you see that?" Midas pointed to a dark splotch on the ground. "It's not burning."

"Let's investigate." I checked the position of the bird, grateful its massive wingspan made targeting the small clearing difficult, then jogged over to investigate. "Weird."

The gap was narrow enough I could turn sideways and scuttle to the warg side, if I didn't mind the risk of catching my hair or clothes on fire. The dark splotch? It was a roach wing. One must have shed it in the excitement to plummet to its doom.

Careful of the heat, I tested the ridged material, found it cool to the touch, and glanced up at Midas.

"You're not serious." He picked up on the drift of my thoughts. "That's a half-inch thick at most."

"Got any better ideas?" I flipped the wing over onto the next section, and it hissed and smoked as it smothered the flames. "Wow." I dusted my hands. "I'm pretty shocked that worked, actually."

Pretending this had been my plan all along, that I hadn't briefly entertained using it as a shield, I grinned.

"How can we get more?" He glanced over at the pit. "We can't let the roaches out without Smythe, and he hasn't so much as twitched. We don't know if his control is fine enough to hold them steady while we pluck them either." He frowned. "There's the risk of infection to consider too."

This would all be for nothing if even one volunteer got tapped as a host. It would start the cycle over again.

"I'm going to distract the bird," I decided. "You make an exit and get everyone out."

"Hadley..." he began and then closed his mouth. "Be careful."

"I will." I rose onto my tiptoes and brushed my lips across his cheek. "You too."

While he got to work, I did the most idiotic thing I could think of, short of throwing myself into the fire and saving the bird the trouble. I charged the outer ring like that was exactly what I intended to do, ideas churning in my mind. Before I could decide on one, the bird squawked and dove for me.

Pivoting on my heel, I ran for the opposite end on pure instinct, steeling my nerves just as the bird decided I was too close to the fire and used a massive talon to knock me on my butt.

The bird was...protecting me?

The coven must be desperate for my skin if they were curbing their murderous tendencies in favor of allowing smoke inhalation to do the heavy lifting for them. Then again, they couldn't work their mojo on a charcoal briquet if I cremated myself, and I was definitely the kind to go out with a bang.

Earning a new sympathy for balls in pinball machines everywhere, I crisscrossed our half of the flaming circle, running flat-out. I kept the bird busy until a stitch developed in my side and I had trouble breathing.

The angle of my next sprint showed me Bishop and Smythe were clear, and the wargs were exiting through the gap Midas made for them. As much as it worried me to release them in such numbers, we didn't know that they weren't here to help. We couldn't let them die just to be on the safe side.

"Hadley," Midas yelled on his way back to me. "We're clear."

"Go on," I panted. "I'm right behind you."

The war of emotions battling across his face told me he knew I was a liar, but he let the whopper slide.

Bishop, however, fought him tooth and nail. He had known me longer, and he could smell a bad idea on me from a mile away.

"You know what to do," I called to him then slid my gaze to Midas to shore up my courage.

One last burst of speed got me to the edge of the circle sealing off the pit, and I erased the line with my foot. The magic fell, but the roaches cared more about the waning music than their sudden freedom. I didn't let myself hope that would remain the case. I didn't let myself think at all.

Arms pinwheeling, I leapt into the pit with them, Ambrose clawing at the air as we fell.

A percussive *boom* shook the world, and brilliant white light filled my vision.

Darkness, thick and copper-tasting, rushed in before I hit the bottom.

TWENTY-SIX

Midas stared at the smoking pit where Hadley vanished and swore his ribs cracked under the strain from his frantic heart. Tongues of fire licked the sky, and rancid debris rained down around them. Dirt and ash and bug. But there was no sign of her.

She had leapt into the void, curls streaming behind her, and she was gone.

Gone, gone, gone.

The bitter word chased itself around his head, constricting his thoughts to a single panicked channel.

Whirling on Bishop, who held his thumb pressed down on a small detonator, he snarled, "What have you done?"

"What she told me to do." His voice came out flat and tired as he pointed. "Make her sacrifice count."

The leathery bird landed near the pit as Midas watched, hopping here and there for a better vantage.

A wellspring of hatred so old he had forgotten its savor rushed through his veins. Not since his time in Faerie had he raged until his body vibrated with so much caustic magic it rose in a blistering wave that threatened to burn him alive. Embracing the beast's strength and righteous anger, he lunged through the gap left on the scorched earth.

The call to the hunt he meant to issue strangled in his throat as he leapt for the bird and sank his teeth in its hide. He slung his head with vicious precision, ripping out chunks of meat. The man didn't shy from the violence, and the beast relished the kinship with his other half, both of them hungry for vengeance.

Rough fur and hard scales brushed his sides as his packmates joined in, but he snarled a warning.

This kill was his, and his alone.

"Wait." Bishop shoved him aside without fear of his teeth or claws and plunged both his hands into the meaty pulp. A slash from his pocketknife, quick and cold, and he withdrew the heart. "Be right back."

Midas shook his head to clear the roaring in his ears. He couldn't have heard Bishop right.

Be right back.

Shadows swallowed him at the edge of the woods, the heart still beating in his hands.

He left her. Without hoping. He just...left. Without trying. *Left.* Without checking.

Midas eased back from the carcass, his sense of self returning, and allowed his packmates to feast.

"I don't understand." Smythe clutched a giant roach wing to his chest like a shield. "What happened?"

The temptation to rip out his throat for caring more about a bunch of mutant pests than Midas's mate itched in his teeth, but he kept his jaw clenched against the urge to revisit his arena days as more than distant memories.

Time stretched, elastic where it bound Midas as he sat on his haunches and gazed at nothing.

"Give it a minute," Bishop was saying to Ares. "It's too hot out there for us to—"

Midas had no memory of how his jaws got wrapped around Bishop's soft throat or how Bishop ended up on the ground with Midas standing over him. He tasted fae blood where his teeth punctured Bishop's skin. Powerful blood. And it didn't make a difference that he was outclassed magically. He could end this with one snap.

"Kill me," Bishop rasped, "and she'll never forgive you."

He didn't fight. He just laid there. He didn't even have the decency to smell afraid.

"Hadley's dead," Ares snarled. "You killed her."

"She's not dead." Bishop rolled his eyes. "Most likely." He shrugged. "Odds are good she's okay."

The memory of finding her inside the safety of a circle in her apartment after the bomb went off shot to the forefront of Midas's mind, and he spat out Bishop. Stumbling clear of him, he shifted onto two legs and ran for the pit.

"Hadley," he screamed over the edge. "*Hadley.*"

Sirens wailed in the distance, drawn by the smoke or the explosion, he didn't care. All that mattered was how hard it made it for him to hear if she called back.

"Use this." Remy hit him in the side of the head with a thick rope. "It's the best I could do."

A burn kit smacked the dirt at her boots, a gallon jug of aloe with it.

"Wait." Bishop shot to his feet. "Wait a godsdamned minute." He raced to them. "The circle she's in is the only thing keeping her from being parboiled." He snatched the rope. "You've got to let it cool down in there, or you're going to kill her."

Midas forced himself to sit, to breathe, to gather his thoughts. "All right."

"Who called the fire department?" Bishop rubbed his face. "This is going to be a headache to explain."

"I did." Remy plopped down several feet from Midas, her shoulders stiff. "I went for help as soon as that idiot bird started vomiting fire."

For her to have monitored the situation, called for help, fetched the dirty rope from somewhere nearby, and purchased medical supplies, she must have sent her other selves scurrying all over the city.

Fae like her were a rarity in this world. For her to come out to Hadley was one thing. The show of trust in also sharing her talent with Hadley's friends, he wouldn't have expected from someone so guarded. But then, he had been guarded too. Before Hadley. She knocked down his walls with laughter and refused to take no for an answer. He had been a fool to walk away from her, even for a second, even for her own good.

Midas would never be the same person he was before Faerie broke him, but he could piece himself back together. For her. For Mom. For Lethe. For the pack. And, he was surprised to admit, for himself.

The days of living apart, of suffering alone, were over. He was ready to rejoin the world, and he couldn't think of a better guide than the woman he had to believe was biding her time in the crater at his feet.

"I should have been faster." Remy threw pebbles across the gap. "I saw that damn bird, and I panicked."

Midas put in the effort since she had too. "I've never seen anything like it."

"Bishop says they're anti-magic flamethrowers, that you can't protect yourself from them through magical means."

And the coven had unleashed the creature on Hadley.

"The roach wing put out the flames," he murmured. "How can that be?"

"I, uh, have a theory." Smythe joined them, but he made no bones about for whom he grieved. "The client who hired me to create the hybrids requested they be immune to a certain type of magic, one I had never encountered until then." He gazed down with sorrowful eyes. "It's not an uncommon request." He wiped his eyes. "Clients often request built-in controls."

This debacle had proven the coven had commissioned the creatures and then stolen them to put the finishing touches on themselves. A theft, of both Smythe's notes and the creatures themselves, meant he would have had to refund their initial investment. The coven had gotten what they wanted at no cost, except to the citizens of Atlanta.

"You're saying the roach wing worked because the coven requested immunity from the creatures, and it went both ways."

"Yes." He gestured with his hand. "There are, however, no such protections against mundane elements."

The distraction was good while it lasted, but Midas couldn't keep his focus from wandering back to Hadley. The pack was a solid wall of comfort at his back as they sat or paced, on four legs and two, waiting for her to emerge.

He hadn't been sure if they would accept her, and then he hadn't cared. She was his. Either they allowed her to claim her place at his side, or he would do the unthinkable and force Mom to choose another heir to fight for their place at the top.

"We arrived too late for it to matter," a soft voice said from behind him. "I regret that, Midas. I truly do."

When he turned, he found Ayla Clairmont standing nude at the apex of her pack, who had kept their fur.

"She was an exceptional woman," she continued, "and we owed her a debt of gratitude for what she did for the warg community." She lowered her head. "She will be missed."

"Thank you," he said, his throat tight with fervent hope these condolences meant nothing, that Hadley was alive and waiting for him to toss that rope and haul her to safety.

The Clairmont pack left the way they had come, and Ayla paused to kiss the cheek of the old man who had hung back to wait his turn.

"She would have been here sooner if I had listened," Garou confessed. "I have fighters, and the numbers are on my side. She came to me for help in order to end this plague on our people, and I haggled with her." He spread his hands. "It's in my nature, but that doesn't make it right." He nodded toward the pit. "Hadley was an exceptional young woman. Linus chose her well. I am sorry for your loss." He scratched the weathered skin over his heart. "Losing a mate changes a man. I hope you weather it better than I did all those years ago."

"Thank you," he said again, glossing over the fact Hadley would have dismantled his corrupt empire, brick by brick, given time.

Garou took his Loups and began the long walk back to the city. Wargs his age were tough, but he was old, and it showed in the way the beta kept flush to his side. Walking out as a man, with no way to defend himself, was a show of power. A statement that he held his people in check through his will alone. But the enforcers required to keep the more eager wargs back hinted that change might be coming to their hierarchy sooner rather than later.

"You're lucky," Remy said once they were alone. "You keep your clothes when you shift." A shudder rippled through her shoulders. "That guy has to flash his prunes every time he changes forms."

Despite it all, Midas huffed out a quiet laugh. "Wargs are more in tune with nature than us."

"Plenty of folks love nature without walking around balls-out in it."

More laughter spilled out of him, a welcome release, and that's when her motive for playing nice with him registered. Remy was doing for him what Hadley would have done in her place, proving Hadley had been right about her.

The sirens, deafening in their proximity, drew Midas's attention toward the ambulance and fire trucks he hoped were manned with paranormals of one flavor or another so he didn't have to work up the energy to explain this. But when Bishop waved him over, he somehow found the strength to move.

"Water will disrupt her ward," the fireman was saying, "but it's the easier fix."

"How about the *safest* fix," Midas growled. "She could be boiled alive."

"We've got a salamander on the squad," he said, eyeing Midas warily. "He can climb down, assess the risk. We're going to do our best to get her out of there without a scratch."

The rumble in his chest was constant, and he couldn't form words around it.

"She's only got so much air in that bubble," Bishop said under his breath. "One way or another, we have to move in the next half hour."

"Send in the salamander," Midas grated out, his ruined voice garbled. "Check her status."

The fireman raised a hand, and a boy with three chin hairs to his name sprinted over. "Do what you do."

The teen saluted him then burst into flames on the spot, burning down until a lizard the size of a cat stood on his boots. Its red skin shimmered as if fire lived in its veins, but its yellow eyes were sharp and determined as it skittered off to the pit.

"Dangerous," Bishop murmured then faced the fireman. "What made you recruit him?"

"Aubrey started volunteering at our old station when he was twelve. He was fascinated by fire, obsessed with it, and his foster mother worried. We put him to work sweeping, cleaning the trucks, helping cook." The man shook his head. "We knew he was a special kid, but we had no clue how remarkable until he hit puberty." Deep lines bracketed his mouth. "He combusted in his sleep one night and burned down his foster parents' house, with them in it."

"That's how it goes," Bishop lamented. "The awakening. He had no choice in the matter."

"That's what we told him."

"I take it he didn't listen?"

"They were the closest thing he had to parents. He still grieves for them." The fireman grabbed his clothes and shook out the ash as if this were routine. "We gave him a permanent bunk after that and let him live at the station. We put him to work to show him he can make a difference."

"You're a good man," Midas managed. "You gave him a shot at having a normal life."

No foster family would touch Aubrey after that, not knowing he was a juvenile salamander capable of incinerating anything or anyone that got him mad. With a teen chockful of hormones, anger was a given. He had to learn control, or he would be exiled to one of the deserts since killing them was nearly impossible.

"It was a group effort," he grunted. "We all wanted him to succeed. Now he's a full-fledged member of the crew."

While they waited, the captain wandered back to his people to check in with them about dousing the fires. Bishop watched him go, a thoughtful expression on his face.

"They're a pride of lion shifters," he decided. "Given how many lizards get eaten by housecats, it's an odd fit for them to have adopted a salamander."

"I wasn't aware there were any new packs in the city."

"There aren't." Bishop half smiled. "They're a pride, and they're unregistered. We'll let it go for now, see how this plays out."

Midas made a mental note to inform his mother. Their pack wasn't opposed to another predatory species in the area. They were strong enough to hold their territory. But any shift in power sent out ripples, and with the coven in town, those ripples could become tidal waves.

A belch of smoke announced the salamander's return, and he burst into flames close enough to singe Midas's arm hair. The captain jogged over to hear the assessment, his arms folded over his wide chest.

"She's alive," the boy reported. "Her circle is holding."

Relief buckled Midas's knees, and he almost hit the dirt.

"There are a lot of bodies between her and the point of origin." He chewed on his lower lip. "They're insulating her, but they've mostly cooked down to their exoskeletons." He ruffled his hair. "They look like..." He shook his head. "It sounds crazy, but giant roaches."

"That's exactly what they are," Bishop told him. "Good work."

Midas bit down on the question, but it escaped anyway. "How do we get her out?"

"We need to get the bodies off her," Aubrey decided. "They'll crush her if she breaks her circle."

"We can't afford to wait on equipment to arrive," the captain said. "We'll have to dig her out ourselves."

"I recommend a pair." Aubrey frowned. "More than that, and there won't be room to relocate the debris."

"I'll go," Midas volunteered at the same time as Bishop.

They looked at each other, and Midas swallowed his anger as best he could until they got through this.

"Here." Remy passed Midas the rope she had tied off on a nearby tree. "Don't get dead."

Shocked by the sentiment, Midas quirked an eyebrow at her.

"I wouldn't want to miss my chance." She scuffed her shoe. "I like to keep my options open."

"Aubrey," the captain ordered, "get started on the outer ring. We need to contain this fire."

With a snappy salute, he nodded. "Yes, sir."

The boy shifted and scurried into the flames...and then he began devouring them. The magical inferno raged around him, but he kept mowing down the blaze with chomps of his wide jaws.

Tearing his eyes from the spectacle, Midas tossed the rope into the pit and climbed down, choking on the smoke. He called up when he was clear, and Bishop rappelled in to join him.

"Aubrey said she's there." Bishop pointed. "We need to shift as much refuse to the other side as possible."

Careful not to put their weight directly on top of her, they began hauling carapaces, dirt, and other debris to the far side of the pit. Their skin burned, and the stench was overwhelming. Their lungs fought to get enough oxygen, and Midas stumbled more than once from dizziness.

An eternity later, they reached a hard shell that, once they dusted off the muck, revealed Hadley curled in a ball on a patch of dirt unmarked by the explosion. She was unconscious, but she was breathing.

"Big spoon to little spoon." Praying for a smile, Midas finished clearing the path. "Can you hear me?"

The shadow pooled beneath her perked at the sound of his voice and slithered over her in a protective black shroud. Midas noticed Bishop watching and understood that he had known about Hadley. Based on the taste he'd had of Bishop's blood, Midas wasn't surprised to learn the fae could see through glamours.

"Ambrose," Bishop said, and the shadow inclined its head. "Break the circle. We'll do the rest."

Midas cranked his head toward Bishop. "Ambrose?"

"That's his name."

Bishop gave him that much but nothing else, and Midas respected that he was protecting Hadley.

The shadow dove into her, weaving in and out, until she cried out in pain, and her lashes fluttered.

"Jerk," she mumbled. "Back off."

"Hadley." Midas pressed his hand to the bubble. "Break the circle."

Her lids raised a fraction, and her gaze locked with his, but she didn't budge otherwise.

"Break the circle," Bishop urged. "Come on, kid. You can do it."

The shadow kept punching through her until tears streamed down her cheeks, but the pain rallied her. She twitched her fingers, dragging grooves in the dirt, until she reached the edge of the bubble. With a grunt of effort, she raked her nails through the line, and the magic collapsed around her.

Midas scooped her up in his arms, but she was already unconscious. The shadow coiled around her shoulders, clinging tight, but Midas held them both as Bishop rigged him a harness from the rope so the others could pull him and Hadley out. With so much manpower, it took a minute. Maybe two. Then he was free of the eye-watering smoke and dragging in heaving breaths of fresh air.

Bouncing on her feet, Remy made grabbing motions. "I'll take her."

She didn't wait for him to agree, just gathered Hadley with help from another Remy, then ran to a grassy patch where paramedics waited with the ambulance.

The beast rose in Midas, its possessive instincts roaring, but he let it go. He had done all he could do. He had to turn her over to the experts, even as he wished for Abbott to tend to her.

The others began hauling Bishop out of the pit, and he flopped onto his back when he reached the top.

Aubrey, who was coiling the rope like he meant to store it, glanced across the clearing. "Who are they?"

Three men stood with three women and watched the paramedics rush to save Hadley's life.

Midas couldn't say how long they had been standing there, waiting, but they must have shown up after he and Bishop entered the pit. Otherwise, he had to believe he would have noticed them. Then again, if Aubrey hadn't mentioned it, he might still have been oblivious.

His brain was stuck in a rut that made thinking impossible.

Hadley. Hadley. Hadley.

"This is exactly what we don't need," Bishop panted. "Gods above, this night just won't quit."

"Ares." Midas located her among the other somber faces. "Send up a call." He stared down the coven. "See if the wargs are still in the area."

Ares filled her lungs and issued an invitation to anyone who heard, who understood, to come and join in.

"I didn't realize you spoke the same language." Bishop scratched his cheek. "Makes sense, given you share common ancestors."

"The language we speak in our other form is a mishmash of gwyllgi and warg, but some things are universal."

The others joined in, strengthening Ares's voice, but no cries rang out in answer.

"They're gone." Bishop exhaled. "Guess it was too much to hope they'd stick around to chew the fat."

"You should go," Midas told Aubrey. "We can't protect you from what's coming."

The youth straightened his shoulders but nodded. "I'll tell the captain."

"They're just standing there," Midas said. "Why don't they act?"

"They might not have figured out the firemen are paras yet, but they will. Bad guys have a sixth sense for that. Or, you know, they'll kill all the witnesses and call it a day."

Midas grunted agreement then glanced back at Hadley.

"We need her." Bishop read his mind. "Her battery is too low, but she can't fight until she recharges."

Alarm swept through Midas as he watched the paramedics struggle to revive her. "What do you mean?"

After checking their surroundings, Bishop asked softly, "How much do you know about her...condition?"

"Only what I can see," Midas admitted, unable to out her birthname to explain he knew more than that. "She has to recharge?"

"Not her." Bishop's gaze bounced from her to Midas. "Ambrose."

The alarm clanged in his ears, deafening. "How?"

"Magic."

Midas stared at his burnt hands. "Can I...?"

"Shifter magic isn't enough to whet Ambrose's appetite. We need a battery to hook up to him."

The coven in the distance drew his attention. "Will they work?"

"Yeah." Bishop hesitated. "One of them would be plenty, but it might juice the heart dry."

"I don't care."

"You might later."

"No." He let the beast stare out of his eyes. "I won't."

The deal was his to uphold, and he would. One way or another. Natisha might have been willing to bargain with him because of

Hadley, but taking one heart had almost broken her. It was cruel to expect her to bear the entire burden alone.

"All right." Bishop crackled his knuckles. "Let's do this."

"Hold up," the captain called. "Aubrey says there's trouble coming."

"Trouble is already here." Midas indicated them with a jerk of his chin. "You should clear out while you can."

"The twins told me it was the potentate down there." He shifted his weight. "That true?"

The twin comment threw him for a loop before he noticed two Remys standing together near Hadley.

"She's the next best thing." Bishop failed to conceal his pride. "She's his apprentice."

"I have a proposition for you." The captain rolled up his sleeves. "Hear me out?"

"Make it quick," Midas said, eyes straying to the coven, to the fix Hadley needed to get back on her feet.

"Folks tend to get jumpy after they hear about Aubrey." He wet his lips. "We're getting tired of roaming, and we could use all the help we can get keeping our family together if we decide to make Atlanta our permanent home."

Midas cocked his head. "Why Atlanta?"

"We heard things are better for shifters here, for anyone who's different." He shrugged. "Rumor has it the potentate is fair and doesn't discriminate."

There were factions, necromancers among them, that viewed shifters as little more than animals. That Hadley viewed them as equals and protected them with her life had clearly resonated with more shifters than the gwyllgi.

"I can't make any promises." Bishop spread his hands. "I'm not the one in charge."

"I can give you the word of the beta and heir of the Atlanta gwyllgi pack that if you help us," Midas said, "we will ally with you to help defend your claim on this territory against others of your kind."

The vow was too big for him to make, and under other circumstances, he wouldn't have dared without the alpha's permission. Mom could rescind his vow, and it would damage his reputation. But that would come later. They needed help now. He was willing to risk it all for the chance to bring down the coven and pay his debt to Natisha.

"I can't ask for better than that." The captain stuck out his hand. "Call me Gray. Everyone does."

"Welcome to Atlanta," Midas said with a growl in his voice. "This is what you need to know about the coven."

Quickly, Midas filled in Gray so he could warn his pridemates, but the alpha didn't balk at the task.

Once he left to fill in the others, Bishop cleared his throat a few times.

"That wise?" He clarified, "Giving them carte blanche?"

"We need the help." Midas would have to survive first to regret it later. "Beggars can't be choosers."

"I'll get Reece on a background check." Bishop sighed. "We screen newcomers, so I'm not sure how they slipped through the cracks. That might be on us, or it might be on them."

"They're hiding the boy," Midas reminded him. "They kept their heads down for him."

"They could have presented him as a cub," Bishop countered. "Secrets make me itchy, is all."

Midas cut him a flat look that conveyed the sheer nerve Bishop had in making that claim.

"Other people's secrets," Bishop clarified toothily. "I'm fine with my own."

About to check with Gray, he turned to find the alpha loping toward him.

"We're set," he said. "Give us a half hour to shift, and we'll be ready to go."

They might not have a half hour. That's what Midas was thinking. But he didn't say it. "Okay."

The pride backed off and stripped out of their gear while Aubrey stood watch over them.

Whatever their story, one thing was for sure. That boy loved them like family, and the feeling was mutual. The fiery glint in his eyes promised agony to anyone who tried to come for them on his watch.

The thick snap of bone and vicious yowls of agony made tracking their transformational progress easy.

The earsplitting roar as the big cats emerged clued in the coven that they had waited too long to strike. A ripple went down their line, and they donned skins, each one more hideous than the last. Midas could name only two of them. The rest...he had never seen anything so terrible.

"I'll do what I can to preserve the hearts," Bishop told him. "You don't care now, but you might later."

Midas shoved the debt out of his mind and focused on the hunt. He let the magic claim him, sweep him away on a tide of primal need and hunger for prey between his jaws. Teeth on display, he set about herding a snack toward Hadley.

TWENTY-SEVEN

I hurt. All over. Every part of me. Nothing felt right. Some things I didn't feel at all.

"We need to bring her in," a man said from somewhere to my left.

"Her vitals are good," a woman agreed. "Let's get her out of here."

"What the actual hell," another man murmured, awe and horror in his voice. "Do you see those?"

"Whatever those are," the first man said, "I ain't hanging around to introduce myself."

"Wait." I coughed, but my stupid eyes refused to open. "Wait."

"We've got you," the woman cooed. "You're all right."

"Midas…" I couldn't feel my right arm. No, my whole right side was numb. "Where…?"

Silence filled the area once packed with voices. Whatever they saw, they didn't want to tell me.

"We need to relocate you to the hospital," the second man tried. "We can't stay here."

A trip to the ER didn't frighten me. All major hospitals had paranormal wings. Most had entire floors dedicated to emergency care. I just didn't have the time. Proper medical care was a luxury I couldn't afford right now.

Try as I might, I couldn't nudge Ambrose into action. He was weaker than he ever had been, and it left me too drained to do more than mumble and twitch my fingers as they loaded me into what I assumed was an ambulance based on the antiseptic smells.

As much as I hated to do it, I had no choice. I couldn't leave the others to face what these EMTs were too afraid to articulate.

"*Sip*," I thought at Ambrose. "*Just a taste.*"

They had the doors shut and the engine purring before he worked up the stamina to drink from the nearest person—the woman. She tasted like a witch through our bond, and she gave him enough of a spark to seek out the men, also witches, and drink from them too.

"I don't feel so hot," the woman murmured. "I hope I'm not coming down with something."

The energy animating Ambrose took its sweet time reaching me, but it gave me enough of a boost to open my eyes. I ripped off the oxygen mask, pulled the needle out of my arm, and flung the tubing aside. I felt like death warmed over, but everything appeared to be in working order.

"You shouldn't do that," she whispered drowsily. "Let's both... take a...nap."

Her lids fluttered closed, and she began to snore where she leaned her head against the wall.

The groans from the front told me the guys were on their way to Dreamland too.

Ambrose had taken more than I would have liked, but he hadn't hurt them. That was progress. I would have treated him if I had more than a hole in my pocket where his truffles used to be.

After unfastening the straps securing my waist and legs to the gurney, I swung my feet over the edge and braced my palms on the walls to get to the door. It must have weighed a thousand pounds, and it took me at least fifty years to budge it, but I got it open before I required a walker to shuffle to the rescue.

The view out the back stumped me for a beat, and I rubbed my eyes to see if that helped.

Nope.

There still appeared to be six lions and a chonky lizard interspersed among the gwyllgi.

"What drugs did they give me?" I leapt out, which is to say I flopped forward and hit the dirt with my face. "Ouch." I struggled against gravity to get onto my hands and knees. "Whatever it was, it did jack diddly for the pain."

Ambrose coalesced beside me, shades lighter than usual, and he gazed into the distance with anticipation.

"Oh crap." I got what the EMTs were raving about and totally empathized with their urge to burn rubber back into the city. "The coven."

Six...*things*...charged down the hill toward the line of gwyllgi, and I almost fainted from the rush of blood to my head as I wedged my legs under me. The limp-noodle state of my arms told me sword fighting was a no-go. I could barely shamble toward them.

"Don't make me regret this," I told Ambrose. "Pick one." I kept stumbling. "Drain it dry."

The shadow bent his head and planted a kiss on my cheek then sped toward the biggest, ugliest, meanest I-don't-know-what I had never seen. With the bloated head of a tiger, body of an elephant, and tail like a pug, it was pure nightmare fodder. Until it whirled to snap at a lion that got too close, I hadn't noticed the golden gwyllgi herding it right for us.

Not one to dawdle when food was on the line, Ambrose honed himself into a black spear and struck the creature in its heart. It roared and thrashed as it fell with a thump that shook the ground beneath my feet.

The others glanced around, Team Good and Team Bad, shock bright on their faces, and that's when they spotted me.

Luckily, Ambrose was too busy gorging to thin my cut of the magic to a trickle. That, or it had overflowed him and had nowhere to go but into me. I didn't care. I would later. If there was a later, but it felt good to have my aches and pains fall silent and my body once again following my brain's commands.

"My swords," I ordered him. "Ambrose."

The shadow ignored me and continued to feast. Unfortunately for him, now that I was flush with power too, I had the reserves to yank his metaphysical leash until he had no choice but to heel. He slunk to me, uncaring as the other creatures descended upon my friends. I jerked on Ambrose until his fury singed the back of my throat in a scream he couldn't utter, but I got him close enough to reclaim my weapons.

"Sip from the rest." I pushed as much power as I could spare into the command. "Help us take them down."

The soul of cooperation, Ambrose ricocheted off me and shot across the field to ping-pong off the five remaining creatures.

"I'm a lover," Remy said from behind me, "not a fighter."

"You tried to mow down Midas," I reminded her. "You've got killer instinct to spare."

"That was One." She pointed to another Remy, one of three I counted in the area. "I'm Five."

"Do me a favor then." I aimed her toward the ambulance. "Get them out of here."

"That I can do."

With her commandeering the ambulance, we had removed the innocents from the field.

Dividing my attention between Ambrose, who used his earlier hit of power to defy me and take *more, more, more,* and the battle raging ahead, I spotted my opening and took it. A gap split the line where the lions and gwyllgi met, their fighting styles too different to mesh seamlessly, and I filled it.

One of the beasts wasted no time homing in on me. Its torso was male, but its tail was snakelike, and a cobra's fan flared around its humanesque head. Its skin was all mottled shades of green, and its blood ran black and sizzled where it hit dirt and grass.

"She lives," he hissed between fangs the thickness of my thumb. "Take her."

The remaining four shifted their focus from mowing down the defensive line to capturing me.

Midas fought his way to my side, and I wished I could run my fingers through his fur to reassure myself he was okay, but I couldn't afford to distract him. Or myself. It would suck to die because I paused to give my boyfriend belly rubs. That's the kind of end you never live down, not that I would be alive to enjoy my notoriety.

A lion with silver in his mane shot in front of me, raking his claws across the snake's belly. The plating on its abdomen kept it from being a kill shot, but the snake man hissed and bowed over, and I took off its head with a clean slice.

"Coming through." Bishop punched his fist through the snake man's chest and ripped out a heart with no finesse whatsoever. "Back in five."

There was no time to gawk or protest the sudden violence. Gratitude he had spared me the task warred with fear it wouldn't count if I hadn't done the deed myself. We had no way of knowing what Natisha wanted from me, and I fretted that ignorance would cost us down the line.

The rest of the coven expressed no grief stepping over their fallen comrade to reach me. The pack—and the pride, I guess?—kept the worst of it from me, but it was close. At times I proved how worthless I could be, unable to swing my sword without fear of injuring an ally. Trusting the pack and these strangers to protect me played on all my old insecurities.

I hadn't been enough for my family. How could I be enough for a pack? For my friends? For a city?

There was no choice. I *had* to be.

A nightmare with six arms fell to the pride, but it took every one of them to finish it.

The pack brought down another, but three gwyllgi had been thrown keeping it off me, and they weren't moving.

Ambrose was slowing the beasts down, but they were too much even for him. I was expending the magic as fast as he harvested it to boost my healing abilities and increase my strength.

A piercing howl rose behind us, but I couldn't turn to check. A half goat, half man with bizarre spines similar to a porcupine had stepped into the breach. A woman with silky midnight-blue hair and bright-red skin joined him. Her eyes were trailing comets, and her sensuous voice...

On the ground.

Flat on my back.

Sky overhead.

How did I get here? Why are my ears ringing? Surely even I can't get blown up twice in one night.

Blinking back to myself, I found Midas on all fours standing over me, a rumble constant in his chest.

When had that happened? When had any of it happened?

Wargs by the dozens yipped, dove, and lunged at the two coven members who had cornered me.

"She's awake." Bishop hooked his hands under my arms and hauled me to my feet. "Hey, kid. You had us worried there for a second."

The questions frothing in my head refused to bubble out of my mouth. "What...?"

"A siren." He checked a rising goose egg on my noggin then nodded, satisfied. "An old one."

Age matured into power, which explained why she had so thoroughly rung my bell.

"I have the worst headache." I clutched my head, but it didn't help. "Goddess, that was brutal."

"They must have been holding her in reserve." Bishop kept me steady. "She whammied you real good, then she fell back. Thank the old gods her range is limited."

Whammy was definitely the right word. "The wargs?"

"The Clairmonts and the Loups." He smiled out at the carnage. "They came back as soon as their alphas managed the shift."

"Oh." I had no memory of them leaving in the first place. "That's good."

"Hold still." Bishop placed cool hands on my temples, magic seeped into my skin, and he gave me the worst brain freeze known to man. "Better?"

"Ow, ow, ow." I swatted him away. "No, that's not better." I glared at him, noticed my vision was singular instead of plural, and laughed. "Hey." I straightened. "That is better."

"Gotta go." He turned me loose. "The wargs are about to bring down that naga."

Until he mentioned it, I hadn't noticed the blood and gore caking his hands, or that it had transferred to me. Elbows, wrists, and hands. Crimson smeared them. I imagined my face looked much the same, my temples anyway. The smells and itch as it dried turned my stomach.

And speaking of my stomach, Ambrose was too glutted to care what happened next. He had gotten drunk on power. Again. He lounged on a tree limb, watching the show, too bloated to give me any trouble. Or help. It was a trade I was willing to make.

I scooped my swords off the ground where Bishop had tossed them in favor of catching me and joined the gwyllgi front line again. This time, they let me work for them, luring the coven then dogpiling them.

Bishop drifted in and out, not fighting, but plucking hearts after fatal blows fell.

The Remys ran interference for the most part, but I caught them hauling out wounded too.

The final coven member standing wasn't nearly as terrible as the others had been. It was a simple manticore. Simple but effective to have lasted this long.

With the others down, and four packs converging on one witch-born fae, it stood no chance. They killed it, ripped it apart in seconds, and Bishop shook his head when the heart came out too damaged to salvage.

Given there were things, not many but enough, that could regenerate a heart, I made the rounds and decapitated the dead. Their bodies would be burned and their ashes scattered to be certain they weren't coming back.

But the coven we fought today had wanted to bring me back with them. Their leader was waiting for me to be hand delivered like a gift. That meant there were more witchborn fae in my city that needed weeding out before we could pat ourselves on the back.

Midas shifted then collapsed in a heap beside me. "How did we do?"

"Five hearts," Bishop answered him from behind me. "Not bad for a day's work."

"Those are all from this?" I did the math in my head. "That gives us six total."

One heart more, and we could call our deal with Natisha done.

Assuming she accepted those Bishop had gathered on my behalf.

"Do you think Natisha will count them?"

I cringed from my own voice. I hadn't meant to ask out loud. I hadn't meant to lessen Bishop's service.

"I got to thinking about that," Bishop mused, and he sat on my other side. "We won't know for sure until she comes to collect, but I've got a feeling it doesn't matter who removes the heart."

"How do you figure?"

"Natisha has come across witchborn fae, or she wouldn't have known to covet their hearts. That tells me she's aware of how they operate and how powerful they can become in large numbers." He grimaced. "She knew no one faction could take on a whole coven and survive, let alone win." He shook his head. "Their magic lets them call up all manner of creatures. They're too diverse, able to turn on a dime." He shrugged. "Shifters have one form, and no witch could cast a transformation spell at their speed. Even if they could, they don't become the creature their glamour mimics. They might look like an ogre, but they wouldn't have its strength, its bad breath, its body odor... You get where I'm going with this."

"Yeah." The coven didn't imitate their marks, they embodied them.

"Factions don't work together," he continued. "They don't cooperate. Not on this scale."

"Hadley is a wild card," Midas murmured. "She rallied enough of us to her cause that where one faction failed, another succeeded." He thought about that. "Natisha didn't assign the task to me because the gwyllgi weren't versatile enough."

"That's my take," Bishop agreed. "It was a group effort, but Hadley was the linchpin."

"Thank you." I took his hand, sticky and warm. "You didn't have to do this for me."

"Kid, I've got enough black marks on my soul I can't see the writing on the wall anymore." He squeezed my fingers. "You might get that far, you might not, but you're not there now, and you won't be on my watch."

Bishop killed to feed. I had always known that about him. He beat himself up over it each time, the loss of control, but he had to eat to live. I hadn't asked him about it, and I doubted I ever would. There were some burdens that no two shoulders can support more easily than one.

"I still appreciate it," I said softly. "You're a good friend."

"I'm learning to be." He slanted his gaze toward Midas. "We good?"

"You blew up Hadley," Midas rumbled. "What do you think?"

"Tell your man to toughen up if he's going to date you." Bishop chuckled. "He ain't seen nothing yet."

Uncertain if he meant it as a compliment or a warning, I thinned my lips and watched him walk away.

"Briefing at dusk." He lifted a hand. "Until then."

"I'm out too." Remy padded over, her skin dull and gray. "I have to find where the rest of me went."

"Get some rest." I pointed a warning finger at her. "Do not open the store at dusk. Take the day off."

"Yes, boss." She grinned at me. "I have inventory waiting anyway."

Midas nodded to her, and she nodded back. It wasn't much, but I was impressed by their progress.

"Gray, this is Hadley." Midas introduced a very naked man with silver in his beard. "Hadley, this is Gray."

"Nice to meet you." I kept my eyes glued to his face. "Thanks for the assist."

"I'm the alpha of the Kingsman lions." He gestured to the other super-naked guys covered in gore. "I would like to sit down and talk to you about making our move to Atlanta permanent."

"Call the office." I reached for a card and forgot I was charred, bloodied, and drenched in ichor. "Well, this is awkward. How about I call you? Midas mentioned you're with the fire department?"

"The city wanted new blood in Station Thirteen after the old captain retired and his coven left with him, so we took the posting. We're used to working in tandem with the cleaners and the sentinels on the police force. We've been fielding paranormal calls in Tucson for about fifteen years now." He studied me. "I've heard good things about you. Otherwise, I wouldn't be standing here."

"I take my job seriously." I averted my gaze to keep myself honest. "I take the safety of my citizens even more seriously."

He crossed to me, which made it even more awkward, given I was sitting and he was standing.

Goddess, I did not want a face full of his junk as he shook my hand, but there you go.

Today was just a face-full-of-junk kind of day, I guess.

The warg packs gathered their wounded and left with nods to Midas and me, and the gwyllgi did too.

Once Midas and I were alone, waiting on the cleaners to arrive, I worked up the nerve to face him.

Chewing my bottom lip, I got down to it. "How mad are you on a scale of one to ten?"

"They haven't invented a number that high."

"I'm sorry." I pulled my legs up to my chest. "It was all I could think to do."

"You saved our lives."

"So..." I flexed my toes in the dirt, unsure where my shoes had gone. "Are we okay?"

"Hadley," he said on a put-upon sigh. "You can jump into as many roach-filled pits as you want, get exploded as often as you like, and shake hands with naked men until your arm falls off. As long as you still come home to me, in one piece, with a pulse, I'm good."

"Good." I leaned my head against his shoulder. "Midas?"

Gently, he pressed a kiss to my hair. "Hmm?"

"I love you." I ignored the way my stomach wrung itself tighter and tighter until I wanted to hurl on him. "I didn't mean for this to happen, but you didn't leave me much choice. Really, if you think about it, it's all your fault."

"I did trick you into the courtship," he admitted, his expression remote.

"Yeah." I linked my hands in my lap. "You did."

"The way I see it," he said slowly. "This is all *your* fault."

A laugh halfway to my lips, I gawked at him. "What are you talking about?"

"I've been broken a long time, and you're the first person who hasn't tried to fix me." He sighed. "You've made me better by example. I see you fighting your demons, and it's given me courage to swing at mine too."

"We've both got work to do. I can't very well shine a spotlight on yours when I'm under construction."

The thumping of my heart grew more painful as it sank in that he wasn't going to say *I love you* back.

"We should go." I kept it casual as I drew away from him. "I owe Linus an update before I crash."

A thin excuse, but it beat the others out of my mouth.

"That's it?" His gaze roved my face. "You're leaving?"

"I feel like a total idiot," I confessed, cheeks burning, "so yes. I'm leaving."

The mate thing must come with an expiration date similar to the courtship deal. It would be great if someone printed a handout for us non-gwyllgi to help us avoid whiplash and awkward declarations.

Midas twisted until he faced me, and he stared until I blinked first. "I love you."

"Are you sure?" I blurted. "I'm a mess, and I joke all the time, and I don't think before I act, and—"

"You're not going to talk me out of loving you." He traced my collarbone with a finger. "Nothing will."

"Are you *really* sure?" I shivered under his touch. "You don't have to say it just because I—"

"Hadley." He cradled my face in his palms. "You can't scare me away."

Throat tight, I had to push out the words. "You would be better off with—"

"I love you." He brushed his lips over mine. "Even your warped sense of humor."

"You're the warped one." I kissed him back. "You like it."

"Let's go home." He got to his feet and pulled me to mine. "Linus can wait. You need rest."

"You're just trying to get me into bed," I teased with a quiet laugh.

"Yes," he said with heat that threatened to melt my bones. "I am."

TWENTY-EIGHT

A heat wave jarred me awake at dusk before my alarm got the chance. Sweat coated me head to toe, and I was sticky with it. I showered before collapsing onto the futon, but I still smelled...well-done. Probably my hair got burned. I might not have minded so much if I hadn't registered the cause for my hot flashes.

Midas was wrapped around me like a blanket. His strong arms locked around my waist, and his muscular legs tangled with mine. His chin rested on my shoulder, and he snored lightly in my ear. He was boneless against me, utterly relaxed, and I could have stayed like that with him forever and been happy.

As if sensing I had woken, Midas growled and tightened his grip, reminding me last night had taken its toll on me.

"Good morning to you too." I reached back, ignoring the twang of pulled muscle, and patted his cheek. "You don't have to get up with me."

"I need to report to the den," he mumbled. "Gotta update Mom."

"I need to report to HQ." I tapped his hands where they rested on my tender ribs. "And I have to pee."

Slowly, as if considering the merits of ignoring me, he let me go. "Come back when you're done."

Sitting on the edge of the mattress, I had to force my legs to get with the program. Midas in bed, his lashes fanning his cheeks, was more tempting than anything on my docket for the day. "No."

Another growl slipped from between his lips, and he swiped out his arm to grab me. I leapt onto my feet in the nick of time, laughing at his frustrated snarl when he closed his fist over air, then hissed through my teeth as a wave of stabbing pain blindsided me.

Midas stood in front of me in a blink. "How bad is it?"

"I've had worse." I got my breath back and straightened. "Abbott warned me to take it easy."

Worry pinched his features. "I didn't hurt you, did I?"

"*I* hurt me." I rubbed my side and regretted it. "I shouldn't have forgotten I'm not an Olympic gymnast."

"I held you all day," he fretted. "Maybe we should drop in on Abbott, get your x-rays done again."

"You're the only reason I slept all day." I shoved him and regretted that too. "And besides, Abbott is mean to me."

"He didn't throw that bedpan at you."

"It hit at my feet," I reminded him. "He could have crushed a toe."

"It slipped out of his hand." Midas kept his face blank. "It was an accident."

"An accident?" I yanked down the collar of my tee to expose my clavicles. "What about this?"

Scrawled in black permanent marker were the words *Highly Flammable.*

"You did get blown up twice in one week." Midas tried and failed to hide his smile. "He's under a lot of stress."

"I'm not going back to the infirmary, and you can't make me." I jutted out my chin. "So there."

"How can I counter such a mature and rational argument?"

"It's impossible." I shrugged. "I win yet again."

"Can you get to HQ solo?" He checked the time. "I can take you to the general area if you need a lift."

"I bet you fifty bucks Bishop is on the fire escape waiting for me to let him in."

Remy had been out there when we got in last night. She wanted to check and see if I was alive. Bishop hadn't been letting me out of his sight since Natisha entered the picture. I didn't see him relaxing his vigil now that we had declared all-out war on the coven.

"That's a bad bet." Midas shook his head. "I'll take it if you take mine."

"What's on offer?"

"I bet you the same fifty dollars Ares is waiting for me in the hall."

"How weird is it we've got people waiting to walk us to work like we're children? Do they think we'll bolt without adult supervision?"

"I notice you're implying we're not adults or able to supervise ourselves." His lips pulled to one side. "That lends weight to the argument we should be walked to work."

Peeling my lips away from my teeth, I growled at him until my ribs protested the vibration.

"I really do love you." He kissed the corner of my mouth. "Even if newborn pup growls are scarier than yours."

"I'm offended, but I'll let you get away with it this time because you kiss pretty good."

"Pretty good?"

"Eh." I rolled a shoulder. "It's been so long since you kissed me, I forget."

"I just kissed you."

"My grandma kisses deeper than that." I wrinkled my nose. "Gah. I had to go and make it weird."

"You always do." He rested his forehead against mine. "It's one of the things I like best about you."

"That I'm weird?"

His eyes sparkled. "Yes."

"Then you're in luck." I flung my arms around his neck and hid my grimace. "I was blessed with a lifetime supply."

"A lifetime sounds good." He took me by the elbows and lowered my arms gently. "Where do I sign up?"

"I'll have my people call your people. They can fax over the details." Smiling, I started down the stairs from the loft into the living room. "Ignore the fine print, and I'm sure we'll be fine."

As soon as my feet touched the downstairs floor, Midas was there, hemming me in.

"You're not scaring me off, Hadley." He ducked his head to put us at eye level. "I mean it."

"I know you do." But it was hard to believe he knew what he was getting himself into with me.

Voice low and gritty, his jaw set, he asked, "Do you think you can ever trust me again?"

"I do trust you." I did my best to let him read it on my face. "I also worry one day you'll regret this."

Regret *me*.

"Do you know how many *one days* have passed since I came home?" He drew back, and his past darkened his eyes. "You know what dating was like for me. You saw me at Joelle's." He cupped my face in his hands. "Do you think I would choose another decade of staring out a window across from a stranger over you?"

"I have issues." I bet that shocked him to his core. "Mostly in the self-esteem department."

"I've noticed," he said carefully. "I don't understand them, but I want to, when you're ready."

A knock on the glass ruined the moment, but Bishop was clearly tired of waiting on me.

Supernatural hearing meant he might as well have pulled up a chair to listen to us pour out our hearts. Linus might not have gotten around to making copies of the penthouse key to pass around, but it was clear Bishop had no qualms in climbing the fire escape to achieve the same direct access. Along with everyone else.

"That's my cue." I backed away from Midas. "Do you get more privacy at the den?"

"You've been to the den." He quirked an eyebrow. "What do you think?"

"I hear it's nice." I mashed the button to raise the curtains. "Or that's the rumor."

"I've heard the same rumors."

"Well?" I flung open the window on Bishop. "Where do you stand on privacy?"

"Currently, I'm standing on the fire escape of the woman who would be potentate." He climbed in and shut it behind him. "Anyone who lobbies for an office can expect to pay for it with their privacy." He flicked Midas a glance. "Same goes for anyone born into a dynasty."

Squinting at Bishop, I got the drift. "You're saying I only have myself to blame for this."

"Pretty much." He shrugged. "You can walk away." He stared at me earnestly. "There's still time."

Curious about the tension in his shoulders, I wondered out loud, "Is that what you think I should do?"

"Hell no." He ruffled my hair. "Who else would sign off on my expenditures?"

"You're talking about the flamethrowers again, aren't you?"

"I will never not be talking about the flamethrowers. If we had to campaign for you like the mundanes do, I would have cartoon versions printed on your propaganda." He slung his arm around my shoulders. "Seriously, kid. I'm glad you're okay. You're what this city needs right now." He wrinkled his nose. "You smell crispy." He withdrew. "Are you going to work in your pajamas or what?"

The reminder I had to buy clothes at some point unless I wanted to wear my remaining outfit, which was dirty, until it fell apart at the seams wasn't entirely unwelcome. Now that Midas and I had ironed out a few wrinkles, I could picture us trying this cohabitation thing long-term. That meant I needed cute undies. And, you know, shirts

and stuff. But mostly sexy sleep attire to coax him out of his pants...
and into mine.

"Actually, yes." I wrinkled my nose at him. "I'll have to borrow
some sweats to go shopping in."

The fresh reminder as my hair crunched when I pushed it out of
my face made me regret the earlier cuddling session as I absorbed the
gorgeous blond with warm, blue eyes on mine. The smell had to be
eye-watering for him. "See you at dusk?"

"I'll be here."

After making a quick mental note to get yet another haircut
before I returned home tonight, I attempted to exit without assaulting
his poor nose again, but Midas drew me against him for a lingering
kiss.

"Be safe," he murmured in my ear, "and I'll bring you chocolate
for dinner."

"That is a bribe I can respect and accept." I wiggled my fingers at
him. "See you at dusk."

"You already said that." Bishop herded me from the penthouse
into the hall. "You two will have to be cutesy on your own time."

The ride down to the lobby gave me an eyeful of the smile I
couldn't shake in the silver panels.

"As a person burdened with my own peculiar dining habits," he
said quietly, "I believe you should know Midas handpicked a meal for
Ambrose. He fed him to heal you." He read my expression with ease.
"I wasn't sure who else to trust or how to get you what you needed."
He frowned. "I hope what I told him won't make trouble between
you two."

Leaning against the wall, I recalled Midas herding the creature,
but I hadn't grasped the full ramifications.

Midas knew about Ambrose, thanks to the sight. Now he knew
Ambrose ate magic, thanks to Bishop. He had stayed with me,
though. Through it all, he was right there. As promised. According to
Bishop, he had been willing to feed Ambrose. That...changed things.
How, I couldn't put my finger on, but then I did.

The shift in my perspective was an emotion I had so little experience with, I had trouble identifying it.

Hope.

Midas's swift rejection upon learning about me had been expected. I was used to that. It still sucked, but I could process it. I knew how to climb back to my feet after taking a brutal hit. But this was the opposite of that, and it confused me.

Midas wasn't spouting crap about mating and love to slap a patch on us until he decided if he was in or out. He wasn't pulling the same shenanigans as he had with Ford and me. He was showing me, and my friends, he was willing to accept the ugly parts of my nature, even the ones that scared me.

And let's be honest—Ambrose, and my bond to him, terrified me.

Bishop and I didn't talk much on our way to HQ, but the whole team was present when we arrived and chatting amongst themselves. I stole a moment to drag on sweats and a clean tee, but the chatter had turned to a roar by the time I emerged, ready to face whatever the night held in store.

"Tell her," Lisbeth urged. "Tell her, or I will."

"We *might* have the green light on the antidote," Reece announced matter-of-factly. "Doughty and I have done all we can do short of launching a clinical trial. We've got Smythe checking behind us before we do that, but it could mean a cure in hand within the next week."

"That's amazing." I did a little dance. "Do the gwyllgi know yet?"

"I sent Tisdale my notes," he confirmed. "She's cautiously optimistic, but she won't share the news with the parents until we're ready to ask for volunteers."

"You deserve all the cookies," I told him. "Thank you for your tireless efforts."

"I'm plenty tired. Now that Smythe is on board, I'm going to sleep for a few days."

The screen went dark before any of us could pat him on the back any harder.

"He's been active for the last thirty-six hours," Anca told us. "The poor thing is exhausted."

"One more thing," Milo added. "We ran down the location Remy gave us for the coven's roach farm. No surprise, they've abandoned the facility. We can't be certain if they brought any of their livestock with them."

Exhaling through my nose, I managed a smile for him. "I figured we couldn't get that lucky."

"I also have news," Lisbeth announced. "I've accepted a position with Abbott, working in the Faraday's infirmary."

There was no doubt in my mind what motivated her to accept a position that could get her killed: Ford.

"Wow." I kept a smile tacked on my face. "Congratulations."

"I start next week," she said, almost bouncing in her seat. "Abbott said to come to him or you if I have any questions."

What are you thinking? Are you crazy? Is a guy you barely know worth this? Do you have a death wish?

Those were the questions running through my head, but I was impressed when none of them escaped.

Humans weren't allowed in the Faraday for a reason. One slip, and they were lunch for one of the predators in the building. But Lisbeth had a clearer picture of the inner workings of the Faraday than most thanks to her time nursing Ford back to health. She was a grown woman, and she was aware of the risks. She was choosing to accept them. All I could do was support her and pray acting on her crush didn't get her killed.

"Ask away." I resisted the urge to lecture. "I'm happy you're happy."

Mentally, I warned Abbott I had a foot enema with his name on it. I was going to kick his butt for this.

"Thanks to you guys," I said, getting us back on track, "we dealt the coven a major blow."

"This won't be the end of it," Anca warned. "I'm worried the worst is yet to come."

A call interrupted our meeting, and I would have let it go to voicemail if it hadn't been Addie. For the fifth time. Gah. I must have left my phone on silent again.

"Give me a second." I took the call into the kitchen. "Hey, what's up?"

"I wanted to warn you."

The bottom dropped out of my stomach. "What's wrong?"

"We're coming to Atlanta to see you."

"Okay?"

"There's an art installation Dad really wants to see, and I thought it would be a great opportunity for us to spend time together as a family."

Code for see and be seen as the Whitakers. "Why the panic?"

"Boaz wants to come with me." She hesitated. "He wants to see..." She left a long pause where my name once would have fit. "Anyway, he asked if I wanted company, and I said yes."

A giddy thrill shot through me at the chance to see my brother, and my sister. "That's great news."

"Except his mother is interested in the art installation too."

A chill traipsed down my spine. "Oh."

"She noticed him packing a weekend bag and asked where he was going," she explained. "Boaz only told her to get her off his case, which backfired. Big time. When she heard I was going, she launched into one of her lectures on familial responsibilities and keeping up appearances. She said he was too old and too engaged to be running off to party in the big city, and she, well, invited herself along. To chaperone us."

"Did you point out your—I mean, *our* dad—was coming too?"

"She implied he would be too drunk to make sure Boaz didn't slip into my room at night. She also hinted at how I was expected to be a virgin on my wedding night and provide an heir within the year, but the math better work in my favor." She snorted. "I stopped listening at that point."

I thumped my head on the table. "I don't blame you."

"Are you okay?" Addie fretted. "We can cancel if it's too much."

"You're fine. It's fine." I sighed. "I'm fine with it."

Regular visits from Addie and her dad went a long way toward cementing our legitimacy as a family.

"Call if you change your mind." A happy note rang in her voice. "See you next week, sis."

"See you then."

I ended the call to make banging my head easier. The noise must have attracted Bishop, who sat opposite me and let me dent my forehead to my heart's content. I only stopped because my ribs hurt, not because I wanted to, and I leaned back with a pained groan.

"Anca was right," I told him. "The worst is definitely yet to come."

ABOUT THE AUTHOR

USA Today best-selling author Hailey Edwards writes about questionable applications of otherwise perfectly good magic, the transformative power of love, the family you choose for yourself, and blowing stuff up. Not necessarily all at once. That could get messy.

www.HaileyEdwards.net

A Time of Dying #3

A Kiss of Venom #3.5

A Breath of Winter #4

A Veil of Secrets #5

Daughters of Askara

Everlong #1

Evermine #2

Eversworn #3

Wicked Kin

Soul Weaver #1